Praise for Jenna Bayley-Burke's
Compromising Positions

"With sensual love scenes, flirty repartee, and a man and woman clearly meant to be together, you get everything you could ever want in a romance novel. Overall, I have to say that Compromising Positions is a must read!"

~ *Long and Short Reviews*

"Compromising Positions would have to be one of the best contemporary romance novels I have read in a long time. Jenna Bayley-Burke delivers it all, romance, humor, and great chemistry between her hero and heroine. It is so well written. The pace is great, and the story line fantastic."

~ *Fallen Angel Reviews*

Look for these titles by
Jenna Bayley-Burke

Now Available:

Her Cinderella Complex
Par for the Course

Compromising Positions

Jenna Bayley-Burke

A Samhain Publishing, Ltd. publication.

Samhain Publishing, Ltd.
577 Mulberry Street, Suite 1520
Macon, GA 31201
www.samhainpublishing.com

Compromising Positions
Copyright © 2010 by Jenna Bayley-Burke
Print ISBN: 978-1-60504-312-8
Digital ISBN: 978-1-60504-477-4

Editing by Heidi Moore
Cover by Scott Carpenter

First Samhain Publishing, Ltd. electronic publication: March 2009
First Samhain Publishing, Ltd. print publication: January 2010

Dedication

A big thank you to Immi, for being my friend before, during and after.

And to Heidi, for sifting the muck from the mire and never once complaining about it...to me at least!

Chapter One

This is what you get for opening your big mouth, David Strong said to himself as he pulled his baby blue Corvette Stingray in front of Working It Out. The gym occupied the street level of a high rise in the trendy Pearl District of Northwest Portland. He'd actually scouted the spot for a Strong Gym three years ago, but the space was too small and the rent too high. Somehow, the location worked for the women's fitness center, even though it excluded half the population from the clientele.

He grabbed a bottle of water from his bag and got out of his car, setting the alarm. He'd been lucky enough to find a spot on the street. Here he would be able to keep an eye on the car. At least the wheels. The front of the building was lined with windows, but Working It Out had etched all but the bottom foot of glass. It gave the illusion of mystery, and probably saved them a ton on lighting.

The corners of his mouth turned up as he held the door open for two beautiful redheads leaving the gym. Two red heads, had to be a good omen. Though he had a hard-and-fast rule about only dating blondes over five foot ten, he could appreciate the rarity.

Craig was going to really owe him for this one. If his best friend hadn't sounded so panic stricken on the message, David might have thought it nothing but a joke. Help lead a couple's yoga class at a rival gym? He shook his head. He'd never been part of a couple and hadn't trained anyone in years. Only loyalty and curiosity had fueled him to show up.

David stepped into the empty lobby. He'd been here once before, at the grand opening two years ago. Craig's wife,

Daphne, had barely acknowledged his presence even as he'd congratulated her. Daphne had worked as a yoga instructor at Strong before going out on her own. David had even offered her the start-up capital, but she'd refused. For some reason the woman just hated him. It put some distance between him and Craig for a while, but when Craig needed something he knew who to ask. And not just for money, though David had funded the last two years of their fertility treatments. David didn't let anyone down. He didn't disappoint. So, even though Craig's message had been short and completely void of details, he was here. In a lobby so stuffed with foliage it looked like a small rainforest. His gyms smelled like sweat and leather and chlorine. This place smelled like laundry day.

The studios flanking the lobby sported the same floor-to-ceiling windows as the exterior, complete with the thick, hazy stripe running horizontally across the glass. Past the reception area lay a hallway with doors on either side. The locker room and office, he remembered. On the other side was the gym equipment. Equipment he'd sold Daphne at half the wholesale price. He barely got a thank you.

A few women pounded treadmills as they watched CNN and MTV. A leggy blonde pedaled a stationary bicycle and eyed him over her book. His radar shot up—blond, fit, pretty, might be tall enough. Maybe this wouldn't be such a chore after all.

"You can't go back there," a peppy voice squeaked as he walked toward the beauty on the bike.

He spun on his heel and saw no one. Puzzled, he looked down. Emerging from the hallway was a tiny young woman, more than a foot shorter than him. At six five he was used to people being shorter than him, but not by this much. He doubted she was even five feet tall. He stared as she approached the desk; setting down the huge bowl of fruit she carried. Maybe it wasn't so massive, just that she was so small.

Plucking an orange from the bowl, she looked up at him. Her heart-shaped face made her big blue eyes seem even larger. The icy blue gaze was shocking beneath her dark brown ringlets and gave him the strangest sense he's seen her somewhere before. He thought he heard her gasp before she stared down at the orange.

"Craig's not here yet," she said in her cheery voice. She peeled the orange, skillfully removing the rind in one twirling piece. "You can wait for him out here or in the office, but the workout areas are ladies only."

His stomach growled, reminding him he hadn't eaten since lunch. He was headed out to grab something to eat when he'd gotten Craig's message.

"Actually, Craig's not coming. What makes you think I'm looking for Craig?" He peered down at her, trying to place where they had met.

An orange segment stalled in front of her pouty, heart-shaped mouth. "What do you mean, Craig's not coming?"

The scent of orange peel hit his nose, making his stomach growl again. "Would you mind if I had something?" he asked, motioning for the bowl.

"Go ahead," she smiled wide.

He grabbed a stem of grapes. Was she giggling? David's brows pulled together. "What's so funny?"

"Nothing." Her curls danced when she shook her head. "What were you saying about Craig?"

He plucked a handful of grapes from the stem and popped them in his mouth. He stared at her while he ate. She knew who he was, and she looked familiar. Maybe she'd worked at one of his gyms before coming here.

"He doesn't want to leave his wife. She's not feeling well. I'm supposed to ask for Sophie Delfino." Maybe Sophie was the blonde on the bike. Daphne was tall and blonde; her sister would probably be the same. Good thing this sprite stopped him. Hitting on her baby sister would really piss Daphne off.

"Sophie?" she mumbled around her orange.

"Yes, she's the owner's sister."

"Daphne's the co-owner." Sophie's heart pounded in her chest. At this rate she'd have a heart attack before she even got to the bottom of this nightmare. A minute ago she'd been minding her own business, studying for the class she was about to teach. Thinking it wouldn't be so bad, really.

It was mostly stretching. She could do that in her sleep, and often did for the sunrise yoga class she taught. Stretching,

11

a few strengthening moves and a couple of minutes demonstrating difficult sexual positions. All laid out in a series of note cards back on her desk. Very technical, probably very tame if she'd already had sex in any of these positions. But since she hadn't experienced any position at all, it was a little out of her comfort zone.

When she'd studied the notes, she'd imagined *him* in every position she'd detail for the students tonight. And now she sat before the star of every one of her late-night, adult fantasies. Who needed a cardio workout when David Strong could walk into a room and send you right over your target heart rate?

"Really?" David's eyebrow arched over a cocoa brown eye. "And what do you do here?"

"Why are you here exactly?" She plugged the rest of her orange into her mouth to keep it from going permanently dry. The man had a body that made her want to learn how to carve marble. He was as big as a tree and as broad as a house. Even through his charcoal T-shirt she could see the definition in his wide chest. His biceps bulged beneath the hem of his sleeves. A package of lean muscle and brooding good looks that made her insides melt.

"I'm here because Craig asked me to fill in for him." David's voice echoed inside Sophie's head. Her heart leapt around her ribcage. *No way.* She'd been mortified at the idea of demonstrating sexual positions with Craig, but with David? No way. She couldn't do it. She'd die of embarrassment. Contorting herself into such suggestive positions with the man whose body she fantasized about every night. She could never. *Never.*

"Fill in for him?" Breathe in tranquility, exhale tension. Breathe in—

"There is some co-ed class that he and Daphne teach together. Sophie's filling in for Daphne, and I'm supposed to fill in for Craig. If you could tell her I'm here that would be great." David popped a handful of grapes into his mouth, his eyes never leaving the bowl of fruit.

Sophie's gaze darted across the reception desk. She hadn't bothered to ask if there were any messages after her Pilates group. There were never any messages. She ripped three pink notes off the desk.

Craig. Please call.

Craig. Use diagrams, he won't be coming.

Craig. Found a replacement, David Strong.

She plopped down in the receptionist chair and rolled back toward a potted palm. Her stomach reeled.

As she looked up at David, the fear that swamped her was drowned by a much warmer sensation. *Why not?*

She was a professional after all. And she'd been in positions with him far more challenging than the ones they'd be demonstrating in class, even if it had only been in her dreams.

She knew more on the subject than she ever thought possible. Every move of each of the classes was diagramed on note cards Daphne had left. She just had to get through it one by one. Without thinking that this was the closest she had ever come to actually having sex.

He met her stare and grabbed an apple from the bowl. She laughed, harder this time. *So predictable.*

"What now?" He crunched into the Red Delicious.

"Nothing." Sophie tried to stifle her giggles and peeled a banana off the bunch.

"I know, the wedding." He looked pleased with himself, as if he'd just solved the mystery of life. "You wouldn't dance with me."

"That's me." Sophie peeled the banana halfway down and smiled at its phallic resemblance.

His eyes clouded over. He looked her up and down once more. When his eyes cleared, he cocked his head to the side. "Are you Sophie?"

"Two for two, ace." She bit the top off the banana. Was there a sexy way to eat a banana? She shook her head. She didn't care. Daphne had complained so often about Craig's womanizing best friend Sophie felt she knew him. Enough to know she wanted him to remain a fantasy. He was way too much for her limited experience to handle. The class would just flesh out her dreams a bit.

"I was expecting someone like Daphne." He devoured the rest of the apple. "Though the attitude should have been a clue."

Sophie shrugged. Let him think she hated him as much as Daphne did. It was much safer than him knowing the truth. She finished the last of the fruit and tossed the peel in the wicker garbage basket. She lifted the basket so he could toss in his apple core.

He eyed her again. "I didn't eat dinner. Are you going to laugh again if I eat another piece?"

"Depends on what you pick."

His eyebrows lifted further up his forehead. Never taking his gaze off her, he grabbed another apple, almost daring her to comment.

She smiled. *Too easy.* Sophie rose from the chair and walked back to the office. She could feel him behind her. Right behind her. She stopped, laughing as the front of him bumped into the back of her. It was fun to tease him.

"Too easy," she said aloud this time. Playing with him was too much fun to resist. She turned into the office she shared with Daphne. Two desks faced each other in the middle of the small room. She perched on top of hers.

"What's too easy?"

"Nothing." She flipped through her cards. "What did Craig tell you about the class?"

"Not a thing." David stood in the doorway, not quite entering the small office. "He just left a message on my voicemail. He wanted to stay with Daphne, but she was insisting he come to this class, so he needed a replacement. So what is it? Partnered stretching? I'm not the most flexible person."

Sophie turned, hiding her face as she choked on her laughter. She should tell him. It wasn't his fault he'd been set up for a most embarrassing situation. The temptation to see his face when he figured just what they'd be doing was big. But he could also run screaming and leave her humiliated in front of the class. Better to prepare him and give him the option to run now, in private.

She picked up a binder and flipped through the pages until she came to the flyer. Turning the binder to him, she pointed. "This is the class."

Chapter Two

SENSATIONAL SEX!
Committed partners explore the similarities
between yoga and The Kama Sutra.
Learn how to stretch and strengthen your body
for better sex in just five weeks.

"Okay," David said slowly, handing the binder back to her. Just what had Craig gotten him into? His mind spun back to the voicemail message. The only thing he could recall was "Ask for Sophie. I trust you". *Damn.* Craig trusted him not to use the class to make game with Daphne's sister. The little sprite sitting on the desk. No problem. She was nowhere near his type. He'd probably break her in two.

"I'll understand if you're not comfortable enough with your sexuality to participate in the class." Sophie's fingers traced up and down the black sweats covering her thighs. The heavy fabric hung loosely around her, making her seem even smaller beneath it. "I can use diagrams if you want to back out."

She was giving him an out. *Or was that a challenge?* "What makes you think I wouldn't be comfortable?"

"The fruit," Sophie answered quickly. Too quickly. Was she psychoanalyzing him because he was hungry?

"What are you talking about?" He watched her ample chest rise and fall as she took a deep breath. She wasn't very proportional.

"Instant gratification." Dimples pressed into her full cheeks and her teeth gleamed in the fluorescent lighting.

He sat down in an office chair. Funny, with him sitting in a chair and her on the desk they were almost eye-to-eye. It was those eyes that had made him ask her to dance at Craig and Daphne's wedding. They'd pulled at him all during the ceremony, pierced right through him. She must have been standing on a box or in some very high heels because he would have remembered she was this short.

"You've lost me." David shook his head and looked down at her feet. They were bare, except for a coat of crimson polish and a silver toe ring on her right foot. Even her feet were miniature. They had to be smaller than the palms of his hands.

"Grapes are the ultimate in instant gratification. Fast, easy sweetness. No mess afterwards. Apples are next. Just a core to discard."

He tossed his head to the side. She had to be joking. "So you think what fruit I like to eat tells about me sexually."

"Yes." Her voice rang in triumph. She flipped through the cards she held.

Refusing to be goaded, he scooted closer, trapping her against the desk. When he heard her gasp, he smiled. "Or maybe you just want me to think about what oranges and bananas say about you, sexually." Two could play at this little game.

She drew in a ragged breath. "That I take my time to get what I want? Go ahead and think about that."

Her feet found the chair between his legs, and she pushed him back, hard. Propelling him into the opposite wall. She jumped down and was out the door before he could even get to his feet.

Sophie rushed down the hallway to her empty yoga studio. Her room. Her turf. She'd feel brave enough here. She'd been doing so well, and then he went and called her bluff. *Bastard.*

She took a deep breath and tried to collect her thoughts. It stood to reason that he might know something about her. He was Craig's best friend. Maybe he knew how inexperienced she was. She'd had to tell Craig and Daphne she was a virgin when she offered to be their surrogate.

"What? Where did that come from?"

"You said you weren't very flexible. I was just wondering if you'll be able to make it through all of the positions tonight." Sophie forced a smile, reminding herself he was just a man. He couldn't possibly know she'd had him in every position in her dreams.

"Where are the cards?" He rolled his eyes and stepped farther into the room.

"Have you ever read *The Kama Sutra*?" She pointed to the raised platform where she'd set the cards.

"Nope." David sat on the platform, stretching miles of leg in front of him, and picked up the cards.

Sophie kept him in the corner of her eye to catch his reactions as she walked to the door and locked it. She didn't want the students wandering in until she was ready for them. She began her deep breathing exercises and returned to the platform.

"Close your mouth," she said, sitting down cross-legged next to him.

"Why would anyone want to come here and go through this in public?" His eyes never left the diagrams.

"Not an exhibitionist?" She smiled up at him, biting back the desire to tease him further.

He ignored her taunt. "The idea of assigning a sexual position, it's very procedural. Good sex shouldn't be that mechanical and structured."

"Maybe it's just a starting point to get them in the mood, like an aphrodisiac."

He turned to face her, finally gifting her with a devious grin. "Or these folks have a group sex fantasy and are using your class to find other couples."

"Yuck! I'm sticking with my viewpoint, thank you. Though maybe that is why some of the students tried to set me up when I sat in on the class last month." She shuddered at the thought. "Besides, you haven't even met any of the students. I was uncomfortable with the idea at first, but the last session changed my mind. All of the couples are in long-term, committed relationships. I think the class helps them spice things up."

He groaned. "It's sad sex gets so boring you have to take a class to maintain your interest."

"Maybe it gives them a starting point to talk about sex. Communication is the key to a healthy sexual relationship." So she'd heard. "Anyway, Daphne thinks it's more about the touching."

David shook his head and stared into her eyes. He had the thickest eyelashes she'd ever seen.

"It's about the sex. Trust me. At least for the guys. They show up because they know they'll be trying out a new position each week."

Thank goodness she'd made most of these arguments to Daphne when she sat in at the last session. She could just reiterate Daphne's answers. Sophie couldn't think straight with him this close, smelling so good. Clean, soapy and warm. Not a trace of the biting cologne most men slathered on at the end of the day. He must have showered instead.

"Maybe at first the women use the sexual element to get their husbands to attend with them. But beyond that it's about reintroducing nonsexual touch to the relationship. Once couples stop dating, they often stop holding hands or hugging. The majority of the session is partnered stretching. Daphne thinks the students stay with the class for the closeness the touching provides."

He shrugged his broad shoulders and finished his bottle of water.

She wanted to keep quiet, but her mind was taunting that this might be the only conversation she'd ever have with him, no matter how trivial. "It's a very popular class. Daphne has enough people on the waiting list for a year."

"Really?" He arched his eyebrow as he turned toward her. Was he teasing now?

"It's a big trend, combining sex and exercise. We're trying pole routines and belly dancing."

"I'll have to look into that."

She looked away to hide her frustration. She shouldn't care if someone else were pole dancing for him. She'd have to watch herself. One conversation and she was already getting possessive.

Sophie got up and walked back to the closet. She liked him, liked him enough to give him another out. "If you're not comfortable with this you can go. No hard feelings. Tell Craig I made you leave." She lifted the sweatshirt over her head, pulled off the sweatpants and slid on her non-slip yoga shoes.

It was his decision. She crossed the room and unlocked the door, peeking out to see the receptionist back at the desk. She opened the door. The first few couples wandered inside. For the next few minutes she busied herself with greeting the students and getting them ready. She didn't want to watch her fantasy walk away.

David wasn't sure if he was staying until Sophie took her clothes off. Somehow, he lost his ability to think. Without her sweats, she looked like a different person. The toned expanse of belly between her sports bra and low-slung yoga pants magically made her seem taller. The curves on the woman were dangerous. Her hips flared wide beneath an impossibly small waist. He swallowed hard to keep himself from drooling.

He watched in amazement while Sophie ran the class through the warm-up. He stood along the back wall, his arms folded across his chest and just stared. She was doing a good job of warming him up.

He kept reminding himself to keep his mouth closed as she modeled moves for the students. The rest of the class must have mimicked her movements, but he didn't notice. This warm-up looked like the main event to him. This was why the men showed up for this class, to watch her.

He closed his eyes and tried some of the deep breathing she'd been doing earlier. Sophie was not his type. Not even close. He had rules about women. Rules that had kept him from having a woman for almost five months.

That's what this reaction was about. It was a steamy situation and his libido was rebelling because it had been ignored. He'd take care of it this weekend, maybe later tonight

21

with that blonde on the stationary bike. He could handle this. He opened his eyes slowly, and winced. *Maybe not.*

He couldn't take his gaze away. She thrust her pelvis forward and back, her hips swayed from right to left, up and down, circles, figure eights. He sucked in a ragged breath and tried to think of the quarterly report he'd read this morning. *No good.* She moved to lie on her back and repeated the same sweet torture again.

Her voice was perky and sweet. "Try and run through these stretches everyday. It will loosen your hips and help the movements feel more natural during lovemaking."

He could run her through those stretches every day. No problem. *Where had that come from?* He stared at her smooth skin. She was young, early twenties, way too young for him.

"Finding which movements work best for you in each position is the key." Sophie flipped onto her elbows and knees. He closed his eyes against the image burned forever there.

Craig trusted him. And all David could think of was running through every position with her later. There had to be a catch, or a hidden camera. *Had Craig punked him?*

From memory, Sophie went through the history of *The Kama Sutra*. Thankfully she could do it without thinking, because having David Strong stare at her that way was frying her brain cells. He looked at her like, well, like he did in her dreams. Maybe this was all a very vivid dream.

No. If it were, the students wouldn't be here, listening to her every word. And he wouldn't be all the way across the room. Sophie crooked a finger at him, beckoning him closer as she picked up the remote. Dimming the lights, she turned on the projector and an image of a couple illuminated the wall behind her.

"*The Kama Sutra* teaches about lovemaking as an experience, not an event. It illustrates how to slow down and make the most of your partner, to bring you both as much pleasure as possible. And that means starting at the very beginning, with touch."

Sophie swallowed hard as David stepped up onto the raised platform. She looked out at the class, instructing them to stand as she tried to find her bearings.

"In *The Kama Sutra*, the man is the pursuer. But that's due more to the age it was written in. Now, women are free to make the first move." Sophie reached out, running her hand down the length of David's arm. The coarse hairs tickled her palm.

"Instead of racing to the main event, start slow. With a simple touch. It's important to start lovemaking outside of the bedroom. It's the glancing touches, holding hands, embracing as you walk, moving together as one that builds the intensity of what's to come."

Sophie stepped closer, leaving the class behind for a moment as she slipped her arm around David's waist and pulled herself to him so they stood side by side. She didn't even come up to his shoulder. The realization made her smile, and brought her back to reality.

"Some embraces can be done throughout the day, with no one knowing what you're up to. Other embraces will escalate things. Like the pressing embrace where the man presses his body against the woman." Sophie clicked the remote so a new image appeared behind them.

David turned so they were face to face, their height difference making the embrace ridiculous. Sophie grinned, her mind daring her on. She pressed the button and a montage of the remaining embraces covered the wall.

"*The Kama Sutra* has ideas on every pairing, ways to make lovemaking more accessible and exciting for every couple. It's up to you to experiment and find the ones right for you. For lovers with height differences there is the Climbing a Tree embrace, where you place your foot on his, your thigh on his, wrap an arm around his back, place your hand on his shoulder and boost yourself up for a kiss."

Sophie illustrated the embrace until she and David were eye to eye. In his gaze she saw something akin to panic, which evened the playing field quite a bit. She slid back down.

"Like climbing a tree, hence the name. There is also the Twining of a Creeper, where you snake your way around his body like a vine until your hand is behind his neck and you can pull him to you for a kiss."

The back of his neck was hot beneath her hand. When their eyes met this time she saw something else there, something she'd never experienced. *Dear God, he could read her mind.* She released him, shaking her head as if it might help clear away the clouds of lust.

"*The Kama Sutra* has a lot to offer in the way of lovemaking preparations—bathing and massage, kissing and oral sex." Sophie prayed her blush wasn't as heated as it felt as she flipped quickly through the slides. "But those are techniques for you to explore on your own. Here, we'll focus on positions you might find awkward at first, or might not have the stamina for. We'll show you how to get in position, and how to condition your body so you can stay there."

Working It Out closed sometime during the class. David stepped out into the empty lobby, marched to the receptionist desk and sat down hard in the chair. There needed to be some physical space between him and Sophie. His reaction to her had been all too real. No matter how technical she kept it, he'd always been a second away from tossing her over his shoulder, carrying her out of there and finishing the act. He couldn't help but overhear some of the students tease Sophie.

"If you would have told me you were going home to *that,* I never would have been after you about my nephew," a kind, matronly voice said.

"No harm, Kathy. I'll see you at yoga tomorrow," Sophie replied.

"When we try this tonight, I'm going to fantasize about that one," a gruff voice said. David really hoped it was a woman. "I hope you won't mind."

He heard Sophie laugh. He sunk his heavy head into his hands. He should bail. Run now and never have to look the woman in the face. *Except he might.* She was Craig's sister-in-law, so she would probably be popping up unexpectedly for the rest of his life. Just like a part of him had popped up unexpectedly.

He listened to the sounds of the students filing out the front door. He battled between being a coward and apologizing. He didn't have much practice at either.

"David, are you okay?" Sophie's voice was laced with honey. She even smelled sweet. *Why was he so aware of her?*

He raised his head from his hands and saw her, dressed in her sweats again, standing next to him. Every fiber of his being wanted to grab her heart-shaped face and kiss her breathless.

He pushed his feet on the ground roughly, sending the chair backward "I'm fine, just fine."

"Okay then." Sophie retreated to her office. He kicked himself.

She'd gotten him through that class without embarrassing him, and he was acting like a child. He shook his head and told himself to sack up. Sophie emerged from her office a moment later wearing sneakers and a backpack. He stood as she walked into the lobby.

When she approached him, he remembered how small she was. He'd completely forgotten. Strange the way someone so diminutive had commanded a room, controlled his body just moments ago.

He swallowed, forcing the words out. "Thank you for covering for me in there. I appreciate it. I apologize if I made you uncomfortable."

Sophie raised her hand. "You don't owe me any apologies, David. Thank you for helping me with the class."

David stared into those pale blue eyes. Was she really going to make this easy for him? He'd seen the look of surprise in her wide, innocent eyes when they were going through the positions. She'd given him every opportunity to walk out of the class, and now, after he had practically molested her in front of a room full of strangers she was going to let him off the hook?

Sophie walked toward the door, pressing numbers on the keypad to set the alarm. He followed, but not too close.

They stepped outside into the cool night air.

"Let me walk you to your car."

"Oh," she turned to face him. "I didn't drive."

He nodded. "You live around here?"

"No, just up in the Alphabet district. I usually go grocery shopping with Craig and Daphne and they drop me off after class."

"You don't have a car?"

Her cheeks pinked. Was it cold enough for them to color? "I have one. It's just a beast to park. It's really not worth the hassle for two miles."

"I'll drive you home." It wasn't an offer.

"Really, you don't have to." She tucked a stray curl behind her ear. "I'm just going to walk up to the grocery store, then head home. I'll be fine."

"I'll take you." She obviously hadn't heard him.

Her smile was so wide, dimples pressed into her cheeks. "To the grocery store? Are you trying to earn a merit badge or something?"

He couldn't help but grin. "No. One man has already accosted you tonight. I just want to make sure you make it home safe."

"You didn't accost me." She rubbed her arms through her sweatshirt in the cold October air. "But if you want to play the Boy Scout, I'll let you."

"Good," he smiled, his alarm beeping as he stepped to the curb.

"This is your car?" He was used to the response. She was a beauty. A very expensive beauty, but he had a soft spot for her.

"Yes," he said, opening the door carefully. Sophie eyed him strangely as she slid inside. Circling around, he let himself in.

"I can't believe you actually fit in here," she said once he closed his door.

Sophie squeezed her thighs together and tried to think about anything but sex. Which of course didn't work. Even though David had been just going through the motions with her in class, she'd been right on the brink of climaxing. Now she was walking a razor's edge of desire. If Sophie knew how, she'd seduce David right there.

But she didn't. Their brief interlude in class had been the closest she'd ever come in reality. Her fantasies were vivid, her dreams lucid, but she had no tangible experience. It had been fantastic, the feel of him over her, and the sensation of him hardening between her legs, filling her body and mind with thousands of blissful sensations. Sophie always wondered if she could provoke that kind of response from a man. She smiled, pleased at her new knowledge.

She watched his hands gripped tightly on the steering wheel. Even his hands were big. She covered her mouth as the smile broadened. She was going to have to buy a new vibrator. Her fantasies of him would not be complete without a more accurate substitute.

Leaning her head back she closed her eyes, breathing in the smell of him that permeated the car. Soap, skin and a touch of cologne. She wanted to remember the smell for later.

Sophie decided to take him up on his offer of a ride for the same reason she did most anything these days. She would have regretted not having done it. Her mother's last words to her were, "A full life, no regrets". She'd barely been lucid at the end, so whether she was talking about her own life, or a wish for her daughters, Sophie wasn't sure. Either way it seemed like a good motto. Ever since, Sophie took a mental check each night. Just as she'd decided to swallow her fear and teach the class with him, she'd climbed in his car when he offered.

Not that she was reckless with her impulses. She'd fantasized about David Strong ever since Daphne had shown her a picture ten years ago. The picture was of David and Craig. Daphne had meant to show off her new boyfriend, but it had sparked a crush in her teenaged sister.

Her sister's disgust with David's womanizing didn't put Sophie off. It only made him safer as a fantasy. Men like him didn't have anything to do with short, chubby wallflowers. She couldn't do anything about her height, but taking over Daphne's classes melted the chub, and now that she had the time, she was starting to have a life.

Sophie inhaled his scent again, memorizing every nuance. She turned and watched him as he drove, his brown eyes staring intensely forward. She fought an urge to reach out and trace his prominent brow, cheekbones and the square of his jaw. He was painfully handsome. Lenore wouldn't be the only one fantasizing about him tonight.

David tried to remember the last time he'd been to a grocery store. College maybe? If there was anything at all in his fridge, his sister put it there. Kelly was wonderful about leaving ice cream and chips in her wake.

"If we split the list it will go faster." Sophie smiled up at him.

"Okay," he shrugged, taking the torn piece of notebook paper from her hand. He scanned the items. All produce. "What's on your list?" he asked, taking it from her hand. More produce. He knew it. Women ate weird. His sister was the only sane woman in the entire world.

"The joy of having a nutritionist for a brother-in-law. Craig's using me to test his latest diet plan," Sophie explained.

David took a step back and looked at her again. Even in sweats she looked fit. "Why?"

She waved her hand. "Who can keep track of Craig's reasons? I just indulge him. To a point."

"You should do his Deliver-Ease. It actually has real food, not just vegetables." And since the plan was run through Strong Gyms, utilizing the plan let him do a little quality control.

Sophie raised a dark eyebrow. "You're on his diet plan?"

"You're not the only one who indulges Craig. Besides, it's easy. Comes right to the office. I don't even have to think about it.

She looked at him in disbelief. "But why are you on a diet?"

"I'm not." David pushed the cart forward, away from the lettuce. "Craig decided twenty years ago that he knew better than I did what I should be eating. It's a habit from way back." He didn't want to get into his bodybuilding days. It had been an obsession for him for a while, something he and Craig did together. But it was not an arena he had ever excelled in, just gotten by. He wasn't comfortable being average.

Sophie began to study the different lettuces so David attacked his list. How did one pick out a cantaloupe? He looked at the melons piled atop one another. Do you just grab the one on top or did you study the specimens the way Sophie was now sizing up the citrus? He picked up two, weighing each in his hands. How could a person possibly know which one to buy? He moved his hands together eying the fruit, trying to squeeze them to find some difference. They looked exactly the same.

Sophie was suddenly in front of him, taking away the cantaloupes and replacing them with grapefruits. "This is much more realistic David, unless you're into fakes." It took him a minute to realize her insinuation.

"I was not, not..." he stammered

"Feeling up the fruit? Sure you were. It's okay; your secrets are safe with me." Her smile told him she was teasing as she turned the cart toward the apples.

He stomped after her. "I thought you weren't into apples." He smiled as she blushed, obviously recalling her earlier lecture.

"Apples can be good. As long as they are part of a whole bowl of fruit and not the only thing in the dish." She gave him a cocky grin.

He laughed, full and deep. This girl was a piece of work. "You handle the fruit since you are the expert. I'll stick with the vegetables." He couldn't help himself. As he brushed past her he leaned in and whispered, "Just how big do you like your cucumbers?"

Chapter Three

"This is it," Sophie said as David turned his car into the driveway. The Victorian house had been converted into numerous apartments. Sophie sighed at the look of disapproval on David's face. She knew she didn't live in the nicest neighborhood, but it was far from the worst.

She had planned on using the profits from the sale of her parents' house for a new condo downtown, but Daphne had needed more money for the gym. Sophie had set aside her plans and became the majority partner instead.

She didn't really feel like an owner in spite of her comments to David earlier. The gym was Daphne's brainchild, not hers. She was just there to help out until Daphne returned to run the show. Then she could finally get on with her own life, wherever that was going.

Before joining Daphne at the gym, Sophie had been a forensic accountant. It was a good job, paying more than twice her current salary, and she was good at it. But it was just a job, and the hours were horrendous. Which was probably why it had been so easy for her to agree to join Daphne at Working It Out.

"You certainly are a full-service Boy Scout," Sophie said as David carried the grocery bags up the staircase leading to her apartment.

"You really should have your landlord install more floodlights. It's not safe for you to be out here alone in the dark."

She waved her hand dismissively as she used her key to open the door. She only ever saw this place in the dark. She left for work before the sun came up and came home once it was down. Flipping on the light, she kicked off her sneakers, glad for the warmth of the apartment. She was usually cold, which was why she left the heat on in her apartment and wore sweats over her work clothes.

David paused inside the doorway and looked around. Sophie scooted around him and closed the door against the cool breeze blowing outside. She wondered how her apartment would look to a man. She turned, trying to gauge his reaction to her sparsely decorated home.

All of the furniture was new. She hadn't wanted to keep much from her parents' house. The crocheted red blanket her father had kept over his leg once he was in the wheelchair was draped across the white micro-fiber sofa. She'd taken the two pictures over the couch herself for a photography class in college. Haystack Rock and the Cape Meares lighthouse loomed over the ocean. She liked them more for the way she remembered feeling that day than for what they actually looked like. She'd been free that moment, just a day at the beach. No in-home healthcare nurses to deal with, no doctors appointments to attend.

The TV and DVD were angled in the corner, a twenty-year-old family portrait sat on top of the entertainment center. Her lease mandated the walls stay white, so she added color with a crimson rug on the dark wood floors. It should look nice enough, not that she wanted to care what he thought. "The kitchen is over here," she said, turning into the narrow room.

David followed right behind her. "It's small." His voice was so soft she barely heard him.

Sophie shrugged. "So am I," she teased, trying to lighten the mood as she unloaded the bags into the refrigerator. Shopping with David had been fun, quite the opposite of Craig's usual lectures. She was grateful Craig helped her get healthier and actually have enough energy to make it through her long day, but he wasn't much fun.

"This place smells like apple pie," David said, leaning against her kitchen table.

"Mmmm," Sophie agreed, shoving a bunch of celery into the crisper and closing the refrigerator door. "Apple butter, I've had it cooking all day." Opening the freezer, she pulled out a plastic bag of cornmeal waffles. "Would you like some?" She slid two waffles in the toaster.

"If it's not too much trouble," she heard him say. She'd never had a man in her apartment before. Just Craig, and he didn't count. Her place was too small to entertain, and she didn't have the time anyway. It made her anxious, having him step out of her fantasies and be here, watching.

Sophie kept busy, ladling the apple butter from the slow cooker into small plastic containers. She'd placed the apples and spices in before work, knowing she would come home to comfort. Her mother had taught her dozens of different slow cooker recipes. She loaded up the crock almost every morning. Coming home to the wonderful smells made her feel less alone.

When the waffles popped up she spread one with apple butter and handed it to David. "Even Craig would approve. It's completely fat free." She quickly turned around, not wanting to watch his face in case he didn't like it.

A minute ago she had been hungry, but now her stomach was dancing around so fast she wasn't sure if she could eat. Setting the plastic containers aside to cool, she washed out the crock-pot. Clearing a space on the counter, she pulled herself up to sit on it. This way she wouldn't have to look up at him. "You want another one?" she asked, noticing his empty hands.

"Sure." David stepped forward taking the waffle spread with apple butter from her fingers. It took him one step to cross the room. She laughed under her breath and placed two more waffles in the toaster.

"What?" He finished his treat in two bites.

"I never realized how small my kitchen was until you crossed it with one step."

"Sorry," he said, his shoulders slouching slightly.

She hadn't meant to make him self-conscious. But it was hard not to think about his size when he was that close. He was massive, and carried it with such confidence she hadn't thought it possible to deflate him.

"There's nothing to be sorry for." She let herself stare at his deep brown eyes. A dark espresso brown, so dark she could barely notice where the irises began. She would kill for eyelashes that thick. She reached up to brush a few crumbs from his stubbled cheek, but let her hand linger there as her eyes locked with his.

Get the hell out of here before you do something you'll regret. Warning lights flashed in David's mind, but he ignored them. He was fixated on the feel of her soft fingers against his cheek. *Ah, hell.* He leaned closer, jumping as the waffles popped out of the toaster.

He closed his eyes and took a deep breath. Thank God for small favors. He'd been seconds away from ruining Craig's trust in him. His oldest friend, someone he loved like a brother. Though right now he didn't like him very much. David didn't like the way Craig controlled what Sophie ate. She had curves women paid thousands of dollars for. Damn Craig for making her think she shouldn't.

He took the waffle she handed him and ate it greedily. The crunch of the cornmeal and spicy sweetness of the apples was a great combination. Without a word she offered him the rest of hers but he shook his head. Careful not to touch her, he took the last two waffles from the bag and placed them in the toaster. The space was so small there was barely room for them both. But he didn't want to move away. She smelled good, like oranges and almonds and spice.

He watched her take a glass from the open cupboard and fill it with water from the tap. She drank half, and then caught him staring. She tipped the glass toward him, offering him some. He shook his head. It wasn't water he was thirsty for.

"I don't have cooties," she said with a laugh, setting her glass down beside her and reaching for a second one.

"It's not that." He stalled her hand with his own. Her eyes were so blue it almost hurt him to look. Across a room they seemed so light, but when you stared into them up close they seemed to darken. That's what he liked most about them. That's what he remembered from the first time he'd seen her.

Why hadn't Sophie been a bridesmaid in the wedding? Daphne had five bridesmaids march down the aisle, while he and Craig stood up there alone. Not one of them had been her sister. Wasn't there some kind of rule about that?

His heart stopped as the toaster ejected the waffles. His hand recoiled from hers. There was way too much adrenaline in his system. He just needed a few deep breaths and he'd regain his composure. So she had pretty eyes, so what? She was so not his type. She was much too short, with even shorter legs. And her hair was the color of dark chocolate. He had discovered long ago that tall, leggy blondes were what did it for him. Never once had he even thought of straying from his MO.

This odd feeling was just low blood sugar, he decided as he wolfed down his fourth waffle and eyed another.

"Are you still hungry?" he asked.

"Be my guest," she said, offering him the last one. While he ate, she finished the water and refilled the glass. This time he took it when she offered and drained it. Setting the glass on the counter he stared at it and took a deep, satisfied breath.

He shouldn't be hungry anymore. Soon, this weird feeling would pass. Maybe it was just embarrassment from being turned on in class. He'd decided that was nothing to be ashamed of. There was no way any straight man would be able to be in those positions with Sophie and not react. Which was probably the real reason Craig backed out.

Craig, his best friend, who would want him to leave right about now. He should thank her, say goodbye and get out. No problem. Then he felt her fingertip tracing his bottom lip. His eyes shot to her face as she sucked something off her finger. His mouth watered, and while he watched he caught her gaze. Again, she moved her hand toward him and inched forward.

Time seemed to stall when he felt the pad of her thumb brush across his upper lip. Fisting his hands at his side, he sucked in a rough breath. He watched her eyes flutter closed and she leaned toward him.

He felt her before her lips ever brushed his. Felt his resolve wash away as she kissed him. A kiss softer and gentler than he had ever known, yet it somehow deepened the ache in his belly. Her kiss was tentative. He parted his lips, wanting to remove any unease. Whatever this was they both felt it, he was sure now. He deepened the kiss, thirsting for her. She tasted of sugar and spice and everything nice. The soft pleading sound she made in her throat made him groan. His tongue played with hers, finally dancing together.

David moved his hands to the counter on either side of her. Stepping forward, he parted her willing legs with his body. He opened his hands and grabbed hold of that magnificent curve of hip that he'd been admiring all evening. He pulled her to the edge of the counter, against him. Just the right height so she could tell exactly what she was doing to him.

Sophie spread her fingers over his chest and then ran them up until she twined her arms around his neck. He felt her full breasts press against his chest. His own skin had become so sensitive he could feel her hardened nipples. His throbbing need extinguished the last of his arguments. They were two consenting adults. Their bodies definitely agreed on what they wanted to be doing.

He kissed her hard, the way he'd wanted to in class, the way he'd been thinking about all night. He felt her fingernails on his scalp as she pulled him down, deepening the kiss. He wrapped his hands around her hips and pulled her closer still. She wound her legs around him as he ground against her. He heard her breath catch in her throat, and felt her stomach flutter against him as her breath changed to tiny pants. He cupped her buttocks pulling her as close as she could be, almost lifting her off the counter as he pressed the kiss further.

He felt her head hit the cabinet before he heard the thud. He must have knocked her off balance when he lifted her up.

"Ouch," she said, her hands releasing him, rubbing her head.

"I'm sorry," he said, stepping away.

There was a glazed innocence in her eyes that jolted him back to reality. She looked dazed. She'd hit her head, but not that hard. He gulped for air, panicked at how close he'd just come to ruining the strongest relationship in his life.

"I was really out of line. I'm sorry," he repeated as he made the two steps to the door.

He looked back at her again. Deer in the headlights, absolutely stunned. Not a reaction he understood. She must be shocked. He must have read her completely wrong. David bolted through the door and flew down the stairs. He couldn't be trusted anywhere near her.

"Wow," Sophie said to the empty room as the door slammed. She listened to his feet pound the stairs behind her and heard his car start, the tires squealing as he pulled away. She thought about getting off the counter, but her legs were still jelly.

Even with her limited experience she knew this wasn't how it was supposed to end. But wow, that man could kiss. She'd come right there, and he had only kissed her. Granted, there had been some serious grinding involved, but still. Wow.

After a few deep breaths she slid off the counter, her legs balking at having to support her. Flipping off the lights, she made it to her bedroom and collapsed onto the bed. She had dreamed of how it would be with him hundreds of times over the years. It was never that good.

She peeled off her sweats and yoga pants and climbed under the white down comforter. The smooth pima cotton against her skin provided such a blend of sensations she was still reeling.

If only she hadn't bonked her head. Silly, klutzy Sophie. She could be lying beneath him right now, feeling every inch of him inside her. Her body warmed again at the thought. She closed her eyes and wrapped herself around the idea.

It wasn't fair really. Daphne had told her he had a rule about only sleeping with women once. It would be awful if she had wasted her turn with David Strong for a few seconds on her kitchen counter. She rolled over, sinking further into the feather bed.

It had been fantastic. Remembering the feel of his powerful muscles beneath her hands, his broad fingers pulling her closer onto his impressive sex made her clench her thighs together. It was no wonder her body had exploded. Her mind grew foggy as she imagined what might have been. She moaned as her thoughts drifted to sleep.

David slammed the door of his condo behind him and threw his keys at the table in the entryway. He sank down into the couch and his heavy head immediately fell into his hands. There was something seriously wrong with him. Physically wrong.

When had he completely lost impulse control? He'd accused his father many times of thinking with the wrong head, but even dear old Dad had never been this wrong. Craig's voice, tinny from the voicemail, echoed in his ears. *I trust you.* Yeah, right. Trust him to act like the old man and nail everything in sight.

David knew he liked women a little more than most. But he controlled it well. He had rules. He followed the rules. Only dated women who knew the score.

Groping Craig's sister-in-law in her kitchen was wrong on so many levels. He could make a list. Do a cost benefit analysis. It was just wrong. He knew better.

But he also knew how it felt to be there. How she felt beneath his hands. As if she were molded just for him. Which was ridiculous. She was so small he would have split her in two.

David groaned as he got up and walked into the kitchen. It was nearly midnight but he could maneuver about the condo with ease because of the lights reflecting off the river. One entire side of his condo was walled in glass facing the Willamette. The lights of the city and the docks reflected off the water, into his living room and kitchen.

Opening the fridge, he selected from the microbrews inside, slamming the top against the granite countertop so the cap went flying. Standing in the window he drained the beer in one long draw.

Sophie probably thought he was a grade A ass, the way he had ran out of there. The way she was looking at him had knocked him completely off-guard. He couldn't even say what it was about the look, just that it had scared him. Scared him because he liked it so much.

There was definitely something wrong with him. The only thing David wanted to do right now was get back in that apartment and finish what he'd started.

"You are one weak bastard," he told himself as he marched to his bedroom. He peeled off his clothes as he went, until he finally wound up naked in his bathroom. A cold shower, that's what he needed. Then maybe there would be enough blood in his brain for him to think straight.

"Got a minute?" A familiar voice said from behind David's office door.

He glanced at the digital readout on his laptop. Nine thirty. He'd been here four hours already. Taking a deep breath, David prepared for the beating he was about to receive.

"Good morning, Craig. Come on in."

Craig kept half of his body behind the door. "Are you still speaking to me?" David's eyes widened. Craig must not have talked to Sophie, yet.

"Seem to be." He leaned back in his chair and tried to decide what he was going to say about what happened. He'd been trying to figure it out since he got home last night. "How's Daphne?" he asked, stalling for more time.

"It's not good, man." Craig collapsed in the chair opposite David's desk. "She says it'll be fine, but I don't know. I'll find out more when we go to the doctor tomorrow. She has to stay in bed from now on."

"All the time?" David asked, leaning forward. That didn't sound good.

"Yeah, if this doesn't work she might have to stay in the hospital where they can monitor her more closely." Craig seemed smaller, his gaze intent and yet lost. Absolutely terrified.

"It'll all work out, Craig. Daphne is in terrific shape. She'll be okay." David hoped it sounded convincing.

"She can't handle it if it doesn't. Neither can I, to be honest." Craig shook his head. "I'm not here for sympathy. I wanted to talk to you about working from home." Craig was the SGI corporate nutritionist. He worked out diet plans, wrote a column for the newsletter and consulted with the personal trainers who passed the information along to the patrons. The Deliver-Ease program he designed, which delivered diet friendly meals to clients, was a big hit in the area. It was supposed to go regional next month. Not a good time to be stepping back.

"Every day?" David asked, hoping the answer was no.

"I can get all my calls forwarded and I'll always be reachable. I don't want Daphne alone in case something happens."

David forced a smile. "Isn't there someone who else who could stay with her a couple of days a week? If not, we might have to push back the Deliver-Ease rollout in Washington and Idaho."

"I could see what Sophie could arrange. I couldn't concentrate unless it was someone I could trust. It's just until she's due."

"And you are scheduled to take paternity leave." David hated himself for sounding like such a hard ass.

"You're absolutely right, man, I know it's not good. I know if you were talking to anyone else you'd say no. But I need this David, or I wouldn't ask. I'll make it work."

"Okay. Keep me posted on whether or not Deliver-Ease can roll regionally." He'd explain the delay to the board somehow. Maybe start looking for someone to manage the program separately, letting Craig design the menus and have someone else supervise it day to day.

"Thank you, for everything." Craig let out a loud breath and leaned back in his chair. Checking the cell phone on his belt he turned his attention back to David.

"How did Sophie do with the class?"

"Great," David said quickly.

"Good, I was concerned. And you were okay with helping her?"

It was only the most torturous experience of his life. "It's a tough job." He tried to sound casual.

"It's a little out there, but Daphne swears it works better than marriage counseling."

David snorted a laugh. He could see why.

"I know it's a lot to ask, but would you be willing to finish it? I could try and find someone else, but you can see why I can't ask just anyone."

There was no way David was going to let someone else bend Sophie around. "Yeah, I'll finish the class."

"Thank you. I really owe you." Craig checked the phone again. "Sophie was okay with you helping? She wasn't too embarrassed?"

Embarrassed? That would be him. "No, she was very professional."

"Good," Craig nodded. "She's so inexperienced I wasn't sure she could pull it off. Daphne must have really worked with her a lot."

"Inexperienced? I thought she taught a bunch of classes there."

"She does. Sophie is a wonderful yoga instructor. I just wasn't sure she'd be able to handle the material." Craig leaned in closer. "Sophie's a virgin."

"Sophie's a virgin." David repeated in disbelief. "Are you sure?"

"She was that convincing, huh? Well, good for her." Craig's eyebrow arched slightly.

Alarm bells started to sound in David's head. He forced himself into a poker face. Craig did not need to deal with anything else right now.

"Sophie hasn't had many opportunities for a social life," Craig explained. "She insisted on taking care of both their parents long after Daphne wanted to have them in nursing homes, and then she worked crazy hours at her last job. She was working a hundred hours a week when she quit. And she was thirty pounds heavier, so guys probably weren't asking her out as much."

David felt his temperature rise. What was it with Craig and Sophie's weight? She'd looked just fine at the wedding. He'd asked her to dance, she'd shot him down cold, but he'd asked.

"I know she dates," Craig continued, "but she has the worst luck of any person I've ever known. She could have a stand up routine. One guy was on his cell phone all through dinner."

Craig checked his own phone again. "Another time she went out with the nephew of one of the women in her yoga class—the guy told her she was too short."

"That's awful." David squared his shoulders. Sophie couldn't choose how tall she was.

"And this from a man who only dates blondes over five foot ten." Craig smiled. "Which is why I knew you wouldn't read too much into the class. Someone else might take it the wrong way. Sophie's book smart, but she's naïve. I don't want someone to take advantage."

David's stomach turned sour. He'd done exactly what Craig was afraid of. Maybe finishing the class wasn't such a good idea.

They both jumped as Craig's cell phone chimed to life. It played "Here Comes the Bride", or would have if Craig had let more than four notes out.

David's heart stalled. He knew Daphne's ring.

"Anything else?" Craig asked, laughing. David relaxed the muscles he didn't know he'd tensed. Craig turned off the cell phone and looked back at his friend. "Staccato Gelato's tiramisu," he explained.

David's eyes widened. "That's one specific ice cream craving."

Craig shrugged. "If Daphne isn't happy, nobody's happy."

Once Craig was off on his ice cream mission, David spun in his chair to face the wall of windows behind him and closed his eyes. *A virgin.* He shook his head. Craig could be wrong. Sophie had worked him all through that class, and she'd been the one who kissed him in the kitchen. At least at first.

Maybe he'd done just what Craig was afraid of, taken her actions in class as a come on and then taken advantage of the situation. Thinking about Sophie and the class sent images of her lithe body dancing across his mind. It made his head and groin ache in equal measure.

He jumped up from the chair, knowing exactly what he needed. A good hard workout, something so intense he wouldn't have the energy to think. The best gym he'd ever built was just over fourteen floors away.

"Mr. Strong, the architects are here. I've put then in conference room A."

David glared at the phone issuing the announcement from his PA. "I'll be right there."

Chapter Four

David hadn't called. Not that Sophie expected him to, really. She'd wanted him to, sure. But with the way he ran out of her apartment she knew seeing him again was unlikely. She wasn't sure quite how she felt about the entire episode, but she'd gladly replayed it in her head the last two nights. In her new version things didn't end so abruptly. She sighed wistfully and snuggled deeper into her down parka as she stepped off the bus.

Sophie checked her watch. Eight forty-five. She quickened her pace, wanting to get to Diprima Dolci Italian Bakery by nine. She hadn't had *zeppole* in six months and she was not waiting another one. The bakery only made *zeppole*, a rich yeasted ricotta doughnut, on the last Saturday of the month. She liked to get there at nine when they set them out and they were still warm. That way she didn't risk the bakery running out and having to wait another month for a taste.

She'd been abstaining, sticking to Craig's latest set of diet rules. But she didn't feel like denying herself anything right now. She'd been working hard. She'd already led two yoga classes today. And now Craig had her rearranging her schedule to sit with Daphne two afternoons a week so he could go in to work. Not that she minded lounging around with her sister. That was a nice break, actually. She just hated the way he had assumed she had nothing better to do.

That she didn't was beside the point.

Her breath rose in front of her in little puffs as she made her way to the bakery. She didn't care that Craig would say she was using food as a reward, she'd earned this. Closing in on the shop she felt her stomach clench. There was a line, but there was usually a line. Only making *zeppole* once a month increased demand for them.

It wasn't the line, or fear they'd run out of doughnuts that suddenly made her anxious. Even from behind, and fifty yards away, she knew it was him. Sophie shook her head. She could be the man's stalker. Taking a deep breath Sophie stood up as tall as she could manage in her cross trainers. A nice four-inch spike heel would be good right about now.

Sophie sidled up next to him, ignoring the glare from the disapproving woman she cut in front of.

"I won't tell if you won't."

David's expression melted almost instantly from shock to a cocksure grin. "Sophie," he whispered.

"Ah, you remembered. How sweet." She stared up at him as she chewed her lower lip. She tried to read his face. Was he glad to see her or annoyed at the intrusion? She couldn't tell. "I never would've guessed you had a thing for *zeppole*."

"Who doesn't like fried dough covered in powdered sugar?"

She grinned, "Craig."

"Don't let him fool you. The guy used to eat two dozen doughnuts a day trying to bulk up. It didn't work, but he tried it. Have you had the *pignoli*?"

"Almond and pine nut cookies? What's not to love?"

"I know. The *cannoli* is amazing too."

Sophie's head bobbed in agreement. "That's because they don't fill them until you order it. It's essential to have them stay crispy." She smiled, thankful for the comfortable banter.

"Why don't you grab that table?" David gestured to a table that opened up as they made their way inside. "Coffee?"

"Chai tea would be great." Sophie sat down and hugged herself in her coat. She smiled, relieved seeing David wasn't as awkward as she'd feared. He made it easy, but then he made everything easy. There was an effortlessness about him she envied. She would give anything to be that comfortable.

He came to the table loaded with goodies. *Zeppole*, *pignoli*, *cannoli* and three flavors of *biscotti*. Sophie snatched a *zeppole* and moaned as the fritter dissolved in her mouth.

"I have waited so long for this."

"A month is a long time." David agreed as he reached for his second.

"It's been six." She raised her right hand. "I solemnly vow never to commit such a grievous sin again."

They both laughed as David swirled an almond *biscotti* in his espresso.

"You are such a bad influence on me," Sophie said taking a *cannoli*. "I like it."

"About that," David began, leaning back in his chair and sipping at his drink. "We need to talk about the other night."

Sophie's stomach sank, not a good thing with so much fried dough inside. She set down her half-eaten *cannoli*. "About me kissing you, or you running away?" She might be terrified, but he didn't have to know that.

He shook his head, then looked her straight in the eye and whispered, "Craig told me you're a virgin."

Her eyes widened. She was scared before, but now she was mortified. Daphne would have her head for kissing David. "You told Craig that I kissed you?"

"God, no," he said, leaning closer. "You're not denying it."

"I won't deny it. Lying is too much work. I may omit from time to time, but I never lie." She folded her arms over her chest and stared back at him.

"I don't know what you thought was happening Sophie, but you can't play those kinds of games with men. If it weren't for my friendship with Craig, I wouldn't have stopped."

"Really," she smiled, uncrossing her arms and leaning closer.

His eyes narrowed. "That look. Don't do that."

"What?" she asked innocently.

"You know what, the big eyes and that smile." He shook his head. "You don't understand. I would have *hurt* you, Sophie."

"How?" she asked. He obviously had no idea how good she'd been feeling.

"What I had in mind wasn't nice, or gentle." His eyes darkened as he peered down at her.

She stretched her leg under the table until it found his. "I knew exactly what you had in mind."

She could tell he was trying to keep away from her, but his legs were too long and she quickly trapped one of his between her own. His gaze met hers and she held it. She may not know how to get it, but she knew what she wanted.

"Damn it, Sophie," David hissed. Playing footsie was not on his agenda for this conversation. He swore under his breath and tried to ignore the way her feet wrapped around his ankle. He shouldn't be trying to be nice about this. Cold, indifferent, apathetic was what he was going for. But she wasn't having any of it.

He shouldn't have smiled when she first approached him. It had set the wrong tone, but she'd taken him completely by surprise. He'd been standing in line, minding his own business, thinking that maybe he would stop by Working It Out and bring her some *zeppole*. It was a bribe, but he'd been trying to come up with a reason to talk to her all week. Phoning to say "sorry for groping you" didn't seem appropriate.

He'd been practicing the conversation for days, and finally thought he had it down. He'd explain that nothing was going to happen, she'd agree and they'd both move on as if nothing had ever occurred. Why couldn't Sophie just do her part? Why did she have to pop up out of nowhere, just as he was thinking about her? Why did she have to know about his favorite bakery? And why, oh why did she have to keep looking at him like that?

"You need to play fair." He tried to free himself but only managed to bring her closer, so that only the table separated them.

"Play fair? You're the one trying to forfeit the game." She somehow managed to tighten her grip on his ankle and run one foot up his leg.

"This isn't a game, Sophie, this is your life." Her feet dropped to the floor with a slap.

"Fine." She huffed, her pink lips forming a perfect heart-shaped pout. "You are no fun." She unzipped her parka and peeled off the layers. Beneath the jacket was a silky wrap top in a shimmering pink exactly the color of her cheeks when she blushed.

David swallowed hard as he stared at her ample cleavage. *She did not play fair.* "I'm not the kind of fun you should be having."

"Says who, Craig? I'm a healthy twenty-six-year-old woman. I deserve a little fun."

Twenty-six? He was thankful because she barely looked twenty-one, and defeated because she was still nine years his junior. Not that it mattered.

"Sophie," he said slowly, wishing she would put her coat back on. Though being covered up hadn't helped him resist her before. It must be the sugar, or maybe the caffeine. There was *ricotta* in the *cannoli.* Protein, maybe that would help. "I don't believe you'd still be a virgin if all you wanted was a little fun."

"What do you mean?" Again with the big eyes. He was going to get her a pair of sunglasses.

"You're gorgeous. If you wanted a fling you could have had a bunch of them. People don't wait this long unless they are waiting for something." His eyes drifted from her face to her breasts. She knew how to use her assets.

She waved her hand dismissively and picked up her Chai latte. "My sexual development stalled in junior high when my dad got sick. I was going through some pretty deep stuff teenage guys didn't want to deal with. During high school they were both ailing. Dad passed away my freshman year of college, Mom the year after I graduated.

"I didn't have wild high school romances or frat party flings. I was giving insulin shots and changing catheters. It sucked, but it needed to be done. I was the one who didn't want them in a home.

"Once they were gone I realized I don't exactly have the dating skills expected of someone my age." She wrapped her tiny hands around the cup. "I've tried, but no one has even interested me as more than a friend. Plus, mention you're a virgin and some guys don't think you're worth the effort or expense.

"And then Daphne was having fertility problems, so I left my job and came to work with her so I could help her with the hormone treatments." Her curls tumbled as she tilted her head to the side. "Then there was the surrogacy option, but thankfully she got pregnant on their last round of in vitro.

"Now the pregnancy has her on bed rest so I'm still helping out at the gym." She sat up straight and smiled. "I haven't had sex because I haven't had the time or opportunity."

David felt a lot of things. Sad, guilty, strangely touched that she'd even considered sleeping with him. Her honesty was amazingly refreshing. The more he found out about her the more he liked her. Which was another reason to keep his distance. "You should be with someone you care about. I don't have relationships, Sophie. I don't do complicated. I don't have room for it in my life."

Her eyes narrowed as she looked at him. He suddenly felt his stomach get queasy. *Too many zeppole?*

"I know. You never go out with the same woman twice. Only super tall blondes with brown eyes. They have to have a career and understand you will not be calling tomorrow. Never women from the club since your father got sued for sexual harassment, never anyone you might have to do business with later. No one who's married, though engaged or divorcing is okay. No fake breasts or obvious nose jobs. You'll only talk about the weather or the news, no discussion of your business or your family is allowed, ever. Always at their place, never at yours." She cocked her head to the side. "Does that about cover it, or did I miss a rule?"

David slid back in his chair. He didn't know how to respond to such a barrage of truths. This was nowhere near the conversation he'd planned on having.

"For someone who doesn't do complicated you sure have a complex set of criteria."

"Who told you all that?" he asked, knowing the answer as soon as the words came out of his mouth.

"Daphne isn't your biggest fan."

He was relieved when Sophie's eyes softened. He wasn't sure how much more of the slanted look he could take. "So she's told you about me. That's how you knew who I was when I showed up at your club." He'd wondered about that. He'd hoped she'd asked about him at the wedding. He shook his head. It didn't matter what he hoped. What she'd said was true for the most part, he just hated that she knew it.

"I knew you from pictures mainly. And from Daphne's venting."

"Yeah, I bet." David wrapped his hands around the paper cup, cool because it was nearly empty. "She really hates me, doesn't she?" He watched Sophie bite her lip and remembered that she said she didn't lie. He wondered if that was true.

"It's not you necessarily. It's what you represent."

"What is that supposed to mean?"

"You have a part of Craig she doesn't. The two of you are such good friends, but you lead very different lives. Daphne isn't the most secure person. I think she worries Craig might decide he wants your kind of freedom, and you would make it easier for him to leave her."

David took a deep breath, pondering her insight. "Craig would never leave Daphne."

"I know that, and you know that, but Daphne's insecure and she projects her fears onto you. Not that you do much to help matters."

"I never would have thought Daphne was insecure."

"Everyone has a fatal flaw."

He didn't like the way that sounded, as if she had him figured out as well as her sister. This was about Daphne, not him.

"Is that why you weren't in the wedding? Because you're prettier than she is?" Daphne was pleasantly pretty in a typical way. Sophie was head-turning. You wanted to look again to see if her eyes were really that blue, if her gypsy curls really the bouncy shine you thought you'd seen.

"I thought you *weren't* trying to charm me out of my panties."

Sophie's smile was infectious and for a minute he didn't fight it. It felt too natural to fight it anymore.

"My mom had vascular surgery two weeks before the wedding. She was really weak, and if it hadn't been Daphne's wedding I wouldn't have taken her out of the house. I was too busy to be a bridesmaid, too busy to do a lot of things."

"Like dance with me?" He was relieved.

"That really stung your ego, didn't it? I must be the only woman who has ever turned you down."

"What? No." *Pretty much.* "I just wondered that's all."

"I know something that would make you feel much better," she said, her voice deep and throaty. He knew right where she was going, and as much as he wanted to go there, he wouldn't.

"Sophie, it's not going to happen, ever. Craig asked me to help you with the class because he trusts me."

"The Sensational Sex class." She said the words slowly, just to taunt him he was sure of it. "But you didn't tell him what happened after."

She had him there. "No, he has a lot on his mind right now."

"Exactly." He felt her feet on either side of his leg again, but he didn't have the heart to pull away yet.

"I know all your rules, and none of them apply to me. No one ever has to know you didn't hold to them this once."

When Sophie leaned across the table all he could see was her. How could someone so small completely block out his view of the outside world? She was offering an arrangement no man would walk away from.

"Sophie," he hissed, "be good. Play fair."

"If you'll play." Her tongue peeked out wetting her lips. His gut clenched.

"I can't," he whispered, closing his eyes. He heard her slump back in her chair, listened as she zipped up her parka. "Where are you going?" he asked, opening his eyes.

"Back to work, I have a class at noon." He watched as she stood in line, buying six more *zeppole*. He shoved what was left of his treats in the bag and offered to walk her to her car.

"I took the bus," she said, clutching her bag.

"Sophie, are you sure you have a car?" he teased, glad to lighten the mood again.

Her shoulders squared as she looked up at him. "I have a full size van with a wheelchair lift. Not exactly something you drive around for fun."

David winced. He'd deserved the hit, but it still stung. A reminder of how much she did for other people. He reminded himself he was helping her more by keeping his distance than he could by giving in and letting himself touch her.

"I'll drive you back."

Sophie stared down at her bag. "I was going to eat them all on the way. I was hoping the sugar buzz would kill the sexual frustration you're giving me."

He laughed and looked at his own full bag. "Does it work?" he asked as they walked out the door together.

"Yes," her voice rang with honesty. "That's how I got fat."

He stopped dead in his tracks. "Sophie, you weren't fat."

She turned and smiled. "There you go, trying to charm me out of my panties again."

"I am not. I just don't like the way Craig makes you feel about your body."

Her eyebrow arched and she touched his arm. "Craig means well, really. I actually like the way I look now, and that's what matters." He looked down into her crystal clear blue eyes and was glad. Glad she was happy in her own skin, glad she was standing so close. "You know there are other ways to get rid of sexual frustration."

"Really?" he asked, putting his hand on the small of her back and urging her toward the car. He was picturing a couple, and if they made it to his car before the logical side of his brain kicked in they'd both feel a lot better.

"Yes," she said as he opened her door. "That's why I bought a vibrator." He froze for a minute, before slamming her door as hard as he could manage. The smile on her face showed that she had won this round. She didn't play fair.

Chapter Five

Taunting him seemed to work better than a full frontal assault. Sophie had four Sensational Sex classes left, four chances to get him to follow her home and try out the moves she taught him in class.

She'd taken extra care getting ready today. Daphne traded classes for beauty treatments with the day spa up the street, and for once Sophie took advantage of the perk. She'd squeezed in everything she could in the last few days. She showered after her last class and slathered her body with lotion, hoping her skin would be soft. All the prep work made her feel ready, prepared for her crusade of seduction.

She even dressed better. She wore yoga pants again, but replaced the sports bra with a push up bra and low-cut, scoop-neck T, much more suggestive, but still appropriate. She was ready. If the poses affected him half as much as last time he might just be weak enough to let her take advantage of him. As long as he showed up.

Sophie had thought of almost every contingency, except David not showing up. Last week he'd been forty minutes early. Class began in twenty minutes, and there was no sign of him. In a flurry of nervous energy she had already prepped the room. Sitting on the platform, she tried to do the deep breathing she practiced before every class. It was no use trying to relax, she couldn't calm down. She wanted him to be there too badly. He was her best fantasy—her only fantasy really—come to life.

Sophie rose and marched through the door toward her office to get the slides depicting the positions. She could teach the class with those in case he didn't show up. Or worse, if he backed out and Craig came. There was no way in hell she was getting into any position with her brother-in-law.

She turned into her office, grinning from ear to ear when she saw David stretched out in her chair with his feet on her desk. Her grin faded as it registered that she didn't like how he appeared to own the place. Still, she was glad he was here, looking just as yummy as last week in his black track pants and T-shirt.

"I thought maybe you forgot." Stepping closer to stand next to his feet on the desk she smiled, watching his eyes look her up and down, settling on the cleavage visible above her top. He swallowed hard then raised his gaze to meet hers.

"I don't disappoint. I was just looking for the cards so I knew what to expect. I see you prepared for tonight." His eyes darkened in a sinister way she wasn't sure she liked.

"I prepare for all my classes," she said coolly, still trying to figure out just what his stare might mean. He stood up, towering over her and she sucked in a hot breath. Standing toe-to-toe she wound up with an amazing view of his hard chest that made her want to reach out and touch him. Soon enough, she reminded herself. She could fondle him all she wanted in class and say she was just doing her job.

"Sophie, Sophie, Sophie. I see you decided not to play fair."

"What do you mean?" she teased, looking up at him, hoping he was referring to how she looked.

"Maybe I should level the playing field." His voice was gravelly and low, his eyes growing impossibly darker.

"Oh, please do," she taunted, wondering just what he had in mind.

She gasped as he reached down and pulled his shirt over his head. The ripples of bronzed muscle stretched out in front of her, making her mouth water. It was obvious he was still working out every day, still keeping his body builder shape.

She raised her hand on instinct, touching the smooth skin of his bare chest. He was sexier, more masculine and somehow even bigger than she had imagined. Pressing her hand flush against his chest she could feel his heart beating, going just as fast as hers. Sophie looked up, meeting his seductively heated gaze.

"Hey you two lovebirds, it's time for class," a nasal whine interrupted from the open doorway.

"Right," Sophie said spinning around. "We'll be right there."

David chuckled. "Why do you let them all think we're together?"

She turned back to him and was instantly disappointed. The moment was gone. David's expression had gone from smoldering to business as usual. *Why indeed?*

"Some of our patrons think matchmaking is their civic duty, and I'm sick of blind dates." She shrugged. It was true, not the whole reason, but part of it.

"So I save you from nephews who talk more on their cell phones than to you?"

"How did you know about that?" *Craig.* She smiled, not sure whether she wanted to kiss him or kick him for that smug expression on his face.

"What's in the cards for tonight?" David whispered once Sophie motioned for him to join her on the stage after the warm up.

Sophie grinned slyly. "You just lie there and look hot."

David's face fell. He was used to women treating him like a sex object, and he'd invited it by taking his shirt off, but for some reason it bothered him when Sophie did it. It was about the only thing she did that bothered him.

"Calm down, it's a bunch of female superior positions. You really don't have to do anything. Just lie back and think of England, it will all be over soon." She patted him pertly on the arm and turned to address the class.

"For some couples experimenting with new positions can help them find greater sexual fulfillment. For a lot of women, female superior, or woman-on-top positions can do just that. We're going to transition through a series of positions, in which we hope you'll all find satisfaction.

"Gentlemen, you will find your role in these positions is largely to relax and enjoy. I know that sounds simple, but relinquishing control can be very difficult for some men. Most of you here are more open minded than that, but if you are having trouble with letting your partner be in control of your lovemaking you can start slower, letting her be in charge of kissing, then foreplay, then afterplay and finally the act itself. Remember that you are making love to each other, but sometimes it can be nice to just be in the receiving end."

David watched in awe as she directed the class. Sophie had an amazing ability to make everyone feel at ease with the understandably delicate subject matter. She was completely professional, and yet all he could do was wonder what she had in store for him next.

He liked this game they were playing, even though he knew it was dangerous. He'd lost control once, but he had the upper hand now. Sophie wanted to push him, to test herself. He'd let her, and push back until she found her boundary. He knew her now. You didn't make it this far in life as a virgin if you were as open as she was pretending to be. He'd just call her bluff, and she'd call it off. He wouldn't even be the bad guy because it would be all her idea.

"We'll begin with one of the most popular positions in *The Kama Sutra*, Butterflies in Flight. Men, find a comfortable position on your back with your arms out to your sides. Ladies, lie atop your mate belly-to-belly, chest-to-chest, thigh-to-thigh. Use your arms to stretch your shoulders up, and press your toes on his feet for leverage to help you move. You can see how the joining of the two bodies looks like a butterfly.

"Gentlemen, you won't have much movement unless your back muscles are strong and your partner is light." David undulated beneath her, and she looked down. Her expression evolved from surprised to pleased instantly. "Thank you for the demonstration," she said in her teacher voice. "You can all understand why I was stressing the back exercises earlier.

"The next position, Cat and Mice Sharing a Hole, flows smoothly from this one. Men move their legs together while women drop your knees to the outside of his legs. Release his hands and push up, straightening your arms. Alternate between pushing with your hands and feet to create a rhythm. For men, your movement is even more limited than before, except your hands are now free." On cue David lifted his hands to cup her buttocks. Sophie grinned and he reminded himself that he really was in control here. Just in case, he recited the alphabet backwards in his head.

"Again you can see the symbolism behind the name. Courtship is often a game of cat and mouse, of the hunter and the hunted. The game always ends the same." Her grin made him wonder if she thought he was the cat or the mouse. He was always the cat.

"If at any time you feel tired, transition into the Inverted Embrace. Just relax your arms to grip his waist. As long as you are smaller than him he should be able to support your weight. You can rotate your hips in every direction, resting your head on his chest or raising your head to look into his eyes. Again his hands are free."

The twinkle in her eyes showed she knew she really wasn't playing fair at all. He raised his hands up her back and tried to list the fifty states in alphabetical order.

Sophie rolled off him slowly, using her body to shield his response to her from the rest of the class. David was grateful she never tried to embarrass him about his reaction. He was only human after all.

He stayed behind her as she stretched the class and reminded them of the importance of not straining themselves. By picturing the faces of the presidents he was trying to name in order, he was able to calm himself enough to put the mats away while she answered questions and said goodbye to the students.

The way she doled out advice amazed him. These people were looking to her for wisdom, yet she had no practical experience of the topic. They respected her, trusted her and presumed she was an expert on the subject.

Her knowledge was extensive. The classes were making David feel like he had a limited repertoire even with his vast experience. He'd only ever shared a night with a woman. The students were sharing a lifetime together. He was beginning to understand how you might want to know more if you were trying to communicate something more than physical need, than instant gratification. How sex would need to mean different things at different times.

He shuddered at the thought. He was getting it.

Sophie enjoyed the way she felt around David. She had a heightened sense of awareness whenever he was in the vicinity. It made her feel more confident, sexy and secure than she ever had before. This was a strange combination of emotions elicited by a man slipping from her fantasies into reality. Her ability to arouse him delighted her more than she thought possible.

She'd wondered if his reaction last week was just a fluke, a physical response to the material. She knew now. It wasn't her or the racy nature of the class that was exciting him, but the two of them, together. There was something heady and electric, something she always felt buzzing below the surface. The more time they spent together the louder it became, thundering so loud even David couldn't ignore it now.

Sophie turned the manual lock on the door after thanking the last of the students and turned to the empty reception area. David sat on top of the reception desk, a wide grin across his face. He'd left his shirt off all through class, to the noticeable delight of the female participants and chagrin of their husbands. He was the epitome of masculine beauty.

Sophie had cautiously enjoyed touching him all night, careful not to let herself get too carried away. But now there was no audience, nothing to stop her. She saw his eyes darken as she stepped closer, watched his chest rise and fall with each rough breath.

"I put the mats away."

"Trying to earn another merit badge?" Sophie kept her voice light, not sure if she wanted him to know yet just what she had in mind.

"How do you do that?" he asked from his perch on the desk. His posture relaxed, his legs wide apart, hands in front of him on the edge.

"Do what?" She stepped easily between his legs. With him sitting on the desk they finally came eye to eye.

"Talk about sex so openly without getting embarrassed."

They were so close Sophie could feel his warm breath as he spoke. She shrugged. "It's a natural act, everybody does it." She looked down as she felt the color rise from her shoulders clear up to her cheeks. "Well, everybody but me, anyway." She steeled herself against her moment of insecurity and met his gaze again. "I've never really understood what there is to be embarrassed about."

"Most women are."

"I'm not most women," she smiled. "Besides, I'm talking about sex in theory, not in practice. I think sometimes women get nervous because what they're saying tells about them emotionally. Here, it's just physical." She leaned closer, breathing in his deliciously spicy male scent. "What did you think of tonight's class?"

His head cocked to the side. "Are you fishing for more compliments? Really, Sophie."

"No, I'm not. I was just curious how you felt about the topic."

"Woman-on-top positions? Nice show." His grin leered at her.

"I'll remember that." She placed her hands on his knees and slid them up his thighs. She smiled, hearing him suck in a harsh breath as she found his hips.

"Sophie," he warned.

"I meant, what do you think about giving up some control?"

"When have you ever let me be in control?" His voice was gravelly and solemnly serious.

Her hands retreated to mid thigh. "I don't let you, you just take it." Not that she minded.

David cleared his throat and slid forward, his toes tapping the floor. "If you're referring to when I kissed you last week, I should remind you that you started it."

"But you wouldn't let me finish it," she pouted.

He shook his head. "Sophie, I warned you about that."

"You don't understand how frustrating it is to be kissed."

"Frustrating?" he smiled. "That wasn't the response I was going for."

"You couldn't do it." Her fingers again began their march north.

"What?"

"Be kissed. You'd never allow it to happen to you. You would have to control even that."

He shook his head. "That's ridiculous."

"I dare you."

"We're not children. You don't need a game if you want to kiss me," he winked.

She licked her lips. "You'll let me?"

"Only to disprove your hypothesis. Purely for the betterment of science."

"How unselfish of you," she taunted, flattening her palms against his bare chest. "Are you sure you can do it?"

"I'm not a control freak. I can do it."

It was intimidating, kissing a man who could clearly kiss so well, who had kissed so many. She wasn't sure if he liked kissing someone with her limited repertoire. But she felt a primal need to feel his lips beneath hers, to know how his mouth tasted on its own.

She lightly brushed her lips against his, breathing in his scent. Closing her eyes she went further, placing tender, soft kisses against his slightly parted lips. She pressed her mouth more firmly against his, and then gently nibbled his upper lip. She slid one hand up his body, the heat of him warming her cool fingers. Threading her hand through his hair she pulled his head in closer.

She moved on, planting soft kisses on each of his cheeks, brow, ears and finally his eyelids, forcing his eyes to close if only for a moment. She pressed her forehead against his.

"Do you always keep your eyes open?"

David nodded slowly, his eyes fixed on hers.

"You should close them, just focus on the sensation." She smiled at the thought of giving him advice on kissing. Absolutely absurd. As if the man had anything to learn.

He shook his head. "There's no way I'm missing the show."

She revisited his mouth, gently licking his lips with the tip of her tongue, tasting her way across his mouth. Clean and cool, as refreshing as water. Growing bolder she took his lower lip in her mouth and sucked it gently. He responded in kind to her upper lip. She pulled back slightly and smiled, rejoining him by sucking his upper lip. She danced her tongue inside, slowly beginning her exploration of his mouth. He sucked her tongue hard, and she pulled back, silently reminding him who was in charge.

Chapter Six

The hardest thing he'd ever done. Letting her kiss him and not take control, not throw her on the desk and do every wicked thing he'd been dreaming about all week.

From time to time she would pull away and gaze up at him, watch him watching her. Then her eyelids would float slowly down as her mouth returned to his.

David loved to watch her when she kissed him. Her soft moans mingling with the sound of lips meeting and the exquisite feel of her mouth were causing a sensory overload. For the first time in his life he closed his eyes and just let himself be kissed. Moments later, his own sigh startled his eyes open. He'd never done that before, let his guard down even so subtly. Had she noticed?

He reminded himself that he was doing all this for her. He was going to let her push until she found the boundary and called it off. The feel of her hand drifting down his chest blurred his mind. He just hoped she would find her wall soon, before he'd gone past the point of no return. Her fingers slid beneath the waistband of his track pants.

"Sophie, play fair," he hissed.

"What?" she asked, batting her eyelashes. Her smiling cheeks pushed her big eyes into semi circles. "This is against your rules?" Her voice was low and throaty as her fingertips advanced another inch into his pants.

He grabbed her wrist to protect himself. "You are playing with fire, Sophie."

She smiled wickedly and reaching up with her free hand, ran her fingers along the stubble at his jaw. "Not yet, but I'm trying to."

Something about her touch moved him. The way she looked at him was different, less hungry and more reverent than he anticipated. He shook his head at the romantic notion.

"You should get your coat."

"Really? And where are we going?"

"Home." He slid off the desk and stood up as tall as he could manage without displaying just how affected he had been by her kiss.

"My place or yours?"

"Very funny." David pulled on the T-shirt he'd rescued from her office. "Do you need a ride?"

She circled her arms around his waist and looked up. "I'm going to walk home unless you promise to come with me."

"And do what exactly, Sophie?" It was now or never. David swallowed hard and began his onslaught. "What do you want to do once we get there? Are you going to kiss me again? Are you really prepared for what happens next? Are you ready to peel my clothes off and work me through all of the positions you tried tonight for real?

"What are you looking for Sophie?" He leaned in closer and whispered in her ear, trying to ignore the trouble she was having catching her breath. "Do you want to see how many times I can make you come in one night?" He leaned closer, puffing the heated words against her skin.

"With my fingers, my mouth, my cock? Do you want me to make you scream, Sophie?"

Sophie's stomach clenched and she forced her eyes open. Making her come by kissing her had been one thing. There was no way she was going to let herself climax just from listening to him talk. She did her best to take a deep breath, raised her hands to his chest and pushed him as far away as she could manage. Which wasn't far because what she really wanted to do was take him then and there.

She looked up into his face, surprised that he didn't look angry, but strangely pleased. "I don't want that much pressure. I would end up so preoccupied with the task that pleasure might elude me and ruin my enjoyment of my first sexual experience." She watched as his face fell. If she had to guess, he was now baffled.

"Sex should be more than just the pursuit of orgasms. Lovemaking should focus on the emotional and physical connection between two people. You're putting too much pressure on me to climax. Let's just focus on a mutually pleasurable experience, okay?"

He shook his head and crossed his arms across his broad chest. "And here I was, thinking I had performance anxiety."

"You? You can do whatever you want and I'll think it's normal. I'm the one who has standards to live up to."

His head tilted back as the laughter erupted from his throat. She smiled in spite of her insecurity and swatted his arm. "That's right, laugh it up."

"I'm sorry, I just never even considered you would be nervous. You're never nervous."

She rolled her eyes. "I'm always nervous. I have a low-level hum of nervousness going on whenever you're around."

"Really?" His face morphed into a little boy grin.

She smiled back. "Come on," she said grabbing his hand and pulling him toward the door. "Let's go earn you another merit badge."

David knew Sophie was mad, but there had been no way he could trust himself to get out of that car. Entering his condo, he knew he was facing another sleepless night of cold showers and torrid fantasies. The lights on inside surprised him.

He never bothered with the lights, the glimmer from the water was usually enough to help him find his bed at night and the door in the morning. The warm glow and buzzing television could mean only one thing. Kelly was here.

Tossing his wallet and keys he went straight to the kitchen. Kelly always brought food. Really tasty, party-in-your-mouth food. Maybe she'd brought something sugary. Sophie said sugar was good for sexual frustration.

His baby sister didn't disappoint. Reading "Moonstruck Chocolate Company" on the lid of the crescent-shaped box David dove in. As one truffle melted in his mouth he rolled another between his fingers and wondered which would be Sophie's favorite.

He liked the *Italia Espresso,* but guessed she would be more *The Mayan* with its milk chocolate, almonds and cinnamon or *The Ocumarian.* Yes, he nodded to himself, *The Ocumarian's* dark chocolate and chili pepper suited her perfectly. She looked innocent, but she played with fire.

"There you are," Kelly said from the doorway to the laundry room he never entered. "I called your office. They said you have a standing appointment for seven every Thursday." His sister stepped closer, standing toe-to-toe with him. At six feet tall she could almost look him in the eye. "David, are you seeing a therapist?"

"What? No. Why would you ask me that?" He eyed the remaining chocolates, choosing *Cinnamon Roll Latte* and grimacing at the cutesy candies that remained. *Ivory Cat* and *Chocolate Lab.* He wasn't desperate enough to go there, yet.

"There's nothing wrong with seeking professional help."

David rolled his eyes and leaned his hip against the counter. "And exactly why do you think I need a shrink?"

She waved her hand in dismissal and walked back to the laundry room. "Everyone could benefit from a little analysis. I was just surprised you had a standing appointment on the books. What is it, a poker game?"

"No," he said quickly, running through possible excuses in his mind. What had Sophie said the other day? Lying is too much work. He stomped his foot on the tile. *Enough thoughts about Sophie.*

"Then what is it?" Kelly asked, carrying a basket of sheets with her. Pulling one out, she handed the corners to David. "You might as well tell me because you know I'm not going to stop asking."

"None of your business," he said as she approached him with her two corners, folding the sheet in half.

"Oh, now I really want to know. Golf lessons?"

"I don't need golf lessons."

Kelly took the sheet and finished folding it.

"You should just leave your stuff and let the housekeepers take care of it."

Kelly ignored him, plucking another sheet from the basket. "I know it's not a date, so let me see. Are you meeting with a trainer?"

David cocked his head to the side. "How do you know it's not a date? I date."

"What you do isn't dating. Your attention span is too short, and your list of rules too long for dating." Kelly set the sheets on the counter and dug in the basket for the pillowcases, then slowly looked up at him with wide eyes. "Omigawd, it is a date isn't it? You're finally seeing someone." She dropped the pillowcase on the tile and ran at him, wrapping her arms around his neck. "David, I'm so happy for you. I was so worried you would never let yourself fall in love with anyone because of Dad."

"I didn't say it was a date, just that it could be. And I'm not in love with anyone." *Infatuated and preoccupied, but definitely not in love.*

"Who is she?" Kelly asked, beaming up at him. "How long have you known her? What's she like?"

"Slow down, there's no date."

Watching Kelly's face fall he felt a little sad. Had the morning at the bakery been a date? Maybe they were dating. "I'm helping a friend teach a class."

"A woman friend?" She didn't bother to mask the hopefulness in her voice.

"Craig's sister-in-law. Sophie." He watched Kelly's face as he said her name. *Could she tell?*

"Sophie." Her eyebrow arched. "What kind of class?"

He was not going there. "It's a yoga class for couples." Omit, don't lie. That was Sophie's philosophy. Damn if it didn't seem to be working. "Craig and Daphne usually teach it, but

Daphne's on bed rest for the rest of her pregnancy. Sophie fills in for Daphne, and I do Craig's part."

"Daphne's okay, right?" Kelly asked, putting her folded linens back in the basket.

"Seems to be. Craig's freaking out though."

"That's what he does." Kelly smiled. "Is it at one of Strong Gyms?"

"No, Working It Out. It's a women's only center Daphne and Sophie own."

Kelly picked up her laundry basket and headed back for the laundry room. "In the Pearl District. I've heard of it. You know they teach a class..." Kelly's basket hit the floor and she spun around. "Get out!"

David's stomach twisted as he realized his baby sister had just figured out exactly what kind of class he was helping teach. "It's not what you think."

"That class is for committed couples only! How long have you been keeping this from me?"

David's mind whirled. *Just how popular was this class?* "How did you know that?"

Kelly looked him in the eye. "Kevin and I are on the waiting list." Kelly and Kevin had been together since high school and engaged for three years. If Kevin weren't attending medical school in Washington and Kelly at OHSU, they'd be married by now. David figured they were having sex, but didn't want to think about it. He shook his head and marched into the living room.

"You didn't answer my question." She chased after him. "How long has this been going on?" He ignored her, still trying to block the mental image of his sister showing up for that class.

"No wonder," Kelly said, sinking into the leather sofa.

David rolled his eyes. "What's that supposed to mean?"

"It's just that you haven't been going out lately. You know, on your little trolling expeditions."

David didn't want to think about how long it had been since he'd had sex. Sophie kept showing him that it had been far too long.

"You're reading this all wrong, Kelly. It's not what you think. I'm just helping her, nothing more. She's really not my type."

"That could be a good thing."

He was starting to think so too.

Sophie shifted her weight, crossing her legs beneath her as she sorted through the reports in the file. Her morning Pilates class left her energized, even with last night's lack of sleep, and she wanted to take another look. She'd glanced through the financial statements from Strong Gyms Inc. when she found the file on her desk this morning, but set it aside knowing that David must have forgotten the file.

The forensic accountant in her wanted to look further. She'd noticed something earlier, and on further inspection she smiled, knowing she was right. She scribbled a few more notes, excited to be using her skills again. Sophie genuinely liked auditing, liked the mystery of finding things people hoped would stay hidden. It was the long hours of her old job she could do without.

The intercom rang, pulling her attention away. "David Strong is on line two for you. He says it's important."

She'd been caught. Sophie broke out in a cold sweat. She'd be breaking his no talking business rule, though his rules didn't really apply to her. David wasn't going to be happy that she peeked, but maybe if she helped it wouldn't be so bad.

Sophie clenched her fists to stop her fingers from trembling before she picked up the receiver. *Play it cool.*

"You don't know what you're looking for, do you?" she asked, hoping to take him off-guard.

"What?"

She smiled, it worked. "With the reports you left on my desk."

"Oh, good. I was hoping they were there." She heard him let out a breath.

"How much?"

"How much what?"

"Are you hoping to find?"

"Oh, the reports. I'm not sure. It's just a hunch really." His light, calm voice suddenly turned tense with realization. "Wait, you looked through the reports?"

Did he want her to deny what she'd already admitted to? She needed to redirect him, and end the long, awkward silence echoing through the phone line. "You don't know what or how much you're looking for?"

He cleared his throat. "Like I said, it's just a hunch."

"Very professional. I could recommend a firm," she offered.

"No, no," he said quickly. Very quickly she noticed. "It's private. I don't want to involve anyone until I know what I'm dealing with."

Sophie shrugged. "Okay. I've made a list of reports you should run that will help you narrow down where you should be looking."

His sigh was audible across the phone line. "Thanks. This kind of thing is what you did before, right?"

"No problem. It feeds my brain. I actually miss accounting that goes beyond simple debits and credits. How sick is that?" She laughed at herself. "It's a good hunch, David."

"Thank you. I'll run over and pick them up."

Sophie waited, hoping he might ask her to join him for lunch, dinner, a walk on the waterfront, anything. Nothing. "I'll leave them at the desk."

"I need a favor," David said, holding out the silver crescent-shaped box. Sophie sat crossed-legged in her office chair, pounding away at her laptop. Her curls had been obstructing his view of her face, but when he spoke she looked up. David smiled, watching her sparkling eyes take him in before they drifted to the box he was holding.

"Wow, Moonstruck chocolates. You must need some kind of favor." He smiled, pleased she knew the company. Entering the office he sat on her desk.

"What's your favorite?" he asked, pulling the box out of her reach.

"Favorites are so overrated," she pouted, leaning closer to him. Close enough for him to breathe in her sweet almond scent.

"Come on, play along," he teased, hoping he had gotten it right.

"Don't you mean play fair?" she teased. "Okay, let me think." As she pondered the question she wrapped a dark curl round and round her finger. "*Extra Bittersweet* is fantastic for a chocolate craving." David chewed his lower lip. He hadn't even considered that one. "But *The Ocumarian* is probably my favorite. They get the chocolate from the Ocumare valley in Venezuela and blend it with chili pepper. It's fantastic. Have you tried it?"

David felt his cheeks begin to ache from smiling so hard. He'd known it.

He handed her the box, watching as she opened it greedily. "There's only two kinds," she said, looking up at him.

"Your favorite and mine, *Italia Espresso.*"

When she smiled her cheeks glowed pink all the way to her eyelashes. Sophie looked down at the box, then back up at him. "How did you know which was my favorite? You didn't ask Craig did you? He has a serious chocolate ban."

David rolled his eyes. "Forget Craig. I was making a gesture. If you don't want them..."

"No!" Sophie snatched the box away in her greedy fingers.

David smiled again. "About that favor."

"These are your favorite?" Sophie rolled a truffle between her tiny fingers.

David nodded slowly.

"And these are all mine." Sophie tucked the box in her desk drawer. "You must be dying for a bite. I wonder if I ate this, if you would kiss me just for a taste."

David rolled his eyes again. He grabbed her wrist, plucking the candy from her fingers with his mouth, chomping it down quickly.

"No fair!" Sophie squealed, jumping out of her chair.

David laughed and grabbed her shoulders, pulling her across his lap to steal a teasing kiss. Setting her back on her feet he watched as her eyes slowly fluttered open.

"Wow. That is good." She said licking her lips.

"Don't sound so surprised or you'll bruise my ego."

"You could stand to be taken down a few pegs." Sophie said, not backing away.

David smiled looking into those eyes. He liked the color they were right now. Bright, shining blue, a little glassy from the kiss. He'd done that. "Now do I get my favor?"

Sophie's hands rested on her generous hips, reminding him of what was hidden beneath the sweats she wore. "I'm still mad at you."

"I brought chocolate."

"Sugar to cure the sexual frustration you left me with last night? Too little too late."

He laughed out loud. Leaning into her, he whispered. "If I had gotten out of the car we never would have made it up the stairs."

"You're all talk." Sophie leaned closer and grabbed his tie. "You look nice today. Very nice."

"Sophie," David warned as she pulled him closer.

"David," she taunted.

"Aren't you even curious what I want?"

"Unless it's me, I really don't care." She pressed her forehead to his.

He chuckled. "Wanting you is not a problem we have. But I need your help."

"With your missing million?"

His posture straightened. "It's a million? Are you sure?"

"Yes and no. In that order."

"Damn." David ground out, rubbing his palms on his thighs. He knew that profits weren't as high as they should be, but *that* much money? How had he let it get past him? "You'll help?"

"Actually I'd love to. I can't prove anything, but I could point you in the right direction. For a price." Her hands rested on top of his.

"Can you come in tomorrow? It will be easier on a Saturday. I don't want a lot of questions from the staff until I know what I am dealing with." *And whom.*

Sophie sat across from David at his desk as he furiously plugged away at his computer, printing the reports she had listed, leaving her to ponder the two pictures that sat beside his computer. They were the only personal effects in the huge office which was barely decorated in glass, chrome and leather.

She looked at the snapshot on his desk of two little boys standing in front of a tent. From the way it was sloping, she guessed they'd put it up themselves. Even with the faded color of the photo Sophie recognized Craig's fire-red hair.

"I didn't realize you and Craig had been friends so long."

"Yeah, since second grade. We were neighbors." He answered without looking up.

She studied the picture closer. The brown-eyed little boy grinned proudly up at her, his face rounder and softer than she would have guessed. "You've always been tall." She set the picture back on his desk next to a snapshot of a little girl with white-blond pigtails.

"Thank you for not mentioning I was fat."

"What?" she asked, eyeing the picture again. "You weren't fat. Maybe it's standing next to Craig that makes you think that. I guess he was always a toothpick." He was round, but he was what, eight years old? Kids' bodies weren't supposed to be chiseled like his was now.

"Yeah, and a bully magnet. Guys were always trying to snap him like a twig." He spun around, whipping papers off the laser printer and sorting them.

"You protected him?"

"You don't mess with bulk like that," he said with a sad chuckle. "We helped each other."

"Oh, no. Did he start telling you what to eat back then?" she asked, attempting levity.

He laughed, loud and long and full. She loved making him laugh.

"No, not until high school when we decided to go into bodybuilding like my dad. He read everything about bodybuilding, and we worked out all the time. It worked for me, but the poor guy has never been able to gain an ounce."

She leaned closer. "Bastard," she said, eliciting another peal of laughter from him. She loved the way he sounded when he laughed.

"Craig can't help it, trust me. I've seen him try." He looked up and caught her. She wasn't watching him, she was ogling. She brought a hand to her mouth, checking for drool. She was relieved to find she hadn't embarrassed herself that much.

"Here is the last round of statements." He broke their eye contact abruptly. "You can look at them in here, or I could get a conference room for you."

"No, here is good. Unless it would disturb you." She had to give him an out, though the only reason she was here was to share air with the man.

"No, of course not. Besides, you'll probably have questions."

"Right," she said, pulling the folders toward herself. She just prayed she could find something that would help him. Something that might mean she would have to spend more time here, near him, looking deeper. "You still haven't told me what made you suspect money was missing in the first place."

"Do you need to know?" he asked, his face tense, almost pained.

"Not if you don't want to tell me." She began looking through the reports. It wasn't long before she was lost, the accounts and amounts coming alive in her brain. She liked chasing the numbers around, trying to catch a thief. Sometime between the January and September reports David had actually left the room. Sophie didn't even notice until he walked through his office door, handing her a bottle of water.

"Thanks," she said, accepting the water. She finished her notes, opened the bottle and drained it.

David chuckled. "I thought so."

"Excuse me?"

"You were thirsty."

"Oh yeah, I guess I was."

"How's it going?"

"I don't suppose you'd let me into your network?"

"Have at it." David offered, booting up the program. "How much longer?"

"Depends, why?" Her eyes narrowed as she looked at his face. "I warn you. If you say you have a date, I can't be held accountable for my actions."

He smiled. "I'm hungry."

She rolled her eyes. "You're always hungry."

"Sophie, we've been here for six hours and all I've been able to find is stale pretzels."

"Oh." Sophie checked the time on the bottom of David's computer. Two eighteen. Where had the time gone? "You do know that I'm doing an extremely accelerated search, that usually I would spend months documenting things before I'd get this far?"

He nodded. "Of course. How about if I order a pizza? Do you like Pizzicato?"

Sophie shrugged as the spreadsheets began to dance in front of her. "Hot Lips is better."

"Sophie, you promised no kissing until after."

"Hot Lips Pizza, you pervert. I thought you actually lived in this town. Pizzicato is too gourmet for me, Hot Lips is more New York. They have a store right by the university so I got hooked. They also have one in the Pearl District, way too close to Working It Out." She smiled and looked up at his confused expression. "Whatever you want."

"What's good?"

"The brownies."

"The delivery driver had one of those electric cars," David said, setting the pizza box on the coffee table in his office. The smell of garlic and melted cheese wafted to her nose as he opened the box.

Sophie turned from the printer and smiled. "Maybe that's what I should get."

David shrugged as he started to inhale the pizza. Half Veggie Nirvana no olives, half Omnivore Bliss. "You should get something you're willing to park."

"I know. The van was going to waste so I donated it to a family at my parents' church." Sophie returned to what she'd found, not wanting to hear another lecture on trade-in value like she had gotten from Craig and Daphne.

As good as it felt to be tracking down missing debits again, Sophie never missed this part of the process. No one liked to get bad news, and considering what she was about to say, he really wasn't going to like it. She wondered if it would be easier coming from her, or if he might blame her for finding it.

She shook her head, reminding herself he'd be fair. Most of what she found was purely circumstantial. Hopefully he would put his anger on what she'd found, instead of on her.

"How are you not hungry? You've been working all day."

"One track mind." She forced a smile as she crossed the room. She didn't want to eat, she just wanted to get this over with.

"David, what tipped you off?" She perched on the end of the sofa, watching as he wiped his hands on a paper napkin.

"She bought another house."

Sophie arched a brow. "She?"

"Her third this year. And she went on and on about return on investment and not having to finance. I knew she was into him for the money, but I thought it was his money, not the company's she was after."

"David, she?"

"Tessa, my father's wife. Fifth wife. The same woman who sued him for sexual harassment two years ago. She's a real piece of work. Blackmailed him into marrying her, and now I guess he's trying to make a go of it. I knew she was bad news from the beginning."

Sophie tried to wrap her head around that angle. It was possible she was wrong in her suspicions, but highly unlikely. "What kind of clearance does she have?"

"She's his assistant. I'm sure he's given her carte blanche."

"Does your assistant have that kind of clearance?"

"I'm not married to my assistants."

"What did she do before?"

"Before she became my father's personal vampire? She was an aerobics instructor."

Sophie winced. "Does she have a background in finance? Because the transactions were very complicated."

"You don't think it's her."

"I could be wrong." Sophie handed David her notes.

He looked into her eyes. "Just tell me."

Sophie took a deep breath. Should she sugar coat or go for the jugular? She dove right in. "There are only two people who have clearance on all the accounts involved. One of them is you."

David closed his eyes and slumped back against the couch. "My father?"

"Lance has been very careful. As far as I can tell, he didn't start until April. He's siphoned off profits during transfers, so no one club has been affected, just the company overall. Which is how it's been overlooked. The money went first to the capital account, then into a personal account."

"Can you hide it?" His voice was barely audible.

"Yes." She heard herself say, surprised how quickly she answered. Cooking the books went against everything she'd learned, but it was David's money that was being lost and if he didn't want to shine a light on the infraction, she couldn't either.

He inhaled loudly. "How much?"

"2.6 million."

David opened his eyes wide as he sat bolt upright. "Since April?"

Sophie nodded.

David sunk his head into his hands. "How did I not notice that?"

Sophie knelt beside him and placed a hand on his knee. "You did notice. SGI is still turning a very healthy profit. The only alarms going off were in your head. And each transaction is for a small amount of money, given the size of the company. They've just added up."

He raised his face, resting his chin on his hands. "You're sure?"

"No," she answered honestly. "I'm just telling you what I see at a first look. If you bring a team in they may find less, they may find more. Whether or not they could prove it's him? There's no way to know right now."

His smile was forced and weak. "Thank you."

"You're welcome." She stared into his eyes, wishing Hallmark had a card for something like this.

Chapter Seven

Sophie stared out at the room full of women stretched out on their backs, all breathing in sync. How was it she could relax twenty women into near trance, yet she was so tense her neck felt it might snap?

"Feel your breath as it fills your solar plexus." Lucky for her she was able to operate on autopilot.

She'd been wound up like this ever since David dropped her off on Saturday night. After a few hours of creative accounting he'd driven her home in silence. He'd walked her to the door, let her hug him, kissed her on the forehead and driven away.

Sophie wanted to call him, but didn't have a clue what to say. It was hard to try and find a bright side, especially since she didn't know much about David's relationship with his father. If only she knew him better.

It was a tough blow to her master plan. She had decided to make a play for him. Give it her all and try and live the fantasy. She'd always regretted not trying to dance with him at Daphne's wedding. No more regrets.

She'd been throwing herself at him as best she knew how. He'd been deflecting her less and less, so that was progress. But in the wake of such seriousness their fun banter seemed deflated. Finally making love to the man of her dreams seemed pretty shallow given his present situation. She wanted him, but what was that to him really?

Women wanted him. He'd proved as much to her last week when he'd gone through class with his shirt off. In front of their husbands, the other women had openly ogled him. She'd tried to play it off, not wanting him to see how insane it made her. It wouldn't have been so bad if they were really together, if they shared more than her fantasies.

That fantasy was slipping, evolving into something different. She was beginning to think of David as more than the dating rules she and Daphne had laughed over so many times. He was more than a commanding physical presence, so handsome and charming people simply melted in his company. There was a kindness in his eyes that made her ache. A quick wit that made her hang on his every word. And when he touched her, he found nerve endings she didn't even know existed. She knew she had to be careful because he was rapidly becoming more than just a fantasy.

Sophie dropped down on the platform at the front of her classroom as the students filed out. Maybe she would call to ask if there was anything else she could do for him. Accounting-wise, of course. It would be too insensitive to proposition him right now. Even though all she wanted to do was wrap her arms around him and make him forget everyone who'd ever wronged him.

With him, she forgot that she didn't really know how. She was completely obsessed with sex because of the class. She had read more sex manuals and erotica in the last few months than most women did in a lifetime. It caused a major case of sex on the brain, and the knowledge gave her a confidence she'd never known.

Sophie was waiting for that wall of nerves she always hit with men. The point at which her stomach clenched, guilt and fear squelched all arousal, and she called the whole thing off. The guilt was always a strange sense of betrayal of her fantasies of David. Now she wasn't sure if the fear was gone, or her attraction to him was just so high it overrode every other emotion, leaving her completely at his mercy.

Not that it mattered, because he was dead set on doing the right thing. Sophie actually respected him for it. She liked him more for turning her down. This was one twisted relationship.

Shaking her head, Sophie followed the last of her students out the door. She had an hour until her next class. She hoped she'd be able to pay more attention. If she could only focus on something besides David, she'd be just fine.

Before she even made it to her office three employees gathered around her. "Daphne's been calling since we opened. She says she has to see you."

Sophie's stomach plummeted. "Is she okay?"

Laurie, the masseuse, roared with laughter. "You'd better get over there. But first you might need to prepare your defense."

"My defense?" Sophie looked down at the newspaper shoved into her hands. "The Living Section? Are we in here?"

"Not we honey, you."

"Me?" Why should she be in the Living Section? "Am I a fashion don't or something?" Sophie tried to open the pages but Laurie's hands stopped her.

"On the front, honey, Colin's Column."

"What's that?" Sophie asked as her eyes scanned the page. A side bar on the right side caught her attention. A thumbnail picture of a man she guessed was Colin, followed by five tiny headlined blurbs, leading with *Sensual Merger*.

Strong Gyms Inc. CEO David Strong has been lending his services to competitor Working It Out for their Sensational Sex Couples Workout Series. Is diehard playboy Strong looking to expand his company with a tempting acquisition, or just hoping to merge with the rival club's co-owner?

Sophie's temperature rose as she hissed out the breath she was holding. As if she needed this. David had enough to deal with, and her sister did not need anything else raising her too-high blood pressure. Sometimes this town was just too damned small.

He should have called. But the only thing David could trust himself to say to her the last few days was thank you. He'd already said that, so there was no need to push his luck. He couldn't risk leading her on. She was already testing his resolve. If she suspected he felt more than simple gratitude, he didn't think she'd ever give up her pursuit of him.

He couldn't have gotten through this mess without her. Sophie had swept into his life at just the right time, helping him keep this mess with his father entirely private. Which made her worth her weight in platinum. His father's embezzlement would look bad enough, but he'd only been in place as CEO for two years. There were board members still skeptical someone in their thirties could run a billion dollar corporation. They didn't need any more ammunition.

Sophie had helped him more than simply finding where the money went, she helped cover it up. David had expected her to say no, would have bet money on it. But she dove in, cleaning up his father's unethical transactions, reframing them as capital draws, essentially personal loans. To fix the problem David repaid the loans, making it look as though he knew all along about his father's need for cash.

It had been her idea, a way to clean the books instead of cook them. Not a lie, just a revision of history. Without her, he would have had to let the entire executive board in on his father's disgrace. They would have brought in an accounting firm and the publicity that provided, publicly humiliating his father. Sophie saved him all that.

David's feelings for Sophie had come on so gradually he hadn't even noticed them building. It was as if he'd always felt for her the way he did now. As if she was the only person in the world he'd ever truly trusted, ever really liked completely.

He liked everything about her. Every move she made had him smiling. He didn't trust himself around her with his newfound knowledge. It had been killing him to hold back before, now he didn't know what to do.

He wasn't sure what to do next in his personal life, so he focused on business. He met with his bankers. He practiced and reworded the speech he was going to give his father today. He did everything he could not to think of Sophie. But everything seemed to work back to her.

"We need to talk." Craig's voice jolted him from his revelry.

David looked up at his friend's tight features. Something was wrong. Before he could formulate a question Craig dropped a section of newspaper on the desk in front of him.

"Tell me nothing's going on. Tell me I can trust you. Tell me you're not sleeping with her."

"I'm not sleeping with her." Sophie's "omit, don't lie" theory worked like a charm. Craig's face softened and he plopped into a chair.

"That's good, because Daphne nearly killed me when she read that this morning."

"What?"

"Colin's Column. The gossip guy."

David scanned the paper until he found his name. "Diehard playboy? That stings."

"Truth hurts, buddy. Daphne isn't happy. She wants me to take over the classes."

"No." David realized he'd said it too quickly, but there was nothing that could be done. He was not going to let Craig get his hands all over Sophie, no matter who he was married to.

"Oh, yeah. Turns out, Sophie's had a crush on you for years."

"We can't let this guy's little innuendo change our lives." Wait a minute, Sophie had a crush? On him? For years?

Craig arched his brows, then softened. He seemed to be buying it. "I know. It's not like you're actually sleeping together. Still, Daphne doesn't like the attention."

"No, Daphne doesn't like *me*. Free publicity is good for business."

Sophie sauntered into her sister's bedroom, finding Daphne propped up on tawny pillows with the day's newspaper spread in front of her. Her long blond hair was rolled haphazardly into a clip.

"Why didn't you tell me?"

Without a word, Sophie removed the blood pressure monitor from the nightstand drawer. She effortlessly strapped it on her sister's wrist. Sophie smiled at how comfortably she fell back into her roll as caretaker. As the machine beeped a healthy reading, Sophie joined her sister on the bed.

"This is so decadent. Do you read the entire paper every day?"

81

"Don't try to change the subject."

"I think that's great. Do you read out loud? I read that he can hear you now." Sophie beamed, her mind hyper vigilant. She didn't want to upset her sister, but she didn't want to discuss David with her either.

"What other things are you and Craig keeping from me?"

Sophie rolled her eyes and looked toward the television. "You've started watching soap operas and talk shows haven't you? They've made you completely paranoid."

"I'm very firmly planted in reality. You've been teaching a very provocative class with a man whose reputation even *The Oregonian* knows. And neither you nor my husband saw fit to mention that it was going on."

Sophie had nowhere to go. There was nothing to deny.

Daphne took her silence as an invitation to continue. "Imagine my surprise to find out he's been coming to my club, bringing you gifts. He's trying to take advantage of the situation, isn't he?"

If only he would. "No, he isn't." *Unfortunately.* Daphne must have grilled the staff and found out about David's visit. *His only visit.* "I looked over some accounting reports for him. He brought chocolate as a bribe."

"Sophie please, the man is a total womanizer. I've never seen him with the same woman twice and I've known him for ten years. He has an entire floor of accountants. Why would he need your accounting advice?"

Sophie took a deep breath. How did she get out of this? The truth would betray David, but lying would betray herself. Complete redirection was the only way. "I'm flattered you think he'd be interested in me."

Daphne narrowed her eyes into slits. Sophie held her gaze. *Don't blink,* she chanted in her head.

"You're right, you aren't his type. But still, you should be careful. He probably thinks you are using the class to come on to him. His ego is enormous. Craig can help you finish the class."

"No." *Too fast,* the alarm in her head warned. *Diversionary tactics needed.* "Craig is a wreck worrying about you and the baby. He'll only go in to work when I come over. If both he and I are at the club he won't be able to concentrate and he'll be totally useless."

Sophie began to feel the adrenaline course through her veins as she neared panic. She'd already solved David's accounting debacle. Without the class she had no tie to him, no excuse to see him. Daphne could not take him from her.

Daphne pursed her lips together and stared hard. "You have to be on your guard, Sophie. I know you've had a thing for his body forever, but he is not the kind of person you should be getting involved with. He can't commit. Women are disposable to him. You are much too sensitive to be treated so harshly."

Sophie shook her head. David could commit. He was committed to his friendship with Craig, committed to honoring his father no matter his indiscretions. He'd just never found a woman to commit to. *Yet.* Sophie smiled at her sister.

"Daphne, you make it sound as if he committed a crime. He's just helping out with a class as a favor for Craig while you are on bed rest. Cut him a break for once." Sophie got up from the bed. It was hard to bite her tongue, even harder not to defend David.

"Oh, not you too. His interest in the classes is just to get his greedy paws on my club. He's wanted it ever since I opened."

Sophie felt her temperature rise again. *My club?* The one Sophie owned seventy percent of? Her blood was now on an even simmer. She had to get out of here before she reached full boil. "Let me worry about him. You just focus on staying healthy and picking out names." Sophie pressed a button on the monitor and waited for another reading.

"Sophie, you have to be careful. It is one thing to fantasize about him, it's another to try and play his game. He can't give you the security you need."

"I'd consider myself warned if I had anything to worry about." The reading was four points higher, but still okay. "I doubt he even looks down far enough to notice me." She smiled as her sister laughed. Self-deprecating humor. Had she really been reduced to this?

David stretched his hands over his head and tried to take deep breaths. Those long calming breaths Sophie was always going on about in class. If only he could breathe in serenity and exhale stress right now. If only he could concentrate on anything at all.

His thoughts were scattered, flitting between his father's betrayal and Sophie's loyalty. They'd both stunned him in such different ways. David wanted to stop thinking about the old man. Which was why he was waiting for him now, to get the whole sordid thing over with. Then he'd be able to concentrate on Sophie and whatever was happening between them. On just what he wanted from her, what they wanted from each other.

"You wanted to see me, son?" The warm voice cut through his thoughts. He didn't need to turn around to know it was his father, the man he resembled so closely one of his stepmothers had nicknamed David the clone.

He'd spent the first half of his life wanting to be just like Lance Strong, and the second half wanting to be nothing like him. *As if he had a choice.* David's stomach sank. If he was just like him, what did that mean for Sophie? He shook his head hard to dispel the thought and picked up the folder from his desk. Handing it to his father he let out the breath he forgot he held.

"What's this?" Lance asked, flipping through the file. The two men were exactly the same height, their weight within five pounds of one another. Lance's hair was graying, though his hairstylist kept most people from noticing. The only telling differences were the deep lines on Lance's face and the color of their eyes. Lance's steely blue gaze locked on to David's face.

"A buy out agreement." David answered, thankful he had prepared everything in advance.

"For what?" Lance asked, still smiling.

"My company, the one you've been milking." There. He'd said it. It was out. Game on, old man.

Lance didn't even flinch at the accusation. Instead he kept his face loose as he read over the pages in the folder. "I assume you've been generous."

"Always." David fought his quickening breath. No denial? No apology?

"How much did you find?"

"You've embezzled 2.6 million since April." David struggled to control his breathing. How could he just stand there so calmly?

"Borrowed." Lance tapped a finger against the pale paper. "This says a shareholder's draw."

"Now that I know about it, it is," David snorted.

"I'm impressed." Lance smiled wide, as if there was something happy and warm about this moment. "You found it all."

"I wasn't looking to impress you. Let's just make that clear."

"How will this affect the prenup?"

David closed his eyes and drew in a wistful breath. If this weren't his father, he'd be swinging by now. "The majority of your assets at the time of the marriage were hidden within the company infrastructure. This agreement pays you for your remaining share of the company, minus the draws you have already taken. It will be an arguable issue at a divorce hearing. The prenup set an alimony payout, but she could try for more. But this agreement also states you won't be investigated for any financial issues that may come up."

Lance shook his head slowly as he walked toward David's desk and set down the folder. "Did you finance my buyout personally or is it through the company?"

It was none of his damned business after what he'd done. "Personally."

"Good, good." Lance picked up the folder again. "Where exactly do I sign?"

"Dad, you should have a lawyer go over it. Retain counsel who you can trust with the facts of the situation. Then, we'll—"

"I didn't put you through law school so you could give me some get a lawyer bullshit. I'm sure it's fair. Let's get this over with so we can go grab some lunch."

"We? I've completely lost my appetite." David didn't want to share anything with this man. "This is really how you're going to handle this?"

"Were you looking for a denial or an apology?" Lance asked, the wild scratch of pen on paper echoing through the room.

He didn't know. He'd played this conversation in his head a hundred different ways, but not this one. He wanted to hear that it was all Tessa the Terrible, that the old man needed help exorcising her from his life. "I deserve an explanation."

Lance shrugged. Walking to the couch he sat down and slumped back into the cushions, loosened his tie and then closed his eyes. "Why does anyone do anything? Love and money. I'm in love with a woman who spends too damned much money."

Brutal honesty, but it still didn't add up. "You make a lot of money. A lot."

Lance looked at David and shot him one of the trademarked Strong grins. "I thought so, but I have alimony payments and a young wife with a penchant for real estate." He rolled his eyes and leaned his head back. "I assume the press release will say I retired?"

David nodded. "Voluntarily. I'm not bringing this before the board. It's a personal buy out so there is no need for their approval."

Lance smiled. "You'll have such a majority you won't have to vote on hardly anything. Majority ownership is what you've always worked for."

The man actually looked proud. David felt a tug from the part of him that still lived for that look. "You could have told me. I would have helped if you needed money."

Lance dismissed the sentiment with a wave of his hand. "I asked you to buy me out, twice. You refused so long as I was married to Tessa. Who else knows?"

"Just me, and a friend of mine. She reviewed the books as a favor. No one else has to know."

Lance's eyes opened wide as he sat up straight. "A female friend you let see the financial statements? I didn't know you were serious about anyone."

David suddenly felt sixteen again. "I'm not. She's a forensic accountant, or was anyway. We're just friends."

"Was? What does she do now?"

"She's a yoga instructor. We're not talking about me."

"Isn't that hypocritical?" Lance said with a smirk. "You issue a blanket rule that I cannot date employees, but you take up with one?"

"Sophie doesn't work here. She has her own club."

Lance leaned forward, his blue eyes sparkling. "The girl from the gossip column. I want to meet her. Call her, invite her to lunch."

"No." He folded his arms across his chest. There was no way. "She doesn't need to be put in the middle of this mess you made."

Again, Lance waved his hand through the air. "You can't hide her away forever. Has Kelly met her?"

David would always admire the way Lance could do that, deflect conversations from himself. "Dad, you're making this into something it's not. She's a friend. I don't do relationships."

"Friendship is a relationship my boy." Lance's pearly white grin gleamed beneath the fluorescent lights.

"You of all people know what I mean." David was flabbergasted. The man was stealing from the family company, couldn't hold on to a wife and wanted to give him advice? "What's that supposed to mean?"

"I'm not wired for long-term relationships. I've learned from you they can be very expensive. You know alimony, child support, embezzlement." It was low, but he deserved it. It was the truth. He'd been stealing from the company for crying out loud.

Lance put his hands on his knees and his shoulders slumped. "And here I was thinking there was hope for you now that you got what you've always wanted. I'm disappointed."

"I don't think you get to be disappointed today. You only get to be relieved I was able to save your butt from jail time by catching on to your scam before anyone else, and covering it up. A cover up that could very well backfire on me someday."

Lance shrugged. "There's nothing illegal about a shareholder withdrawal. It's only money, David. I'd much rather my son wasn't such a cynic."

David shook his head. "I am what you made me, Dad."

Looking at Lance had always been like looking into a time machine for David. Most of his life he didn't just want to be like his father, he wanted to be him. A man who it turned out could steal and not even feel any remorse.

"Me? I am forever an optimist."

"With five marriages in your wake."

A soft chuckle breathed its way out of Lance's nose. He stood, walking to where David leaned against his desk.

"You've never been in love."

David narrowed his dark angry eyes to his father's. "Excuse me?"

"Love. It is an incredible sensation. An amazing gift. All consuming and yet as light as a whisper. Once you've been in love you don't ever want to find yourself out of it."

"If love means robbing your kids I'll stay away from it, thank you very much."

"I'm not saying I went about it the right way, but robbery is a bit harsh. I never jeopardized the company, just got a little creative with the accounting. Love can make you a tad blind to reality."

David rolled his eyes. How could someone have so little remorse? His anger bubbled inside. "Is this the way you handled your divorces too? Just a 'too bad' and a few flimsy excuses? If that's your idea of love it's no wonder you can't stay married." David flinched at the sound of his own words. He knew he'd gone too far.

Lance shook his head furiously, swallowed hard and stared at the floor. "I never married thinking I would get divorced. I loved your mother so hard and so desperately that when she died I thought I would never marry again. But I wanted you to have a mother. And Karen was great, but once she had Kelly I couldn't stand the way she treated you differently."

"Don't blame all your divorces on me." One he shouldered the blame for, that was more than enough.

Lance met his gaze. "I'm not. I just want to make you understand. I was loved once, in a way that makes it hard for any other woman to measure up."

"And don't blame my mother either. She probably wouldn't have fared any better than the rest of your brides."

David felt the adrenaline shoot into his veins as his father crossed the office in two long strides and placed both hands on his shoulders. "If your mother was alive I would still be married to her today. If you don't believe anything else about me, you can believe that." Lance loosened his grip, but didn't let go.

"Life is short, my boy. One day I had every man's dream, and the next moment it was every man's nightmare. A dead wife and a crying child who needs you so much you can't just end it all and go with her. I would have if not for you.

"I know I've failed you in so many of ways. If I've scared you into not allowing yourself to love I will never forgive myself. That brief moment of being loved is worth any pain you have to endure at losing it."

David felt a tempest of emotions as his father wrapped his arms around him. His father hadn't hugged him in years. College graduation maybe? And where was all this coming from? Some sort of emotional penance for firing him? "Dad? Are you okay?"

"Yeah." Lance said, pulling away and wiping his eyes. "I'm going to go home and make love to my wife. Let me know when my retirement party is."

Chapter Eight

"Your boyfriend is weird," Laurie announced as Sophie followed the last of her students out of the mat Pilates class.

Eyeing the cello-wrapped tower of citrus on the reception desk, Sophie felt her cheeks tighten in a grin. Oranges.

"He's not my boyfriend," she forced herself to say. Someone here had told Daphne about his earlier visit, no doubt they'd tell her about this. "If you know they're from him there must be a card." Which they'd read. Nothing was sacred around here.

Laurie handed her the tiny white envelope. Sophie took a deep breath, soaking in the moment. A tiny triumph, he was thinking about her. Slipping the card out of its sleeve she read:

Sorry about Colin's Column.

It won't happen again.

David

A little disappointing, but he wasn't the type to wax poetic. Maybe he knew Daphne was suspicious and he didn't want to upset her further. Sophie shook her head, her smile fading. She was reading too much into this. It was fruit, not flowers.

Slicing the plastic with scissors, she unwrapped her gift and plucked an orange from the pile. "Help yourselves, ladies," Sophie offered, marching back to her office.

What she wouldn't give for the message behind a dozen long stemmed red roses, or a bunch of grapes. There was something to be said for instant gratification.

"Where are we going?" Sophie asked, turning in her seat to face him.

"To get your thank you present." David downshifted as they hit traffic. He was trying hard not to look smug. She was going to love it. It was exactly what she needed, what she wanted.

"Give me a hint." Sophie slid out of her cross trainers and tucked her legs beneath her.

As traffic came to a halt he turned and unable to stop himself reached out for her, running a finger down her face. He felt her whole body shudder from head to toe, making his spine tingle. "No." Surprised by his reaction, he turned back around, placing both hands firmly on the wheel. How did she do that to him?

"I can think of a really great present and we don't have to go anywhere to get it."

If only. "No."

From the corner of his eye he saw her teasing smile. "Come on, play fair. Twenty questions?"

No way would she guess. "I thought most women liked surprises."

"I keep telling you I'm not most women. You can't control everything. Just a hint, please."

He inched the car forward, remembering just why he lived on the waterfront. Crossing any of the bridges joining the two sides of town was tedious. "Twenty questions."

She tucked a wayward curl behind her ear as her face suddenly got serious. "Animal, vegetable or mineral?"

"Mineral. That counts as three. You're supposed to ask yes or no questions."

She stuck her tongue out at him. "Is it bigger than a breadbox?"

"Yes." David smiled as he watched her eyes widen, glistening with anticipation. Disappointment filled him as traffic began to move again. He would have to watch the road instead of her. Which was good, because they were friends, nothing more. His meeting with his father proved he couldn't be more than that to her. It just wasn't in his DNA to be the kind of man she deserved to be with. If he indulged with Sophie, she'd wind up hurt and he'd never forgive himself. This was it, his thank you and his goodbye.

"What could we possibly need that's bigger than a breadbox?" He heard her whisper to herself. His hands tensed at the "we". This wasn't leading her on, it was thanking her for her help, he reminded himself.

"Can you play with it?"

"I suppose so."

"Did you pick it out?"

"Yes, but I haven't seen it."

"How did you do that?"

"The internet is amazing, especially when you are too distracted to work."

"Oh. How did it go with your father?"

He couldn't think of anything but what kind of man his father was. And what that meant for Sophie if he tried to have more than a friendship with her. "Yes or no questions remember?"

"David, you know how I feel about your rules," she said, her voice taunting him.

"They don't apply to you."

"Finally you see it my way," she teased.

The silence stretched out as he weaved through traffic, crossing the river and continuing on. "I thought we were playing a game?"

"David, I've been trying to play with you for weeks. You keep turning me on and turning me down."

He groaned. "We're almost there. If you're going to guess you'd better hurry."

"I think I've figured you out."

He almost choked. "Really?"

"You only want a woman you can't have. The thrill of the chase is what does it for you. I've made it too easy."

"You haven't made anything easy, Sophie," he said, turning into the parking lot.

"Why are we at a car lot?" Sophie asked as she pushed on her shoes.

David slid out of the car. Two salesmen with matching greasy hairstyles attached themselves to David before he could answer.

"It's over here," he said as he broke free and propelled her forward.

"What is?" she asked as they made their way toward the tiny ruby red car, the color of her toenail polish.

"It's the Honda Civic Hybrid. You said you were thinking about electric. You can go six hundred miles without having to find a gas station."

She spun around, wrapping her arms around his waist and locking him into place. "You bought me a car?"

He nodded, throwing in a devilish grin for free.

She shook her head. "It's too much. I can't accept it."

"Yes you can. If I'd had to hire someone I would have spent much more. And it would have gotten very messy." He held up the key. "Say you're welcome and we're even."

"But you don't have to. Really, it's too much."

"Let someone be nice to you for a change, Sophie." He let go of the key and she instinctively caught it on the way down.

Giggling, she stepped back and reached for his hand. "Let's take it for a test drive."

"Go ahead," he smiled.

"Come with me." She tugged on his hand as she stepped closer to the car.

David laughed at her enthusiasm. He knew she'd love it. "Sophie, that car is as small as you. I'll never fit."

She looked him up and down as her face fell. It was the truth. He rarely fit in cars without having the seats retrofitted. "You want to buy me a car you don't fit in?" There was an edge to her voice he didn't recognize.

He shrugged. "It's what you want." The keys banged into his chest. She spun on her heel, marching back to his car.

"Sophie," he caught up to her as she pulled her backpack out. "What?"

She only glared at him as she began to walk away.

It was almost comical, her trying to walk away from him. Her short legs had three strides to his one. "What are you doing?"

"I'm going home," she huffed.

"Sophie, you can't walk home from here." He grabbed her arm and held her in place. When she tried to wrench away he tightened his grip.

"I don't want it," she said, pulling at his fingers.

"I'm getting that," he said, not letting her release herself. "Come back with me and I'll drive you home."

"I need some room right now, David," she said, still wrestling with his fingers. "Let go of me."

"You're not walking home from here. It's too far and it's not safe."

Her eyes morphed into a cold bluish gray beneath her squint. "We are three blocks from a MAX station. I'll take the train in."

He still held on.

"Let me go."

"No. I'll only let go if you let me take you home."

She stared hard at him, the battle of wills beginning. Only she broke much sooner than he'd expected, raising her hand to wipe her eyes as she looked away.

"You're reading too much into it, Sophie. I don't fit in almost any car unless I get the seats moved. And it's not for me, it's for you."

Sophie shrugged and hugged her knees tighter to her chest. She knew he was right, knew she was over analyzing the situation. But she just couldn't stop. She didn't want something he couldn't be a part of.

Somewhere along the way she'd crossed a line, no longer able to keep him solidly in her fantasies. She'd felt it as the lines blurred, but they were completely obliterated now. It was the reality of him that she was falling for, not the fantasy.

"Most women would be ecstatic to get a car. I thought you'd be over the moon."

"I'm not most women," she mumbled. She'd been excited, for one brief fleeting moment. Until she saw him arranging a life for her without him in it.

His poor car was taking a beating. David weaved the Corvette in and out of traffic as they made their way back across the river. Her neck ached from all the times he hit the brakes and downshifted quickly. She laid her forehead against her knees and tried to relax.

She tried to concentrate on her breathing. But all she could hear was his, slow and rough, angry. She nearly choked as she pulled oxygen into her lungs. She was being an ungrateful little brat and she knew it. A polite thank you would have been her normal reaction. She'd just expected more from him.

Not that he'd given her much reason to expect it. At every turn he was telling her there was nothing between them. But damn if that noble streak didn't make him even sexier. And the vulnerability she'd felt when she broke the news about the financial debacle. And those gifts—guessing her favorite chocolate truffle, remembering what she'd said about fruit, he even picked out the car because of some off-handed comment she'd made. He gave a woman hope without even meaning to.

Sophie turned her head and rested her cheek on her knees. She could just make out his profile backlit by the streetlights. His jaw was set so hard his teeth must ache.

"Thank you for the oranges." The meekness in her voice disappointed her. She was blowing this big time. This was fast becoming a situation she would regret later, but she didn't have a clue how to fix it.

"You're welcome," he said purposefully. "See, it's not too hard," he muttered under his breath.

"I didn't ask for you to buy me a car, David." She cursed the tears prickling her eyelids. She would not cry again.

"I was trying to say thank you. I never guessed it would turn into a disaster." He jerked the car sharply into the driveway of her apartment.

Sophie searched for a way to turn the whole thing around. He wouldn't look at her, keeping his hands on the steering wheel. Sophie swallowed hard, choking down something that felt like pride. "Come upstairs with me. I want to show you something."

"Not tonight. Let's just forget this whole thing happened."

"I just want you to see something. I want you to understand."

His head whipped around, his eyes pinning her in her seat. "Do you know how many women would love to get a car just for helping a friend out?"

He had no clue. "Then you'll have no problem getting rid of it." She snarled across the seat. Blood pounded in her ears. He just didn't get it. And from the way his hands were squeezing the life out of the steering wheel he had no intention of figuring it out. Sophie leaned over and twisted the keys from the ignition.

"Hey!" David swiped for the keys as she scrambled from the car.

Sophie took the stairs two at a time, hoping it might make up for his long-legged advantage. He'd proven earlier running from him was a logistical impossibility. Panting, she had her key in the lock when his hands came down on either side of her. "Give me the keys, Sophie."

Smiling wickedly she spun beneath him, holding out her keys. "You want to do the honors? "

"I'm not in the mood for games." Her stomach caught at the feel of his breath against her face, fast and shallow. If only he was breathing like that because of her, and not because he'd gone up the stairs in only three long strides.

Reaching her hand behind her Sophie turned the doorknob, swinging the door open. She caught David's hand as it slipped from the opening door and tugged him inside. "I just want to show you something, to explain."

She tugged him through the dark living room, past the kitchen into the hallway. She pulled him through another doorway and hit the lights.

The light from the lamps covered with red silk scarves on the bedside tables reflected off the full-length mirrors nailed to the wall. The room was completely taken up by an enormous bed. Two tiny bedside tables flanked it. The white down duvet and piles of pillows seemed to shimmer in the dim lighting.

David peered down at her, his eyebrows knit together. Before he could speak Sophie braced herself and pushed him as hard as she could. "Lie down."

Startled, he tumbled backwards. The only place to fall was on the bed. He scrambled up to his elbows. "Sophie," he hissed as she bounced on the bed beside him.

"This will be over much faster if you do as I say. Lie down," she commanded, scooting to the opposite side of the bed.

"Whatever game you're playing—"

Sophie shoved him down on the mattress, pulling his legs up onto it.

"There," Sophie said triumphantly. "See?"

David lay on his back against the pillows and crossed his arms across his chest.

"What is it I'm supposed to be seeing?" David's nostrils flared as he ground his teeth together.

Sophie rolled to her side and propped herself up on her elbow. "Comfortable?"

He turned his head and narrowed his eyes. "If I say yes, can I have my keys?"

"How are your feet?"

"What?" he asked, looking down to the bottom of the bed. She smiled as the wheels slowly turned in his head. He sat up, turning his head from side to side as he surveyed the bed. "Where did you get this?"

Sophie pulled her legs beneath her as she sat up. "Getting it in here was quite a task I assure you."

David lay down again and marveled. "I didn't know they made beds this long."

"They're in my backpack, the front pocket."

"What?" He wiggled his feet and smiled.

"Your keys."

David made no move to leave. Instead he closed his eyes. She lay down, propping herself on her elbow so she could watch him. Here. In the bed she dreamed of him in. She wanted to touch him, but didn't dare push her luck.

"I don't want anything you won't fit in." She whispered the words so as not to betray the tumble of emotions she felt.

"When did you get it?"

"Last year, after my mom died and I sold the house. It really helped my fantasy life. You wouldn't believe the limits a twin bed puts on a girl's dreams." She was babbling, definitely not sexy. Not when she finally had him in her bed.

"Is that when it started?" he said without opening his eyes.

Sophie was surprised his question didn't ruffle her. "What? My fantasies about you?"

She watched his Adam's apple bob as he swallowed hard. "Yeah."

"No, that goes way back. Back to when Daphne and Craig first started dating. He has always talked you up to her. I was sold, but Daphne...well, she doesn't like to share."

David laughed. Sophie hoped she saw him start to relax. "I became your fantasy and her nightmare."

Sophie lay back on the pillows. "I never thought of it like that. I just always thought we fit, like kindred spirits, you know."

"That's crazy. We're total opposites."

"Only physically. You know that family comes first. Think about what happened with your dad. Your instinct was to protect him before anything else. You take care of everyone before yourself. I get that, hell I do that. Not everyone respects obligation."

"You keep coming on to me because you see a chance to live out your fantasies." Once he spoke the words he turned his head to face her. They were in such an intimate position anything but honesty was unthinkable.

"At first. But it's more than that now. I'm comfortable with you in a way that I can't even explain. I feel safe and it makes me bolder. It gives me the courage to say things I'd usually stifle, to do things I normally wouldn't dare."

"Is it me, or your fantasy of me?"

She moved closer, pressing her forehead to his. "It's definitely you." Sophie closed her eyes. Slowly, she focused her breathing to match his. She was almost dizzy from the masculine pheromones permeating the air, her lungs, her bed.

"I don't want to hurt you. We can't do this, Sophie," he whispered. "I don't want the things you want. I don't want you to regret it."

"I'll regret never making love to you."

"I'm not getting married Sophie, I'm not having kids. I'm not cut out for it. You'll be great at it. You've waited this long, you should wait for that."

Sophie pursed her lips together as she weighed his words. "I waited for you."

She hated the tremor in her voice, hated the weakness of the admission. But oh, how she loved his reaction.

David's body responded instinctively to her words. Sophie had laid herself open before him in a painfully honest way. He moved closer, finding her mouth and taking it. He didn't have the words to tell her how she moved him, how he was finding it impossible to think of anything but her, how he actually understood why she had gotten so crazy about the car.

He knew kissing her would cure the ache in his gut that ate at him whenever she wasn't around. He claimed her lips with a desperate demand. Her mouth answered back, fulfilling his needs, making him groan as she rolled closer. She yielded beside him, opening to welcome him with a tender, silken demand of her own.

Rational thought was extinguished by a torrential need to possess that he didn't recognize. An entirely new sensation he found both unknown and completely irresistible. Sophie's breaths were as uneven as his, her mouth unrelenting, her kiss urgent. He swallowed her pleading sigh and realized she was no more in control of the moment than he was.

If they both lost control he knew exactly where this would lead. He tried to stay in check. One of them needed to be able to think, to rise above such carnal desires. Trying to pull away he rolled onto his back. He hadn't meant to encourage her, but she rolled right along with him. Now she was on top of him, her dark curls falling forward, framing them in their own world.

They were both adults, obviously consenting. She was warm and willing, and with her legs straddling him she had to know just how much he wanted her. The groan erupting from his own throat startled him to reality.

He cursed every part of his psyche that couldn't just be the man she wanted him to be. How wonderful life could be if he could just trust himself to be who she thought he was. But he wasn't, and he wouldn't. He wouldn't take from her more than he could give back. He knew that as well as he knew he couldn't walk away. Not now.

He just needed to push her further, to make her call it off. It would be easier on her if it were her idea.

"Show me," he whispered, trying to get a handle on his ragged vocal chords.

"What?" Sophie breathed against his mouth.

"Show me what you like." In answer, she ground her hips against him, teasing the ridge of him nestled beneath her.

He groaned again, raising a hand to her hip to still her. He would never be able to hold back if she did that even once more. "No." He brushed the hair from her eyes as she stared down at him. "Show me."

Her eyes sparked with realization. "You want me to...while you... I don't think so."

"Please?" he asked, kissing her softly as her eyes drifted close. She'd never be able to, and he'd be able to walk away without hurting her.

"What?" They fluttered open again, dark in their desire. "Why?"

"So I can see what you like." He tried to focus, to calm himself. Pushing her past her boundaries had to work, he couldn't think of another way. Especially since he was having a hard time remembering why what she wanted would be a bad thing. He rolled her onto her back and sat up.

Sophie propped herself up on her elbows and stared at him. "What are you going to do?"

"Watch you." He scooted to the foot of the bed, wishing the room were big enough for a chair. He needed distance.

"So you like to watch?" she teased, her eyes gleaming. "From way down there?" She wiggled her foot at him.

His grin faltered. She was considering it. If she went through with it, there was no other way out. "I can't promise I'll stay here."

She frowned, her bravado failing. "I don't think I can."

"Why not?"

"You want me to make a list?"

"I already told you what I want you to do," he winked.

She sighed in defeat. "I don't think I can relax with you watching me. And if I can't relax, I won't be able to climax."

"Then we could never sleep together."

"No!" She sprung up to sitting. "I mean, that's different. We'd both be naked, both be vulnerable. This way it's just me."

He bit his cheek, pondering which argument to use.

"Maybe if you were naked."

"What?" he choked, noticing the gleam in her eye.

"To provide visual stimulation. And that way you'll be ready to join in."

David's breath caught. A trap. And he'd run right into it.

David had severely underestimated his ability to hold back. He had to remind himself to breathe. His mouth was completely dry, his stomach in knots. He was actually glad he had compromised and taken his shirt off because he was sweating. He was sitting on his goddamn hands to keep from touching her.

Thankfully, Sophie had closed her eyes. When she'd been watching him he had wanted to scream, groan, devour her. What had he been thinking? Asking her to do what he had been doing every night in his dreams since that first class? And that was all before he'd seen her naked.

He knew she was beautiful, had felt those amazing curves for himself. But always through the safety of clothes. Bare, the woman was downright lethal. And those hands, those tiny hands that wielded so much power.

Her strokes were light and feathery at first, tracing up and down while her other hand kneaded one ripe breast. Her breasts had felt amazing pressed against him through clothes, but in person they were absolutely perfect.

This was such a bad idea. He should end it now while he still had some blood left in his brain. But he couldn't move, mesmerized by the show. Then she dipped a finger inside, spreading the glistening liquid she found across her inner lips she increased the pressure and moved from side to side. He didn't know where to look as she concentrated on her nipple, pulling at the tip while she gnawed her bottom lip.

She picked up speed, the circles of her fingers getting smaller and smaller until they focused on the tight bud of her sex. Her shallow breaths grew rapid as she neared her peak. She rolled her hips, finding all the best positions to intensify her pleasure

Her head fell back, lips parted. He didn't even want to breathe, didn't want to hear any sound but the gasping of her breath. "Amazing," he whispered, unsure if he'd said it aloud.

She smiled. "If you liked that, you should see me with BOB."

He stiffened, lurching forward as if he might be sick. Exactly the reaction she was hoping for.

Sophie placed her still wet fingers against his arm, shooting him a devilish grin. "BOB, battery operated boyfriend. You wouldn't believe how many batteries I've gone through lately."

His shoulders relaxed as he finally let out a ragged breath. David lifted her hand from his arm, brought her fingers to his mouth and inhaled deep. She trembled as if the air he breathed was coming directly from her own lungs.

She was amazed by her own power, and more aroused than she had ever been. She fought against the drowsiness that always followed climax for her, not wanting to miss what happened next.

For once, nothing felt forced or awkward. The fear that usually grabbed at her belly was flooded out by waves of wanting. Excitement began to make her giddy.

You're in control here she chanted in her head. Stay focused, and you'll finally get everything you want. David placed one of her fingers against his tongue, closed his lips around it and sucked deeply. She felt her belly go concave as every fiber of her being focused on his mouth. Heat pooled once again in her stomach as he repeated the act on a second finger. No way was this happening to her again. She closed her eyes and tried to regain control over her body.

"Sophie, look at me," he breathed across her skin. *No way, he had barely touched her.* She felt her muscles clenching, so close.

"Look at me or I'll stop."

Her eyes flashed open. "No," she pleaded with him. She reached out and grabbed his hands, pulling him forward as she fell back on the pillows.

"Sophie, wait." He held himself above her, shadowing her body with his presence.

She ran her hands along the hard lines of his arms. There never were more beautiful biceps.

"We can't."

"Oh, but we can," she said sliding her hands across the rigid planes of his chest, down the ripples of his abdomen, straight to his belt.

His hand formed a vice over hers. Locking her gaze he shook his head. "I don't have any condoms."

"It's fine, I'm on the pill." She smiled, proud of recovering so quickly.

He pulled her hand from his pants, stretching it over her head. "What? Why?"

Now if this wasn't a mood breaker. "So I only have to deal with PMS four times a year. But it comes in handy right about now, don't you think?"

"Damn it, Sophie. You should never let someone come near you without a condom."

"Dually noted," she said reaching her free hand around his neck. She tried to pull him closer but he wouldn't budge. She felt her heart stall as she met his gaze. The enormity of the situation crashed down on her. She was naked beneath this man, a man she'd been throwing herself at for weeks, a man who'd just watched her pleasure herself, and he was telling her no.

She closed her eyes and tried to breathe, tried to think of a way out with a shred of dignity. Her breath caught in her throat as David's hot mouth caressed her there. She melted in the blissful feeling, the physical sensation and the emotional relief.

She arched, pressing herself against him, relishing the sensation of her bare breasts against the hard muscles of his chest. She stifled a whimper as he made his way down her throat, across her collarbone. He held his body above her, too far. She hooked her legs across his hips, tilting her hips off the bed, pressing herself against him.

He dropped his body down, pressing her into the bed. "Sophie, play fair or I stop," he growled against her skin.

Her skin cooled where it was wet from his mouth, heated where his breath caressed it. The sensation was amazing, almost making her forget how he had thwarted her efforts. And that he threatened to stop.

"I was trying to be fair." The throaty tone of her voice surprised her. She arched up into him as best she could, given he topped her by more than a foot and over a hundred pounds.

Using his hands to unhook her legs he rolled off her. "I mean it Sophie. I'm only human, I can only hold back so far."

She rolled against him. "So stop holding back."

He saw it then, the part of her he was trying to protect. The woman behind the bravado, the one whose hands trembled for a moment before she touched him, the one who bit her bottom lip before pushing ahead, the one he was terrified of hurting.

Sure, her words were bold, her actions brazen beyond her experience. And if she kept her eyes closed he could almost forget just what she was offering him. But when her eyes opened, he could feel her fear, all the way to her soul. She knew what she was doing, what she was offering and she believed he'd do right by her. He just didn't deserve that kind of trust.

He'd been wrong to indulge himself with her tentative explorations. He'd pushed too far this time. He squeezed his eyes shut and searched for a safe exit. This was such a bad idea. *Push her until she backs down.* What idiot had thought of that? As if he had more control than she did.

Or was that just the excuse he was using to allow himself the indulgence of being with her? Because he just couldn't seem to walk away. He wanted her more than he'd ever wanted any woman, any thing. But he would not be her regret.

"Sophie," he whispered, pulling her closer.

"Please," she breathed against his ear.

He fought his desire for her with the last of his will. He tilted her head up to look at him. Her eyes were glistening with desire, for him. A woman with more experience would have hidden that look of need, that honest response that was all Sophie, without pretense.

If only she'd lived more for herself. Then they would be two adults enjoying chemistry that could light up the entire skyline. Because he wasn't holding back because of some sense of loyalty to Craig anymore. He was holding back from her, for her. He wouldn't take from her more than he could give back.

"You won't disappoint me," she said, her voice breathy. A statement that robbed him of choice. He growled, flipping her onto her back. He didn't disappoint. Ever. How dare she taunt him this way?

Turnabout was fair play. She had him on the edge of reason emotionally. He'd put her there physically. He set about his new plan with vengeance, determined to set every nerve in her body on fire.

Threading his hands through her dark ringlets, he pulled her to him. He found her mouth, demanding more than stolen, teasing kisses. His demands were deep throated and hungry. As hard as he tried to overwhelm her senses she seemed to intuitively know where he was going. She matched him kiss for kiss, touch for touch until he realized he was playing with fire.

Slowing the frenzy he kissed his way down her neck, savoring every inch of her. He discovered a place where he could taste her pulse as it jumped fast and thready beneath her skin. He let one hand drift down her cheek, over her shoulder until he found the ripe swell of her breast.

He squeezed gently, his thumb teasing her nipple. Her back arched against him, thrusting her breast into his hand. The moans that choked out of her throat surprised him. She was so sensitive. Leaning his head down, he tasted the ripe bud, rolling it along his tongue. Her moans became whimpers as she fisted the sheets and bit her lip. Angling back to her face he asked, "Sophie, relax, let go."

She opened her heavy lidded eyes. "I don't want to yet. I don't want you to stop." The throaty whisper caught him off guard.

"Go ahead," he said filling both hands with her breasts. "I won't stop." As his thumbs skidded across her nipples she arched up off the bed. He slipped one arm behind her, lifting her to him. In one long pull he sucked her nipple into his mouth and heard her cry out. Her responsiveness amazed him as she weaved her fingers through his hair, anchoring him to her as she rode the wave of her bliss.

When her breathing slowed she released her hold, but left her fingers there. Massaging his scalp with her fingers, scratching with her nails. Did she know how close he was? How much he wanted to shuck his principles along with his pants and bury himself inside of her? He couldn't now even if he wanted to. As close as he was he'd never make it. He wouldn't disappoint her with that.

He lavished his attentions on her other breast, memorizing every nuance. He kissed down her soft belly, deep enough so he could feel the muscles beneath. His hands drifted further down, molding to the sides of her waist. He ran his tongue down the curve of her hip. He stared in awe, noticing how perfect his hand molded to the flare of her hip.

He worried his hands might be too rough to touch such delicate skin, but her sigh reassured him. Her sensitive inner thighs were smooth and pliant beneath his nimble fingers.

Unhurried, he inched his fingers beneath her curls, parting her. So wet. His longest finger slid down one side of her clitoris, making a gentle swirl before gliding down the other. His fingers pulsed at her opening. He drew them up along the length to the pearly tip of her. Gently, he pressed a finger on either side of the bud. Her hips rose, begging for more as he squeezed the clitoris and delicate inner lips between his fingers. He kept the speed of his strokes deliberate, varying the pressure until he made her gasp. He pushed inside her then, curling a finger inside looking for the supple pillow that would take her home.

He slowed, realizing his own desire to taste her, to completely feel when she came again. He always avoided it, the act seemed more intimate than sex. Somehow it fit perfectly now. His mouth found the button of flesh he was seeking. The erect little nub he would use to coax her into screaming his name.

His fingers pressed as his mouth sucked, building her ecstasy until her gasps and moans intermingled with his name. It wasn't long until he felt her spasms, tasted the fruits of his labors. He stayed with her, prolonging her pleasure until she shuddered and he felt her body go limp. Climbing back up the bed, he pulled her to him, not willing to walk away just yet.

Curling around her, he pulled the blankets on top of them. He didn't want her to be cold. He bowed her tiny body against his, and held on. Never had he completely sacrificed his own pleasure. That could be what he gave back to her. That and enough mind-blowing orgasms to make her drunk with passion, to make her sleep so deep he could figure out just what was going on.

Chapter Nine

Sunight blazed red beneath David's eyelids. He sucked in a slow breath and squinted in the streaming light. *What the hell?* His eyes flew open. *Too fast.* He brought a hand to shield his stinging eyes. He was still there, still in Sophie's bed and the sun was up. He'd never woken up with a woman before. Never been with a woman who might expect him to.

His heart tightened as he reached for her. "Sophie," he whispered, swallowing hard against the rasp in his voice. Rolling to his side he reached out, shivering at the cool sheets beside him. Sitting up, he looked about the room as his eyes adjusted to the light.

"Sophie?" he called out. She must be in the bathroom, in the shower. He smiled at the thought of her bare beneath the water. His morning erection jumped in response. *Maybe...*

The sensations of last night flooded through him as he swung his long legs off the bed. He was startled by the lush rug at his feet. He curled his toes in the soft red chenille and smiled. Soft and warm and unexpected. He looked out her bedroom window and marveled at the blue sky he could make out above the neighboring rooftops. Such a beautiful morning.

Looking around the room he spied a pile of books on the bedside table. Small red paperbacks with couples in provocative poses on the covers, *Fabulous Fellatio*, a Kama Sutra manual and a tiny pair of wire-rimmed reading glasses. *Cute.* His dreams last night would probably make those books pale in comparison.

Rising to his feet, he listened to the silence. He couldn't hear the shower. Maybe she was taking a bath. His pants jumped again at the thought of her beneath a mountain of tiny bubbles.

"Sophie," he called out as he shuffled to the bathroom. The door opened to a darkened room.

Drawing in a harsh breath, he spun quickly on his heel, racing against the inevitable. By the time he made it to the end of the hall his heart was beating so fast it was hard to stand. She was gone.

He collapsed on the couch, his head falling all the way to his hands. This should make him happy. She'd given him the safest, easiest out in the world. He could just go. So why were his feet on the ground? And why did he feel everything but relief?

Lifting his heavy head, he looked around the room as if he might find her somewhere, hiding beneath the fern or peeking out from behind the palm. She could have at least left...a note. He jumped up, his feet barely touching the hardwoods as he crossed to the kitchen table.

Sunrise yoga.

Didn't want to wake you.

Sophie

His thumb wore a path over the tiny heart between her words and her name until the pencil lies blurred. Not quite what he was hoping for, but still a relief. He made his way to the bathroom and flipped on the light. The bathroom held a claw foot tub, like the one he had imagined her in just moments ago. He shook his head as if the act might dislodge the image. Placing his hands on either side of the pedestal sink he leaned forward and looked in the mirror. Damned if he didn't look well rested. It was as if he was staring into the eyes of a whole different man. *What the hell?*

"Honey, if you think your feelings will freak him out, then you're in the wrong relationship," a dulcet voice said slowly.

Sophie jumped as if the woman were speaking directly to her. She couldn't help but overhear in the small steam room at

Working It Out. But the petite blonde with the Southern drawl on the other side of the partition was obviously talking to the younger woman next to her. The women huddled closely together, too lost in the intimacies of their discussion to notice their audience.

"I know it can be tempting to settle for less when you really want to be with someone," the warm voice drawled on, "but you need to have some respect for yourself."

Sophie opened her mouth to argue, to explain that there were compromises in every relationship, but shut it as the woman continued. *She's not talking to you.*

"Don't feel sorry for him, don't defend him. You just need to raise your expectations. If he thinks you're worth it, he'll rise to the occasion. Men like a challenge."

Sophie's tongue shriveled in her mouth and her heart began to ache. Just minutes ago she'd been humming, actually humming as she made her way into the steam room. Last night had been more amazing than she'd dreamed, not quite all she had imagined, but magnificent nonetheless. He'd literally knocked her out for goodness sake.

It felt as if he'd made love to her, no matter the technicalities. They'd been intimate, even if his pants had stayed on, and he'd held her all night long. Which was the best part. Though it made getting out of bed without waking him a challenge. Still, she'd loved every moment.

And now? Listening in on the conversation of strangers, her stomach sank. She was throwing herself at him, had actually begged him. Had he been with her last night out of pity?

Heat rose from her shoulders to her hairline that had nothing to do with the temperature of the room. Even he was telling her she deserved more. She'd thought he was just being noble.

"You just don't understand him. He loves me the best he knows how," the younger woman pleaded.

The mother shook her head. "Why are you willing to settle for so little? Right now, is this what you want?"

Sophie's heart beat in her ears as she listened for a response. She didn't want the relationship she'd promised

David, the no strings, no one has to know. She wanted to change him, wanted to make him want the same things she did. Which wasn't fair, because she was incapable of doing the same.

The mother continued, "It should feel like what you want."

"It could get better." She heard a voice croak between sobs. Heat prickled her own eyelids as she got up and turned to leave. The girl was her age, her mother holding her now as she cried.

Sophie tightened the towel around her as she made her way to the showers. She had long ago learned how to hold it in, to cry silently so no one would worry. She stood beneath the icy water, letting it ease the puffiness before it began.

She wanted her mother now. Right now she would give anything to just lie down and have her mother stroke her hair and say it would all work out. She'd never once worried her mother with talk of boys, had no idea if her mother might advise her to wait him out or cut him loose. But she did have those words she could never forget. "A full life. No regrets." The words she used to make herself bold enough to do what she dared.

Why did the woman have to be so damn cryptic?

Sophie turned the corner toward her apartment with a sense of dread. She hung her head as she saw it, his blue Corvette still in the driveway. It was hard to believe that only a few hours ago it hurt to leave him. Now she was wishing he was anywhere but inside, waiting for her.

She'd hoped he would be gone, that by some miracle he had a spare key hidden somewhere. What she really wanted to do was rewind time and remember to leave his keys on the table. Sophie had completely forgotten about swiping his keys last night until she'd heard them jangle in her backpack when she reached inside for lotion after her shower. She might have ignored the entire situation if not for the three messages David had already left with the receptionist. The hour break she had between classes left her with no excuse but to deliver them herself.

She climbed the stairs slowly, her feet heavy. She didn't want to have a conversation about what had and had not happened last night. She was still trying to figure out just how she felt about it. The usual butterflies fluttered in her stomach at the thought of seeing him. It just wasn't fair. Every second she spent with him she fell harder, and he was immune.

Taking a deep breath she chanted the words still echoing in her brain. *Raise your expectations. If he thinks you're worth it he'll rise to the occasion.* She blew out the air in defeat. Expectations? She'd have to get some of those.

Pulling off her gloves, she reached in her coat pocket for her keys. Her numb fingers fumbled with the lock. All too soon he was there, pulling open the door and filling up the doorway. Involuntarily she smiled up at him as they stood there, neither of them moving an inch. Her smile widened. She realized he didn't want to have a conversation about last night any more than she did.

"Is your hair wet?" David asked, pulling her inside by the arm. "It's too cold for you to be out with wet hair. You'll get sick."

As he closed the door she reached a hand up to inspect her curls. Her hair had been too damp to pull on her hat before she left, but it was almost dry now. "It's a myth," she said. She plopped her backpack on the table and rummaged through it for his keys.

"What's a myth?"

His rumored sexual notoriety. Where had that come from? "That going outside with wet hair makes you sick. Viruses make people sick, not temperatures." Sophie held up the shiny silver key ring engraved with his initials. "I'm sorry. I completely forgot I had them."

"You mean you weren't plotting to keep me trapped in your apartment all day awaiting your return?" He grinned, crossing the room.

She could only shake her head as he lifted the key ring from her finger, obviously careful not to touch her. Or was she just being hypersensitive? She tried to catch his eyes to see, but he was watching the floor too intently.

"You shouldn't leave someone to wake up alone, Sophie."

Her heart leapt in her chest. Could he be just a little sad, hurt, upset? Please, anything.

He cleared his throat without looking up. "It's not safe for you to leave someone unsupervised with all of your things." He looked up with a grin. "Somebody might try to unalphabetize your spice rack."

Her heart slowed as it sunk lower in her chest. Swallowing hard, she found she actually had a few expectations.

"That's what you want to say to me, David? That it's not safe to leave a man alone in my apartment." Sucking in a hard breath she continued. "Great. Thanks for all of your wonderful advice on dating." She tossed the words at him like daggers. "Never let a guy con you into not using a condom and don't leave him alone in your apartment. You're a wealth of knowledge." She ticked off his rules on her fingers. "Heaven forbid I might actually trust the person I'm having sex with, or not having sex with as the case might be."

David raised his hands. "I didn't mean it like that."

"Exactly how did you mean it then? It sounded pretty straightforward to me." Her blood flowed so hot it was easy to slide her fingers into her gloves now. "I realize I may not have a lot of experience, but I don't need you to critique me at every turn. It's insulting." Her mouth was so dry her tongue was sticking to the roof of it. She knew she was overreacting. She looked to him for a response. At this point she would take any sign of life.

"You're leaving?" he asked incredulously.

"I'm in between classes." She picked up her backpack, but couldn't leave the kitchen with him taking up the entire hallway. "David?"

"I'll drive you," he said, walking to the door.

"No, you won't."

"Sophie, it's cold. I'll drive you."

"Would you please stop telling me what to do? I'm tired of you making decisions for me."

"Me? Making decisions for you?" He blocked the doorway. "I don't do that."

Arching an eyebrow, she wondered if any of the moves she had learned in self-defense class would get him out of her way. "And exactly what would you call what you're doing right now?"

He rolled his eyes and stepped aside. She brushed past him and plodded down the stairs. Between her footsteps she heard him whisper, "Always lock your door when you leave."

She turned on the step. Was he really giving her more advice? "You did not just say that."

Meeting her stare, he glared at her as he slowly replied, "I sure did," slamming the door afterward for effect.

Sophie turned and stomped down the stairs, marching down the street as fast as her short strides could take her. She was still close enough to hear the squeal of tires as he pulled out of the driveway moments later.

What was that about? It was as if she was an entirely different person. Funny, teasing, easy Sophie had been inhabited by one angry woman. David didn't deal well with a woman scorned. He didn't do complicated, never stayed around long enough to have a mess to clean up.

She had no right to be mad. He was the one who had been stuck in her apartment for half the morning. David slammed his car door shut, enabled the alarm and made his way up the stairs to his condo. He should be the one who was angry, not her.

He didn't have time for this. He needed a fast shower and a change of clothes so he could get to the office. He'd already called and checked in, and there were no raging fires that needed to be put out, but he still wanted to get there quickly. He wanted to get to a place where he was in control.

Opening the door, he saw books and papers strewn about his living room floor. *Kelly.* She often used his empty home as a study spot, especially when she needed quiet and a lot of space. He usually liked the company, but he didn't need her questions right now. Making a beeline for his bedroom, David hoped he could sneak in and out without her even knowing he'd come home.

"There you are," he heard her say from the kitchen. Reluctantly, he turned around. "Where were you last night? I brought Pad Thai. There's still a ton in the fridge, but I ate all the peanut sauce."

Luckily, he'd found half a dozen blackberry corn muffins at Sophie's. "I'm just going to shower and change so I can head back to work."

"An all nighter? David, if you're too swamped with Dad retiring I'm sure he'd agree to stay on longer."

David winced. Lance hadn't told her the real reason for his retirement. So be it. He wished he didn't know. "It's nothing I can't handle. Time for a shower."

"Your pimp called."

David whipped around. "Excuse me?"

"I guess technically she would be your madam, right?"

"I don't have a madam. I don't have to pay for sex."

"Really? How much does one of those nights cost you?"

What was she talking about? "I'm not following you, Kel."

"That stewardess. The one who whores out her friends."

He swallowed hard and met her gaze. He wasn't discussing this with his baby sister.

"Call it whatever you want, it's still disgusting. She said to tell you she has some prospects for you."

"Knock it off, Kelly. You know it's not like that." David shrugged. He took two steps toward his bedroom and stopped. He wasn't going to call. He always called. He should, he really should because he could use the distraction. Sophie wasn't the only one undergoing a major personality overhaul.

"Please use protection," Kelly's voice rang down the hall.

David stomped back into the living room. "Not that it is any business of yours, but I'm not even going to call her. I have way too much going on right now."

Kelly's smile stretched across her face. "With Sophie?"

"Sophie is a piece of work," he said, crossing into the kitchen. If he was going to talk he needed coffee. Thankfully Kelly's study sessions required a fresh pot every few hours. Pouring a cup, he helped himself to some of the girlie powder she put in it. He downed half the mug before Kelly started in again.

"What is that supposed to mean? Did you two have a fight?"

"We had her snapping at me about telling her what to do for absolutely no reason. So if that's a fight, yeah."

"What did you do?"

"I left."

"No, not that." Kelly waved her hand. "To make her mad."

Who knew? "I bought her a car."

Kelly plopped into a chair at the kitchen table and sucked in a harsh breath. "You what?"

"What is it with women? Why is that a bad thing? She helped me out with some work stuff, things that would have been very expensive if not damn near impossible, and I wanted to say thank you."

"Did you ever think of flowers?"

David shook his head. "She needs a car." You never know what she might think of flowers. "I did send her some oranges." He shrugged. "She liked that. But it was a big favor, huge."

Kelly narrowed her eyes. "And she didn't like the car because?"

"Oh, she liked it. She just didn't like that I couldn't fit in it."

"Oh," Kelly nodded furiously. "I get it."

"Well I didn't." He drained his coffee cup and set it in the sink.

"You'll learn." Kelly smiled. "Why were you telling her what to do?"

"I wasn't, really. She just took it wrong." He didn't want to talk about last night with Sophie. There was no way he was going to discuss it with Kelly.

"And now she's mad, and you stormed out," Kelly summed up.

"Hey, she left first." David leaned back against the counter. His counter, his turf. Why was Kelly taking Sophie's side? He really needed to get to work.

"She left her own apartment? She must have been all kinds of mad." Kelly shook her head. "You need to figure out what you did and apologize."

"Why am I wrong? I'm not wrong here, Kelly. Trust me on that one. I did the right thing for once." David said, crossing his arms across his chest.

"Right for whom?" Kelly asked, looking him straight in the eye.

"For Sophie." He answered without blinking.

"Aha! But she doesn't agree, and thinks you're telling her what to do."

Was that it? "Or maybe she is just a grouch in the morning," he said defensively. He did the right thing.

Kelly pulled her head back, "Oh wow, was this the first time you woke up together? I forgot you don't do the whole stay-the-night thing. I thought you had rules about that. Didn't you actually write them down when you were in college?"

"Rules don't apply to Sophie." He heard someone say using his voice.

"Why?"

David shrugged. Why indeed. Because she broke them, because she didn't care to abide by them, because she was different. She was rich and textured and completely different from his usual diet of casual women. Women who wanted light and easy as much as he did. It was the difference between hamburger and filet mignon, instant vanilla pudding and crème brûlée. He'd gone gourmet and fast food had suddenly lost its appeal.

"You're in love with her, aren't you?"

"What?" His heart quickened at the ridiculous notion. He may not know what he wanted from Sophie, but he wasn't in love with anyone. "You have the wrong idea about this whole thing. Sophie and I want very different things. And besides, she may not be speaking to me ever again."

"You need to make it up to her."

"I need to get to work," David said pushing himself off the counter. He needed to come up with a plan.

❦

"Plan B. We bring the party to you," Sophie said, settling in beside Daphne for an afternoon of soap operas and girl talk.

"It's not like I can't get up. We could do it at Beaches just like we planned. It would only be for a few hours."

Sophie shook her head. "I'll sneak you in some of the carrot cake from Beaches, but I am not dealing with Craig if I try and take you out of the house. He is wound way too tight right now. Before he left he actually told me to try and make you nap."

Daphne fell back against the pillows. "I've only gotten up to pee, I swear." A slow smile crossed her lips. "Although being this pregnant, that's pretty often." Daphne wrapped her hands lovingly across her stretched abdomen. "We're going to be okay. I wish he could relax."

Craig's anxiety was getting out of control. "Me too." Sophie replied looking down at the notebook in her hands. "We'll do it in the living room and you can sit on the couch. We'll keep it short. I made out a guest list. All the women from your prenatal yoga will come. You're all we talk about in class."

"It probably makes them nervous that I'm having trouble." Daphne said rubbing her stomach.

Being here was just the reminder Sophie needed. Family is what really matters. David kept telling her he wasn't cut out for what she wanted from life. It was her own fault for not believing him.

"Nothing you can't handle," Sophie said, resting her hand on top of her sister's.

Daphne turned to face her. "I'm sorry you have to work so much right now. All my classes plus your own and babysitting me so Craig can go in to work. It doesn't leave much room for anything else."

Sophie smiled and wished she could confide in Daphne. But Daphne had her own stresses right now; she didn't need to be burdened with her baby sister's dating disasters. Plus she would assume the worst about David, and as confused as Sophie felt she didn't want any more negativity.

"You've always put your needs aside to take care of people, Sophie. You need to find someone who'll put you first. Someone who'll show you the world, and how to have fun."

"Work can be fun," she smiled cheerfully. Twisting into compromising positions with David was the highlight of her week. Or had been, until they spent the night together. And after her hormone attack the next morning who knew if he would ever bother showing up for class again.

"Do you mean Sensational Sex with David Strong?" Daphne's eyes darkened.

Sophie had to acknowledge she liked the sound of that, but it was never going to happen. "You must admit, it is a fun class. But I was actually thinking about the prenatal yoga. Hannah brought her baby today. He was so small he didn't even have eyelashes yet."

She watched Daphne's frustration melt before her eyes. Daphne didn't want to talk about David any more than she did. "They named him Sawyer. Do you like that?"

Daphne nodded. "I've been thinking about Lennon or Kinsey."

Sophie grinned. "Kinsey, like the sex researcher?"

Chapter Ten

Two long days. And even longer nights. David hadn't called. Not that Sophie expected him to, exactly. It was just with as often as she was thinking of him, it would have been nice to know he gave her a second thought. Obviously not.

David tended to arrive early for class, ostensibly to review the positions, but Sophie hoped it was to see her, too. Two minutes until class started and he'd yet to cross the threshold. Sophie loaded the slides depicting the positions just in case.

She should focus more on stretching and strengthening anyway. It would be a better take away for the students. Much more practical than watching her grope David for an hour. Twisting her mouth into a smile Sophie took one last look at the room, and the raised platform that always made her feel so small. She let out the breath choking her lungs. When David was here he seemed to fill all the extra space around her.

Scratching her nails through her hair, Sophie shook her head. She'd decided she wasn't going to do this. There was absolutely no balance of power in their relationship. Just her throwing herself at him, him saying no and her not taking no for an answer. But now she would. He was right. Daphne was right. The stranger in the steam room was right. She could not handle a casual relationship with David.

She didn't have it in her to do casual. She'd confused her fantasy of him with the reality, twisting everything until it turned out exactly as she wanted. She'd even deluded herself into thinking she knew what would make him happy.

Sophie took a deep breath all the way to her belly. She could teach the class alone. That would be easy. It was answering the student's questions about David that would sting.

Twenty minutes late and David still had no idea what he was going to say to her. Hell, he wasn't even dressed for class. He was still in the same jeans he'd put on this morning. The same clothes he'd planned on wearing until after lunch when he'd head into the office. But nothing about this day turned out the way he planned.

David was a master at planning. He could organize real estate transactions, monitor financial markets on four continents and manage a billion dollar fitness empire. But for the life of him he couldn't figure out exactly what he wanted from Sophie. Or what he was going to do about it for that matter.

She infuriated him to no end. What really bothered him was that she seemed to understand him in ways even he didn't get. She expected him to be a better man than he usually was. He had a reputation, a history around town. No one ever expected him to be interested in anything but sex. No one except Sophie.

David had an innate distrust of people, brought on by all the transient figures in his life. Nannies, tutors, stepmothers, friends. They all promised to stay, but never did.

Never give someone more than you're willing to lose, he'd learned that over and over. Yet he trusted Sophie in an almost instinctive way. It still struck him as odd that he'd let her sit in his chair and play with the SGI financials like they were a video game. She understood them better than he did. She could've done a little creative accounting of her own. And it hadn't even crossed his mind she would.

Then there was Craig. Craig was family. Not by blood but by time and friendship. And Craig trusted him with Daphne's sister. Trusted him not to take advantage of her. Which he was finding harder and harder to do.

Finally arriving at Working It Out, he had to circle the block searching for a parking spot. Of course, even this would take longer today. After his third trip around he finally slid in next to the curb. Jumping out he remembered to beep the alarm on as he bounded up the sidewalk and into the club.

David inched open the door to the classroom. Slipping inside, he made his way to the back of the room as slowly and as quietly as possible. He didn't want to interrupt, but he didn't want to wait outside either. He didn't want her thinking he had blown off the class for a minute more.

Sophie had the students up in pushup positions, raising one leg up at a time. As he walked past Ramon and Cindy, a couple who always stayed in the back of the room, he watched Ramon's body shake in fatigue.

Ramon collapsed on the floor and rolled to his back. "Thank God you're here. Whatever you did to piss her off, I beg you, apologize now, before she kills us all."

Sophie wanted to kill him. Making her think he wasn't coming and then showing up dressed like that when class was half over. Even from across the room she could tell his jeans were old, so worn they would feel thin and soft. His black sweater stretched teasingly across his chest, the sleeves hugging his biceps. He looked sexier now than he ever had, and was providing quite the distraction to her and the other women in the class.

You're not going to do this anymore, she reminded herself as the class rallied around him for support. The positions tonight were challenging. Sophie had been running the students through some basic Pilates moves to make them aware of the muscles they would be using. They'd be thanking her later, though now they were begging him to make her stop.

Sophie quieted them down, assuring them and herself that David had done nothing to influence the course of the class. Taking advantage of the break, she had the students join their partners on a mat to begin the positions. David's long confident stride had him joining her on the platform in seconds.

"What did you have them doing?"

"Ab work. Sitting postures can be very challenging on the lower back muscles. You should do it to warm up."

"I'm sure my abs are as strong as yours."

"I doubt that." She taught two Pilates classes a day, six days a week. Plus, he was twice her size. "We could find out though. Would you rather try sit-ups or see who can hold the plank position the longest?"

He shook his head with a smile. "Sophie, I hold more on my chest than you weigh when I do sit ups. It's not a fair match. Let's just get to the demonstration."

One of the men taunted, "No way buddy. You don't put in the work you don't get the fun. No foreplay, no play."

Sophie tried to ignore both the comment and David's smile.

"Aren't you going to defend me?" he asked loud enough for the entire room to hear. Sophie knew they all assumed she and David were together. She'd never done anything to make them think otherwise.

Sophie shrugged and addressed the class. "David has no problem—" she paused for effect, "—with foreplay." She grinned from ear to ear as the class snickered. It was petty, but it was fun.

"Sophie," David hissed at her. His jaw was set so tight she wondered if his teeth might break. Sophie shrugged again, cued up the projector and dimmed the lights. As the explicit photo illuminated the wall behind her she watched David's brows knit together. Let him see she could handle things on her own without him trying to rush in and fix everything.

Sophie stood in the center of the platform, crossing her arms across her body and hugging her elbows. "The positions tonight can be more challenging than those we've tried before. I think you'll all understand why we focused on abdominal strength and flexibility tonight.

"This first position is Kama's Wheel. It's one of the more meditative positions, so I want you all to focus on your breathing and sense of balance while in the position. Men, you'll want to sit comfortably with your legs stretched out in front of you."

Sophie heard David moving behind her and knew he was getting in to position. She wanted to prove a point, but like the fool she was, she also wanted to touch him. Her insides knotted as she tried to decide, knowing where touching him might lead. She'd want more, she always did. But she also didn't want to reject him, leave him exposed in front of the class.

"Ladies, you'll need to lower yourself down, stretching your legs out behind him. As your partner gets into position, men, you'll need to place your hands on her back for support. Ladies, hold onto your partner's arms for leverage and support."

Sophie watched as the class struggled with the position. They could look at a picture from a book at home. What they were here to learn was how to get into the position. She felt a tug on her finger as David whispered her name.

She turned, looking down on him for a change. His soft brown eyes looked up at her, unraveling the knots in her stomach as she moved and joined him. She heard the class quiet as they watched her lower herself down to him, achieving the position as easily as if they'd practiced it a hundred times.

Swallowing hard to keep her voice steady, she reminded the class to take a moment to focus on their breathing, to try to mirror their partners. Closing her eyes Sophie realized she and David had already done that. Their bodies ever so slightly rising and falling in time.

She felt David's heavy stare, but found it far easier to move ahead with the class than with David Strong. Reaching for the remote, she clicked the slide ahead, finding the next position.

"This next posture is called The Position of Equals. Men's position remains the same, and ladies you lean back further moving your hands from resting on his arms to his feet. Once your partner is in position, men, you can relax your arms, using your hands in whatever way is comfortable." Sophie leaned back into the position, thankful that with her head back she wouldn't have to look at David.

She listened to the students giggle as they realized just how a man might use his hands in this position. David realized it too, as the thumb of the hand away from the class began to stroke the side of her breast.

Sophie snapped her head up and gave him a warning look. He didn't stop. Increasing the pressure, he stared at her with a cocksure grin. Unsure just what he meant by his little display,

Sophie reached for the remote again, changing the position on the screen.

"Next we transition into the Snake Trap. Ladies, make sure you can support yourself in the position you are in with your hands on his legs. Once your partner is secure, men. lean back and hold on to her feet. You can see that these positions are more about enjoying each other, more about sex play than about achieving orgasm quickly."

David rolled his eyes. "You and your oranges," he muttered under his breath. "Of course if achieving orgasm suddenly becomes your goal," David's voice echoed in the quiet classroom. "Then you simply..." Sitting up quickly and moving his legs, he threw her off balance, landing her flat in her back. She instinctively drew her legs together as he came down on top of her. "But I'm sure you all have that move down."

Sophie felt her temperature rise as she realized just how he'd turned the tables on her. She prayed the move they taught in self-defense class would work when she was so outmatched in size. She moved her legs to the side, then quickly raised them up in the air, perpendicular to their bodies. She swung her legs over, using them as leverage as she pushed him off her. Taking him by surprise, she was actually able to roll him off her and onto his back.

She quickly sprang to her feet, brushing her hands together in triumph. Grabbing the remote she shut off the picture and brightened the lights.

"There is a rule in this classroom. No one should feel pressured into a position that makes them uncomfortable."

She was enjoying the giggles from the crowd so much she barely noticed David hadn't moved from where she left him. Turning to him, she realized his eyes were closed in a wince. Her stomach sank. She'd hurt him. She took the two steps back toward him.

"I'm sorry," she whispered as she knelt down. "I didn't think I could hurt you."

David opened his eyes. "You know better than that."

"Are you okay? Where does it hurt?"

"Mainly my pride," he said, pulling himself up slowly. "And my back." He winced again, bringing a hand to his lower back.

Sophie brought a hand to her mouth. Kneeling down, she said softly, "I swear, I didn't mean to. I just wanted to show you I could take care of myself."

David waved her off as she tried to touch him. Finally standing, he looked down at her. His smirk came close to sinister, his voice low and gravelly. "You're going to be sorry later."

Gone. As if he hadn't been there at all. Sophie turned and looked at the empty gym. She'd finished the class and dismissed the students, hoping David would be waiting. But of course, he'd gone.

Backing against the reception desk, Sophie set her hands on the counter and her shoulders slumped in defeat. Even though she'd decided not to continue pushing things with David, she was still attracted to him. She rolled her eyes. Most of the women on the planet were attracted to him.

She wanted him to be attracted to her. Until tonight, she'd always known he was aroused as they ran through the positions. Tonight there had been no signs of life. The powerful feeling she usually had from getting a rise out of him was woefully absent.

Sophie closed her eyes and willed her heart to harden. He didn't want her, probably never did. As the tears pricked the back of her eyelids she sucked in a deep breath. She wasn't going to cry about this anymore. There was nothing she could do to change things, no point wasting energy on what ifs. Pushing off the counter, she propelled her tired legs to her office.

Turning into the doorway, she heard him before she saw him. "You date a lot." His voice was more curious than accusatory. "A lot, a lot. Much more than me."

Her forehead wrinkled as she saw him tooling with her PDA. "What do you think you're doing?"

David looked up. Reading her expression, he set down the organizer and held out his hands. "Relax. I was looking for some Ibuprofen and saw it. I was bored so I thought I would play a video game. But you don't have any games on yours."

Her eyes narrowed. "I don't have time for games, David." Sophie picked up her backpack and shoved the PDA inside. "Why would you go through my things?"

He rolled his eyes. "I told you, I was looking for some Ibuprofen. Someone wasn't playing fair earlier."

Sophie planted her feet firmly on the ground. "You started it." She had to grin. They'd been reduced to playground bickering. Again.

"I'm sorry. You had my corporate and personal accounts at your fingertips. You could have robbed me blind. You could trust me a little."

"I don't want your money, David." She yanked her coat off the chair behind him

"I know." He muttered, looking at the floor. "I was just surprised. I assumed you didn't date much."

"That's what happens when you assume."

"I don't get it Sophie. Why weren't you with any of them?"

Pausing at the second button of her coat, Sophie met his gaze. "I didn't want to be." The words echoed in the still room. The blood pounding in her ears got louder and louder until she just couldn't take it anymore. She had to break it up with something, even if it meant she rambled.

"Some of them were jerks, some didn't want to deal with my folks, and when I agreed to be a surrogate for Daphne, I stopped all together. It just didn't seem appropriate."

"Daphne's been pregnant for what, seven months now?"

"She's been sick, David. I've had to step in and keep this place going while she takes care of herself. Losing my virginity hasn't been a priority. I didn't see the point in sleeping with one man while fantasizing about another." Finally she'd said it. Fishing her gloves from her coat pocket, Sophie asked, "Haven't we already had this conversation?"

"We need to have a conversation about what is going on with us."

Sophie swallowed hard and charged forward. She couldn't bear to hear some impassioned "it's not you" speech from him.

Jenna Bayley-Burke

"I've been thinking a lot about that, and I've decided you're right."

"I'm right," he repeated slowly.

"Yes. I can't handle a relationship with a man like you. I can't keep putting myself out there and being rejected at every turn. My ego isn't as big as yours."

"I never rejected you, Sophie," David said, leaning forward in the chair. He winced, his hand finding its way to the sore muscles.

Sophie pursed her lips together and continued. "You won't have to worry about me throwing myself at you anymore. I'll respect your decision." She sucked in a hard breath. When had the air in this room gotten so cold?

"I hope you can understand that I can't handle kissing or touching outside of class." She cast her eyes to the floor as she made her confession. "I'll feel you and want more, it makes me think you do too, and that isn't good for either one of us." She could feel her heart splintering apart inside of her. This was supposed to make things easier, why did it feel like dying?

"Whatever you want, Sophie," his voice rumbled quietly.

She looked up and watched him sit, staring at his hands. "I thought you'd be relieved."

He looked up at her, his eyes unreadable brown pools of emotion. "Are you ready to go?"

She nodded, wrapping her scarf around her neck and heading for the door. "You don't have to drive me," Sophie said as they reached the exit. "I walk every other night. I'll be fine."

David held open the door as she walked out, turning and checking to make sure the door locked behind them. "Actually, I need you to give me a ride home," David said, fishing the keys from his pocket. He pressed a button, flashing the lights on a deep red compact SUV, before handing the keys to her. "Surprise."

"What are you doing?" David asked as Sophie followed him out of the truck.

"I'm making sure you get home okay," she said, falling in line behind him.

"I'm fine," he said, turning to face her.

"Don't make me give these back to you again." She dangled the key in front of his face. He realized then that her spare key was already on his key ring. He'd have to give that back. Nothing about this day had gone as he planned.

David still wasn't sure what he wanted from Sophie, but he damned sure knew it wasn't the nothing she was offering. He'd known all along he didn't deserve to be with someone like her. So if this was what she needed, he wouldn't fight her on it. At least not until he figured out what he wanted for himself.

He stared down at her determined expression and shrugged, turned and walked up the stairs to his condo. This was not the scenario he'd thought of for the first time he brought a woman back to his place. She had to be feeling guilty. She'd dumped and injured him, and he'd bought her a car. Again.

Turning the key, he pushed the door open and turned to tell her goodbye. But somehow she slipped under his arm and made her way inside, flipping on the light as she passed into the living room.

Spinning on her heel, she began to take off her gloves and scarf.

"What are you doing?" he asked, removing his own jacket.

"I'm going to make your back feel better," she said, peeling off her coat. She stepped next to him, hanging her coat on the coat tree by the door and dropping her keys on the table beside his.

"I took some Ibuprofen. I'll be fine."

"I'm the reason it's sore. Just let me fix it." Her eyes sparkled as she grinned up at him. She looked like the old Sophie, the playful, fun Sophie he knew before things got out of hand at her apartment.

David shook his head. "I don't think that's such a good idea."

"Why not?" she asked, pushing her full lips into a pout.

"You said we weren't going to go there anymore." And if she kept looking at him like that he definitely would want to.

She rolled her eyes playfully. "You think I'm coming on to you?"

"Aren't you?" His voice betrayed him, cracking as he spoke.

The way her eyes darkened showed him she'd heard it. "You should be so lucky. No, I just don't want you aching tomorrow and cursing me all day."

He cleared his throat to make sure he could speak. "I won't. I'll be fine."

"You don't trust yourself do you?" Her voice was low, throaty, teasing.

"Excuse me?" He managed.

"That's it, isn't it? You don't think you can keep your hands off me." She must have grown because he could swear she was bigger than him now.

"You're the one who wants to get their hands on someone."

Sophie held up her tiny hands. "Purely medicinal, I assure you. Come on, I swear I'll keep my clothes on no matter how much you beg."

It was his turn to smile. "You should be so lucky."

"Fine, then I'll grab some lotion while you take off your clothes."

He watched as she bounced to her bag and pulled out the bottle. Her lotion, the one that smelled like almonds. He turned and walked through his bedroom into the bathroom where he stripped off his shirt. He caught his reflection in the mirror. What was he doing? He must be crazy to be turning down a massage from a beautiful woman. She was right, he was afraid of her a little. She had some physical power over him he couldn't explain. Craig had made him promise to leave her alone, and she just said they weren't going there anymore. And he was trying. Failing miserably, but still trying.

His head cocked to the side as he realized something. He could scare her off. He dropped his pants and stood naked in front of the mirror. Reasoning with her didn't seem to be working. He could march out there nude and she would definitely change her mind. More than a few women had been intimidated by his size, and they weren't virgins. If he just called her bluff maybe she would run for the hills. If he pushed her far enough it might work. He met his own eyes in the mirror.

Unless she didn't. Without the safety net of clothing he'd never recover his senses enough to hold back if she made a move for him. He grabbed a towel off the rack and wrapped it around his waist. He didn't trust himself that much.

He stepped out of the bathroom and stood frozen. She sat on his bed, rubbing her hands together.

"Oh, no. Not in here."

"What do you mean?" Her wide innocent eyes almost had him believing she wasn't trying to seduce him.

"Not you and me on the bed. We can use the couch in the living room."

She shook her head and patted the bed next to her. "Are you afraid of little, tiny me? Come now, what could I possibly do to you?"

Was she batting her eyelashes at him? What could she do? He had a list a mile long that would do for a start. He opened his mouth to object but was stopped short.

"Get over yourself. I'm not going to jump you the second you close your eyes. I told you, I'm done with trying that. Now lay down." His body did as he was told. His brain was still urging him to run at full speed toward the nearest exit.

He lay down on his stomach reaching his arms around the pillow under his head, reminding himself it was just a massage. That his back hurt, though for the life of him he couldn't remember exactly where. Every muscle in his body tensed as he felt her thighs on either side, straddling him. So much for relaxing.

His protests were futile now, she had him. This was what he wanted, her, warm beside him in a bed. It was the rest of the time he was confused about. He didn't say a word, trying to focus on anything but her scent, her weight pressing the bed on either side of him, her hands. One warm hand fanned out between his shoulder blades while another pressed the base of his spine. He could feel the lotion slip across his back. She must have been warming it in her hands because it glided effortlessly, slowing the sensation of her hands so it was like she was everywhere all at once.

Her fingertips lightly stroked his back from top to bottom. Her hands worked in tandem, so that one was reaching the towel across his buttocks as the other began atop his shoulder. Over and over her fingers ran down his back until he could feel the muscles begin to relax. Dancing fingertips were replaced by the steady pressure of flattened palms as she continued the path on either side of his spine. For what seemed like eternity, she kneaded and stroked, rolled and pushed at his tired muscles. Her hands explored his shoulders, neck, the back of his arms, his buttocks, back of his thighs.

He'd experienced thousands of rubdowns in his life. But this was different. Somehow, because it was Sophie, the motions had a different meaning and seemed to trigger a deeper response. Every nerve ending in his back had ached before, so he knew they were there. But never had he considered those same nerve endings to be capable of such immense sexual pleasure. In fact, if this didn't end soon he might come right here on the bed, without her ever having touched the front of him.

He hadn't been this out of control with his responses since junior high. But he was powerless to stop it. Such simple touches shouldn't be affecting him like this, but his body responded in hope that she would keep touching him, not stopping until he found release. At some point he'd given in, relaxed to the point where he was only semi-awake. Or so he convinced himself.

There would be no honorable intentions today. He'd be receptive to anything and everything she had in store. He gave into the push and pull of her warm, strong hands. Hands he'd thought were so small and fragile wielded amazing power over him. His closed eyes felt heavy as her strokes became lighter.

Maybe he would sleep after all. She would be gone when he woke up and there would be no awkwardness, just the pure bliss of the moment. He tried to drift, but the aching hardness urgently pressing against his belly kept him on the edge. Her attentions drifted down his shoulders, back, to his buttocks. She must have removed the towel, but he hadn't noticed exactly when. She kneaded lightly, building the intensity. He knew he should stop her, but he was so close. So close.

She traced his spine from his cleft to nape with her tongue. His eyes shot open as sensuous shivers shot through him like lightning. Her tongue retraced its path and he drew in a hard breath. Was it worth it to try to hold back? His body ached to accept the release she was offering. He closed his eyes again, finding it impossible to think when there was no blood left in his brain. She took mercy on him, removing his decision-making ability as she laid an open mouthed kiss on the triangle of skin just above his buttocks. Her fingers massaged his butt as he came, prolonging his ecstasy as he rode the wave of the spasms.

He recognized the familiar weight of her body resting on top of him, and smiled. This was a perfect way to fall asleep. Relaxed and sated in a room that smelled of Sophie. He moaned as he felt her warm kisses along the back of his neck. He breathed her in, enjoying her ministrations. How in the world did she ever learn to do that? Whatever it was, she should teach it in their class.

His eyes opened as he felt her pull away, rolling off him, off the bed. As she covered him with the comforter he caught her wrist. "How do you know how to touch me?"

Sophie took his hand in hers and knelt beside the bed. "You told me."

He shook his tired head. "I didn't say a word."

"Your breathing, I listen to how you breathe and you tell me."

"You listen to me breathe?"

"Yes, sometimes I hear more when you breathe than when you talk." He closed his eyes and listened to his breath. Ragged, shallow and purposely slow. What did she hear in that? She ran her hand gently through his hair.

"Feel better?"

He nodded slowly, not wanting to open his eyes. He felt her lips softly pressing first one eyelid and then the other, heard himself sigh. His eyes barely opened as she dropped his hand.

"Where are you going?" he asked sleepily.

"You sleep," she said, crossing the room.

Stay, he heard in his head.

Chapter Eleven

David's back didn't hurt at all this morning, making him wonder if it ever did. He was second-guessing every feeling he'd ever had. Sophie had knocked him to the ground. Literally, figuratively, in every way possible. She was a mass of contradictions he couldn't wrap his head around.

She was mad because he got her a car he couldn't fit in, yet a few days later she was ejecting him from her life. He'd been more intimate with her than he'd ever been with a woman, yet she accused him of rejecting her. She'd said no more touching, then hadn't kept her hands off him. Not that he'd minded in the slightest.

Maybe she was just playing a game with him. Jerking him around for sport. Maybe this is what she did, why she went out on so many dates last year. It was easily a different guy each week, sometimes two. He knew she dated, Craig had told him as much. What the hell was "I waited for you" supposed to mean anyway?

David shoved his hands deeper in his coat pockets and willed himself to pay attention. This plan had been his idea completely, and he couldn't even focus long enough to make it through a presentation.

The acquisitions director of SGI was leading David and six board members around the perimeter of the Taylor Center. The high-rise housed Strong Gym's downtown location at street level with offices, including eight floors of SGI's corporate headquarters, on the seventeen floors above. David had decided SGI would buy the building instead of continuing to lease the space two years ago when he took control of the company.

Growing the company through real estate hadn't been popular with the older board members. Now that their holdings included seven high-rises in three states the board was starting to sit up and take notice of the growing profit margin.

Not that he needed their approval anymore. For the first deal his father had run interference and called in favors to get the approval for the sale. But now, for the first time since his grandfather had taken on partners, a single person held the majority of the company shares and made the decisions. Him.

He'd achieved his career goal. There were still projects he wanted to accomplish, but his main objective of majority control of SGI was complete. It was time to reevaluate where he wanted the company to go. David was never satisfied with more of the same.

He tried to listen about equity and growth potential. It seemed interesting enough to the board members, but David had read it word for word in the report last week. His eyes wandered across the street to the row of storefronts. His gaze caught on a sign in the window of a travel agency.

Sophie probably hadn't traveled much. There wouldn't have been much time for that. Her youth had been filled with responsibilities, while his had been peppered with extravagant adventures like the safari for his sixteenth birthday or the summer in New Zealand after graduation. Sophie would like Europe, he decided with a nod of his head. She should take a Mediterranean cruise so she could sample a little of everything.

David froze as the rest of the group turned the corner for a better view of the building elevation. *Where the hell had that just come from?* From the emotional roller coaster that was last night, David could tell Sophie didn't know what she wanted anymore than he did. Or she'd realized he couldn't give her what she wanted.

Falling in step behind the group, David tried to listen to the questions the board members asked. Tried and failed as his attention was diverted by the sparkle of diamonds in a jewelry store window across the street. He shut his eyes tight against the glare. There was no way he was going there. What he felt for Sophie was a companionable fascination, bordering on obsession. No reason for a ring and a complete revision of his life plan.

Before opening his eyes he turned, so as not to risk being tempted by the glare. He opened his eyes to the grocery at the end of the street and a huge display of easy-peel oranges. It was as if the whole damned universe was conspiring against him.

This was never going to work. No matter how she looked at it, she just couldn't make it fit. Something had to give. If the landlord raised their rent even a little, the club would be in the red. They were flirting with the line as it was.

Sophie scrolled through the budget sheets one more time, hoping for a miracle. Her meeting with the landlord was in two days, and the bastard always wanted more. Ever since Daphne had opened he'd raised the rent every six months, per the ridiculous agreement Daphne had signed.

There was really nothing to prune from. All of the programs would be profitable if overhead weren't so high. As it stood, the club would have to close shortly after Daphne returned from maternity leave.

"There has got to be something I haven't thought of," Sophie said to herself, blinking her dry eyes as she continued to stare at the monitor.

"You want me to take a look?" She spun in her chair as David's voice boomed in the doorway. He must have come from work. Sophie mentally froze him there in his chocolaty suit pants and toffee colored dress shirt. In his hand he had a box of easy-peel mandarins. Odd.

"I'm not as great with numbers as you are, but I do know my way around a financial statement."

He looked delicious and she was so hungry. "Are you trying to seduce me with produce, again?"

David smiled and looked at the box. "I do seem to have a citrus thing with you, don't I?"

Forcing her grin away, she turned back to her computer. She'd forgotten herself last night, but in the light of day she'd be stronger. "You don't have to bring me presents."

"Sure I do." David entered the office and cocked a hip against her desk. Just what she needed, a close up view of exactly the treat she was missing. "That's what I wanted to talk to you about. Are you playing some kind of game with me?"

"Me?" Sophie had to force herself not to shout. "You must be joking, but it isn't very funny."

He leaned back on the desk, planting his hands on either side of his narrow hips. "I'm wondering what your no-touching speech was about, since it was immediately followed by some very hands-on time." The man was nothing if not direct.

She hadn't been able to help herself. Guilt had overwhelmed her as she'd driven him home, and she'd honestly thought she could give him a massage without it turning into more. Of course, he'd been right. Subconsciously she'd been trying to seduce him. But she didn't want him to know that.

"How is your back?" she asked, trying to look busy on the computer as she saved her work, again, and powered down.

"Never better. You didn't answer me."

"What do you want me to say?" she asked, shutting the lid of the laptop, looking anywhere but at him.

"Are you trying to manipulate me with sex?"

"We aren't having sex." She shot back too quickly, pinning him to the desk with her eyes. "Are you trying to manipulate me with money?"

"What? Where did that come from?"

"You bought me not one, but two cars in the last week. And even though the truck is in my name, you left instructions with the dealership not to tell me how much it cost."

"You actually called them." He shook his head in what looked like disbelief.

"You had to know I would or you wouldn't have told them not to tell me."

He nodded and grinned. "Just like I knew you would try to wire the money directly into my account because you know I wouldn't cash your check. The truck was a thank you gift. It's rude to ask how much a gift cost."

"Fruit is a gift, David." Sophie said, thumping the blue box for effect. "An SUV is a major purchase."

"You're telling me. I had to try and squeeze into every damn electric car in this town. It took all day."

"Hybrid," she corrected automatically. Just how many had he tested out?

"You drove it today?"

Was that even a question? She nodded and watched a smug expression cross his face. Of course she was driving it. She'd never had a brand new car in her life. She loved everything about it. It was big enough to make her feel safe, yet small enough to park easily. It didn't use too much gas and it was cute. He fit in it and now she realized he'd spent all day picking it out. Of course she drove it.

She watched his fingers walk their way to hers. "Let me take you to dinner and talk you out of this no touching rule you dreamed up." She could feel the heat coming off his hands, but there remained a hair's distance between their fingers.

What had that woman in the steam room said? Raise your expectations so he'll step up his game. Game on. "If you're asking me for a real date, that requires advance notice."

"You're not seeing anyone else."

Thanks for the reminder. "No, but I'm tired, I just want to go home and put my feet up." As his fingers retreated, so did her game plan. She couldn't push her luck, it might push him away. "Come home with me. I'll make you dinner and we can talk."

He raised an eyebrow. "I thought you said you were tired."

"I am, but cooking relaxes me. You can help."

"I can't cook," he said, shaking his head.

"There it is, another item on the long list of things you won't even let yourself try."

David stood. "Should I bring the oranges or leave them here?"

"Are you afraid I can't whip up something appropriate for dessert?"

The driveway was dark as she pulled in. Stepping out of the truck, she noticed shattered glass on the ground. Crazy teenagers must have thought breaking the lights that usually illuminated the parking area was a funny prank. She shook her head and grabbed her backpack. She wanted to get inside and make sure she hadn't left anything embarrassing lying around before David got there.

Too late. The headlights from his car lit up the area. Sophie shrugged. Let him see her trashy romance novels. She had nothing to be ashamed of.

"How long has the light been out?" David asked as he pulled himself and the box of mandarins from the car.

"It was on this morning," Sophie said, noticing the extra key and alarm pad on his key ring as he slipped it in his pocket. She looked down at her new keys and smiled. He had her spare key. That had to be a good sign.

"You're sure the safety lights were on when you left this morning?"

Sophie glanced at the darkened side of her building. "Maybe the power is out." She started toward the stairs, but ran into his arm.

"Do you have your cell phone?" His voice was calm, but the look in his eyes was anything but.

"What's wrong?"

"Did you leave a light on?"

"Of course not." Sophie looked up at her dark apartment windows. Was he trying to scare her?

"I thought I saw a light inside as I pulled in. Why don't you call the police, just in case."

She shook her head. Who was playing games now? "It's just dark, David," she said, stepping into his arm again.

"Fine. You stay here and I'll go check it out." Lifting her hand he pointed to her alarm pad. "If anything spooks you just press the red button. It makes the alarm on the truck go off and I'll come right back."

"You're starting to freak me out," she said, dropping her hand. He shrugged and made his way to the staircase. Two could play at this little game. Sophie dug her cell phone out of her backpack and flipped it open. She would call her home number and spook him as soon as she saw him at the door.

But instead, she heard crashing, bumping, growling, wood breaking, saw the flicker of light in the window he must have seen earlier. She didn't dial her own number, she hit 911.

�֍

Sophie wanted David more than she wanted to breathe. In those long minutes waiting for the police to arrive she'd imagined so many things that could've gone wrong.

Even after he called down to her that he was all right, she still worried. Once the cops handcuffed the intruder, Sophie clung to David as tightly as she could. Wishing it was all over so she could just tell him exactly how she felt. No games, no future, no regrets. Just now.

She hadn't been able to find a thing that had been taken. Stuff was thrown everywhere, but nothing seemed to be missing. Every time she closed her eyes she saw it. The flicker of light in the window, the flashing police lights. What if she'd come home alone? She'd teased him, never thinking anything was wrong. The thoughts buzzing around her head wouldn't let her forget.

Six minutes. That was how long the police said it took them to respond. Six minutes of sheer hell as David held the creep down and tried not to imagine what might have happened if Sophie had come home alone. Into a dark apartment. Where that loser was rifling through her things. Probably waiting. Every time his mind had gone there, David twisted the little snake's arm further up his back.

He was grateful she'd stayed by the truck and waited for the police to arrive. It might have scared her to see him that way. It scared him just to feel it. To feel how close he had come to losing her, losing any part of her.

He was glad Sophie was there now, on the twin bed in his guest room where she insisted on staying, even though he'd offered his room. Her words still haunted him. *Unless you're going to let me sleep with you.* Barely audible, and she hadn't even looked up when she said it. It wasn't a good idea. Even with as much as he longed to hold her close and make sure she felt safe, he didn't trust himself. She'd closed the door over an hour ago, but he hadn't managed to sleep at all.

David heard a noise coming from the kitchen and sat straight up. He knew it was just her, but got out of bed just in case. Pulling on a T-shirt, he walked toward the kitchen. She must be hungry, and she needed him to show her where he hid the chocolate.

Sophie was sitting on the counter, opening a tube of refrigerated cookie dough with a knife. Seeing him, she set her project aside. "I can't sleep," she admitted before forcing a smile. "You don't have any food. Are you sure you actually live here?"

"I live here," he said, opening the cabinet on top the refrigerator where he hid his chocolate from Kelly. "I just don't eat here very often."

Turning to offer her the silver bag, he noticed the tears. "I should have called the police when you asked. I'm sorry."

"It's okay," he shrugged and set the bag on the counter beside her. "I just had a feeling. You couldn't have known."

She filled her hands with his shirt. "I shouldn't have let you go up there. If anything would have happened to you…"

"Sophie, it's fine. I'm a big guy. People don't really mess with that."

"You're not bullet proof." she said, choking on a sob. "The police said he had a gun."

"Hey, it's okay." He stepped forward, wrapping her up in the protective shell of his own body. He remembered the feel of the gun against his knee as he'd held the jerk on the ground. If the guy had been smart enough to go for it, the whole thing might have come down very differently. "I'm fine. You're okay. It's over."

"I know, but every time I close my eyes I see it." She looked up into his eyes. "I was so scared."

"Me too." He inched back to look at her face. He cupped her face in his hands, using his thumbs to brush away the tears. He leaned in and kissed her softly, gently brushing his lips against hers.

He felt her legs wrap around his waist as she reached up and pulled him to her, deepening the kiss. There was no holding back in her kiss. Her mouth provided such a sensual assault he had no choice but to give in. It took every ounce of strength he had to pull away.

"Please," she begged. "I don't want to think anymore. Please."

If he doubted her intentions, her hands removed any doubt. She pulled at the waistband of his sweats, her hands sliding beneath the fabric. David tried to remember why he kept stopping this when it always felt so right. There was just enough blood left in his brain to form one rational thought.

"Sophie, not like this, okay. Not tonight. Your first time should be candlelight and roses."

Her hands released him, drifting to his hips and pulling him closer against her. "We have moonlight, I'm allergic to roses and the only thing I ever wanted for my first time was you. David, I—"

He silenced her mouth with a kiss. He was barely breathing after hearing she wanted him. If she finished her thought he'd melt right into the floor.

He lifted her from the counter and carried her effortlessly to his bedroom. Laying her against the mattress he decided he was going to make love to her. There was a lot he couldn't give her, but he could make her forget her fears for a moment, make her feel cherished and beautiful.

Leaning back on her elbows, Sophie watched as David lifted his white T-shirt over his head. The angled muscles rippled with the movement as he dropped his sweats and stepped out of them. He was magnificent with his unabashedly male confidence. He looked like he could have been sculpted from marble, fit for a gallery pedestal except for the thick member pressing against his concave belly. That was more suitable for one of the erotic art galleries she'd read about.

Yes, she thought as she sat up, this was exactly what she needed to keep her from thinking about anything else. Whenever he was this close her mind shut down and opened up only to him.

"Sophie," he whispered, lifting the hem of her T-shirt over her head. She raised her arms, helping it slide off quickly. She was instantly grateful her obsession with him had made her switch to lacy pushup bras as his gaze stuttered on her breasts. The look in his eyes now was all she ever really wanted from him. He wanted her. Now.

Her body moved across the rumpled cotton sheets as he slid on top of her. In one fluid motion she had gone from having her feet firmly on the floor to her head at the headboard. Fantastic.

"David," she said, her mouth finding his. The taste of him filling her, making her throb for him. Tonight she wouldn't take no for an answer. She wouldn't regret not being with him another moment. She would have him, even if she had to play dirty.

Reaching down, she wrapped one hand around him, rubbing her thumb across the swollen tip. He jerked in her hand. Freeing himself, he pulled her hands over her head and pinned her legs with his shins. With his body on top of hers she was reminded she still had on her pajama pants.

"Slow down," he said, looking her in the eye.

She shook her curls from side to side. "Now."

"If we go too fast it could hurt you, and I still need to get a condom."

She watched his expression freeze before his forehead hit the pillow beside her head. He must not be prepared.

"Good," she giggled, trying to move her legs to the side. He was so militant about using protection she knew he was safe, and besides, she wanted it to be different for him too.

He pinned her harder to the bed. "Don't you dare flip me."

"Don't you dare back out on me again." The way he was holding her down should have scared her. Her arms were stretched above her head, his shins pinning her parted legs on the mattress. But all she could think of was if it weren't for the unneeded layer of clothing, he could be inside her in seconds. Hell, she could probably manage the act herself by distracting him with a kiss and tilting her hips upwards.

"I promise you won't mind a bit." He bent, kissing her neck but not trusting her enough to give her an inch.

"I'll just wait until you're asleep," she said breathily, trying not to moan at the exquisite torture he was ravishing on her neck.

The light reflecting into the room off the water sparkled in his eyes. "You wouldn't dare," he said between clenched teeth. She felt his hands tighten around hers as she arched her back.

He wanted her as much as she wanted him. She could see it in his eyes, feel it in the air in the room. "I'm going to have you. Tonight." She held his gaze.

His head shook slowly from side to side. "That's a lot of bravado from a woman pinned to my bed."

"You can let go. I'm not leaving." Without letting up his hold, he kissed her again, forcing her to remember who was really in charge. For all her bold words she was completely at his mercy. When he kissed her like that, deep and full and hungry it was even up to him just when she could breathe.

He had full possession of her mouth, nibbling and sucking until she purred like a kitten. She didn't even care she'd lost whatever control she had, that they were now moving on his timeline. She only cared that he continue to taste and taunt her. Because she was painfully close. If he would only brush against her once she would be there.

She tried to arch up, but he pressed her back down. With her arms pinned, she couldn't even reach between them and take care of herself. She whimpered as his tongue worked slow circles down her neck.

"Please, just touch me."

He grinned up at her wickedly. "So soon?"

She nodded furiously, biting her lip.

He laughed, he actually laughed as he held her down, torturing her more with his evil tongue. Their size difference was being used against her now, as his impossibly long arms still anchored hers over her head while he tugged down the cups of her bra with his teeth. She could see her pink buds standing at attention. Arousal so deep it was almost painful.

She watched her nipple disappear in his mouth with one long pull. As his tongue flicked across the tip she felt her vision blur and closed her eyes, riding out the sensation as stars prickled the backs of her eyelids. Her body was not her own as she absorbed the pleasure he had offered up. Every nerve was firing. It was as if she could feel him everywhere all at once.

When her eyelids finally fluttered open, she realized her arms were at her sides, her bra undone and loose on her belly as he lapped at her other nipple. Ridding herself of the garment, she threaded her fingers in his hair as he worked her nipples more and more.

She could feel herself slick with wetness. She remembered how he had liked to watch her before and slid her hand inside her pants. Her fingers rubbed at the smooth folds as he sucked and nibbled harder. Sliding her pants and thong down her hips, she kicked them to the floor, giving him a better view of her ministrations. She could feel the pressure building again, but she wanted to wait for him this time.

Slowing down, she dragged her wet fingers up over her belly. Kissing his way between her breasts he grabbed her retreating hand, placing an open mouthed kiss on her palm that sent shivers to the base of her spine. As she watched, he drew her wet finger into his mouth with one hard pull. Breath stuttered in her throat at the building sensation. She couldn't wait. Running her fingers through his hair, she tried to pull him up to her as he kissed his way down her belly.

"Now. Please, I just need to feel you inside me."

"You have to let me. I need to taste you."

"Later, please."

"Later you'll taste like me."

She moaned at the thought, her blood pumping even thicker at the thought of him filling her. She couldn't control her body, her back arching wildly as his tongue pressed against her. She was thankful for his hands on her buttocks, pulling her open, anchoring her down.

His tongue made one long wet pass from her entrance to her clit that sent her soaring. As his lips focused their attentions, she felt her muscles begin to spasm. She could feel him slip a finger inside of her, curling it upward and coaxing her climax to go on and on. Breath escaped her, as the only thing that mattered was the next contraction of her muscles. He removed his finger, allowing her to come back down and oxygen to once more flood her brain. She needed him now—soon—before she was too far gone to notice.

After kissing his way back up her body, he pushed up, his large frame looming over her. Reaching her hand up, she brought his mouth down to hers in search of the taste of her he had talked about. Wrapping one leg around his back she arched herself up.

"Sophie, wait," he said breaking the kiss.

Her heart stopped. He was not going to say no again. She wrapped her other leg around his back lifting her hips completely off the bed and anchoring herself to him.

She felt his fingers in her hair as his kind brown eyes looked into hers.

"Promise me you'll tell me if I hurt you."

"You won't," she said in relief.

"Promise me," he said, lowering his body until her hips again met the mattress.

"I promise," she whispered.

Closing her eyes, she pressed against him, feeling his thumb spreading her lips and his impossibly large member rubbing between them, soaking up her wetness. She should be afraid, nervous, anything but the tightening she was feeling deep in her belly again. It was more than from the stroking of his fingers, the pressure of his cock as he slid against her, the tip of him finding the tip of her. It was the realization that soon they would finally be one.

Very soon, she realized as the swollen head of him pressed against her opening. Splaying her hips wider, she thrust up, pushing him further inside. His hand moved to her hip, holding her back.

She opened her eyes and studied the concentration on his face as he inched in frustratingly slowly. The initial sting melted into a stretched fullness, warming her from head to toe. He was there with her, inside her, filling her completely. It was sensation overload as all of the blood in her body traveled to the source of her pleasure. So close. Closing her eyes, she lived the feeling completely.

She could feel the fire of pleasure and rising passion burning inside, her muscles tightening around him. And yet he remained stoically, perfectly still.

"David, please," she whispered, offering her hips up to help him begin the motion.

He brushed his lips against her temple. "Just a second. I'm not sure if I can."

"I'm close," she whispered, running a hand down the planes of his chest.

His eyes flew open. "Promise?" he growled.

She only got to nod once before his downward thrust smacked into her body, pressing her against the bed. His strokes came at her now, fast and hard as she rose to meet every one. She bit her lip, forcing herself to wait for him though she could feel the dam starting to overflow. She heard her moans echo through the quiet room, mirroring David's panting breaths.

Not able to hold back any longer the dam broke and she could feel her own juices start to flow. His insistent rhythm forced her spasms to continue, drawing them out longer and longer until she thought she might pass out from the sheer intensity.

She was terrified she might have to tell him to stop, might not be able to before she blacked out into oblivion. His rhythm slowed and she could actually feel jets of warm liquid streaming into her body. Wrapping her arms around his neck, she brought him to her, crushing her breathless body with his. She lay under him with her eyes closed, enjoying this intense sensation she was feeling for the first time in her life.

David hated it when women asked to cuddle after. It was just too intimate. But it physically hurt when Sophie rolled away. He rolled closer and wrapped his body around hers. She was curled into a ball, so small that when he wrapped around her, her feet came to his knees. "Sophie?"

She rolled into him, burying her body in his. He felt the cool wetness of her hot tears against his chest. "Oh, no. Sophie, I hurt you. I'm so sorry. Why didn't you tell me?"

She looked up at him, her big blue eyes wide and surprisingly clear as she tried to force a smile. "You didn't hurt me, not even a little."

"Then why the tears?" His hands framed her heart-shaped face.

"I'm just on emotional overload right now. Post-coital bliss and all that."

He wiped another tear with his thumb. "You don't have to be brave Sophie. I'm sorry. You just have to tell me when it feels—"

She silenced his mouth with her finger. "I can't tell you how I feel. You won't let me." Her voice was a rough whisper against the silence. He watched two more teardrops erupt from her eyes as she closed them. His breath caught as he watched them roll down her pink cheeks and onto his hands.

Her mouth found his without looking. She kissed him wet and hungry, deep and demanding as she rolled on top of him. She laced her fingers through his and brought their hands to the side.

Butterflies in Flight he realized too late. "Sophie, we shouldn't."

He thought it would be too soon. For him, for her. But she seemed to communicate with his body better than he did. He hadn't even realized he was ready again until he felt her body sliding against his, the sweat from their last mingling helping her to glide across him. He remembered how this felt the first time, with all their clothes on and a room full of people watching.

He hadn't imagined it right. There was a gracefulness to the position he hadn't fathomed. It wasn't mechanical at all.

The feel of her breasts pressing against his chest as she rocked was amazing. He could open his eyes and watch the swell of them as she moved, aligning their bodies. Watching her, he could feel his own need growing. The need to be back inside her, to be back in the one place where they made perfect sense.

"David," she whispered as the head of him finally kissed her, finding her wet and ready. It almost hurt to look into her eyes as she bit her lip and slid him inside of her. He wondered if she could see as deep into his soul as he saw into hers at this moment. This was how it was meant to be. A man and a woman and a feeling bigger than either of them.

He might not have heard her I love you, but he felt it.

Sophie was here, still here in his bed. Though to be fair, with the hold he had on her she couldn't have moved if she'd wanted to. He had her pinned to the mattress with his arm and thigh. He pulled back slightly. He must be crushing her.

His mind was still groggy from sleep as he began to realize everything that had transpired. It hadn't been a dream, or she wouldn't be here. And it hadn't been just sex. No, that would have been too simple. He'd made love with this woman over and over. He closed his eyes against what that meant.

It wasn't ever like this. When he came, he usually felt like he was letting go, falling apart for a brief second. This felt like holding on, and coming together forever. Sex usually left him sated yet energized. This, whatever it was, had him hungering for more.

He had to think, and to think this early in the morning he needed coffee. Slowly, he released her, turning to the opposite side of the bed.

"Don't move." Her voice was thick and gravelly from sleep. She reached out and pulled him closer. "I'll freeze to death if you leave."

He chuckled and held her close. She was hardly cold. He gave her a squeeze and prepared to make his exit again. She grabbed his arm and looked up at him.

"You're trying to kill me. It's freezing in this place."

"I need caffeine or I can't function." He rolled out of bed and strolled into the kitchen. For the first time he realized how cold tile felt in the morning, how drafty the condo could seem. Maybe she really was cold. Once the coffee machine was on he crept back to the bedroom, wishing he had spare blankets somewhere so she wouldn't feel the chill in the air.

Sophie was tucked beneath the comforter; David could only see her hair from the doorway. Not wanting to wake her if she'd been able to fall back asleep, he turned to go.

"What are you doing?" she asked, tossing the covers back.

David groaned at the sight of her wearing nothing but his white T-shirt, so long it covered to mid thigh and her shoulder almost peeking out the neck. She'd put it on sometime early this morning, the skin-to-skin contact between them had kept either of them from sleeping.

One knee pressed on the bed as he bent down. With her curls tumbling about and her eyes still heavy lidded from sleep he'd never in his life seen anyone so beautiful. He dipped his head, kissing the expanse of skin at her neck that should have been covered by the shirt. He moaned, laying her back down on the bed. And he thought he had wanted her badly last night.

"I thought you needed caffeine," she giggled, pulling the blankets over the top of them.

"I need you," he whispered against her skin as he lifted the hem of the shirt.

"Enough to turn up the heat in here?"

He doubted the pearled nipples beneath his hands were the result of the temperature. "I'll keep you warm."

David should have started sleeping with Sophie a month ago. He accomplished more in the half day he'd been at work than in the entire week. And it wasn't because there were fewer people to interrupt him on a Saturday. He was just finally able to focus.

He was relieved his acquisitions director had come in. He'd been avoiding going over the building proposals, and having him there to answer questions streamlined the process. After deciding together which building to pursue in Seattle, David thought of another project.

"I want to get in on the Pearl District. Not having a gym there is noticeable. We looked at going in when the city was restructuring the area, but the rents were too high to hit our usual margin. It would be costly to buy in, but I think with the success of the other acquisitions behind us, we'll get the board to sign off on it." A shot of glee rushed through his veins. He didn't really need their approval. He still wasn't used to the power of majority ownership.

"We'll get to work on it. Did you have a building in mind already?"

The building Working It Out was in would be a good investment. He'd always thought it was a great location. But the real estate division of SGI was based on having Strong Gyms as the anchor of the building, not a rival women's club. David shook his head, deciding to let the team do what they did best and bring him the best options.

"We'll research it and I'll have a report back to you by the middle of the week." David shook the man's hand as he walked him out the door of his office. Turning around, David looked at his office as if it were the first time. It was empty. He needed to get some pictures, or art, or something. Something to make it look like he did more than just work.

His father's office next door was cluttered with photos. He didn't want it to look like that, but something would be nice. David made his way into his father's office. Flipping on the light, he was not at all surprised Lance hadn't touched a thing yet. The deep green walls absorbed the light, making the snapshots on the walls seem to glow as if backlit.

Tessa had redecorated the office completely when she took over as Lance's assistant. The pictures all hung in matching dark wood frames, arranged artfully. The effect was warm and inviting. David wondered what Lance was going to do with them all. Most of the photos were copies of those hanging on the walls at home.

Tessa arranged the photos by subject. One arrangement was largely she and Lance together. Another block was vacation photos. Kelly dominated the wall by the bathroom. David stepped behind his father's desk and examined the wall where pictures of him filled the space.

There was the gratuitous bathtub shot, first day of school, Little League, a portrait of him and Lance in tuxedos. He looked about ten. Must have been when Lance married Gretchen. There was him and Craig at graduation, a snapshot of them from Greece, him and Lance the day Kelly was born. His heart stopped on the faded eight by ten in the center.

There weren't many pictures of his mother, so he knew this one by heart. His father stood behind her, wrapping his hands over her swollen belly, both of them smiling like fools. Her blonde hair long and loose like women wore it back then. He plopped down in the desk chair and stared at her smile. Did she know she'd be dead within a week? That it could all be over that quickly?

"You should take them." A voice jolted him back to the present. Tessa stood in the doorway with a rolling cart and lidded storage boxes. Her long black hair hung in a sheet down her back. "I'll have someone from facilities move them over to your office."

David met her almond-eyed gaze and wondered why she had chosen to clean out the office on a Saturday. No matter what Sophie had found, or what his father had confessed to, he still didn't trust Tessa with anything.

"Dad with you?" he asked, rising.

Tessa shook her head, pushing the cart toward the vacation collection. Her head was still moving as she turned back to him. "I'm just here to collect some pictures to decorate with at his retirement party."

"I can help you," he said, walking toward her. He'd already removed all of the sensitive files and computer from the office, but he didn't trust her alone in the building.

"Suit yourself." She shrugged, lifting the pictures off the wall and setting them carefully in the box. "I haven't received your card for the party. You are coming." It wasn't a question. As if she had any right to make demands of him.

"I'll need to make an appearance." He set a picture of him and Lance arm in arm wearing scuba gear in the box. He must have been about twelve.

"Will you be coming alone, again?" She didn't change her tone, or stop her hands. Just intruded where she wasn't wanted as if she had the right. As if she were more than a transient figure in his father's life, barely older than him.

It was the "alone" that made him pause. He always attended events alone. Bringing a date implied a level of formality, regularity he wasn't usually comfortable with. But he had to admit, the party would be easier to get through with Sophie there to talk to.

"I'm not sure. Why?"

"You father is hoping you're seeing someone."

David watched her turn to face him, felt her reading his reaction. Was he? Were they? They hadn't exactly gotten around to discussing it. And he hoped they'd never have to.

"Are you taking these too?" David asked, crossing to the collection of newer photos featuring Tessa and Lance together.

"Yes," Tessa said, putting a lid on the first box and opening another.

She pushed the cart to him, then made her way to the desk. David held his breath as she opened a drawer and pulled out another framed photo.

"This one too," she said, slamming the drawer with her hip.

As she walked past David caught a glimpse of it. Lance and Tessa, him and Kelly from the wedding. The one Kelly dragged and guilted him into coming to. He was the only one not smiling.

David had hated that day. He'd begged his father not to go through with it. Marrying a woman so she would drop a sexual harassment suit was like jumping from the frying pan into the fire. But Lance claimed legal action was the only way for Tessa to get through to him. Maybe the two of them were both so twisted they deserved each other.

"Why was it in the drawer?" David asked as she slid it in the box with the rest.

"He was upset," she said, as if that explained anything.

Chapter Twelve

David was surprised to see Sophie's red SUV in the parking lot of her apartment building. She was supposed to be at work. He'd been expecting to see service vans, not her truck. Fishing the gym bag he'd thrown some clothes in from the passenger side of his car, he made his way to the stairs. David nodded to himself, noting the original floodlights had been replaced and new motion-sensitive lights had been added along the stairway. Better.

At the top of the stairs, he inspected her door. The door and the frame were new, reinforced steel. The door had been painted to match the others on the converted Victorian, but an alarm warning and permit were affixed to the bottom corner. Much better.

He knocked, listening for any sound from inside. He couldn't even hear her coming toward the door. "Sophie?" he called, knocking again. His heart started to race. All the workmen were employed by SGI, so they all had passed a background check. But the alarm company, who had they sent? And why hadn't they waited like he'd instructed them to? His fist hit the door again, harder. "Sophie!"

As the door swung open, he stepped inside, lifting her off of her bare feet, crushing her against him. "Don't do that," he whispered in her hair. "Why didn't you answer the door? What are you doing home?"

She swung her legs, reminding him he still had her up in the air. Once her feet were on the ground, she took a step back and looked up at him.

"I live here. Or at least I thought I did before I came home and found a team of worker bees all up in my business. There were twelve people here, David. Twelve."

Sounded about right. The cleaning team, locksmith, alarm company and maintenance crew. All with orders to be done by the time he arrived at six. It was five thirty. He dropped his bag by the potted palm and closed the door, locking the deadbolt in place. "Is that peep hole too high for you?"

"David," she snapped, placing her hands on her hips. "I am not something you can put on project status. I can take care of myself."

"You shouldn't always have to." *Where was his thank you?*

He watched her eyes dance as if she couldn't make up her mind about something.

"The peep hole is fine. I was watching you outside and trying to decide if I should let you in."

He recognized her then, not Sophie, but that animal from the morning when she'd taken his keys. He wanted Sophie back. "Of course you should let me in. What smells so good? There's a lemon and berry thing going on in here."

"I can run my own life. I don't want you to bulldoze over the top of it. You can't make these kinds of decisions without me. I won't let you tell me what to do."

"That's not what I was doing," he said, stepping into the kitchen. It was a muffin explosion in there. His mouth watered in anticipation.

"Hey!" she shouted, following him into the kitchen. "We're not done." Sophie slapped his hand as he reached for a muffin.

"You hit me!" He looked at his hand in disbelief.

"Sit," she demanded, scooting one of the kitchen chairs against the wall.

"You can't tell me what to do." Why was it that whenever this side of her came out he sounded like a petulant child?

"You don't like it either? Imagine how I felt, coming back to my own home, already nervous because of the break-in, to find my apartment swarming with people who refused to tell me anything until I threatened to call the cops and showed them ID."

He sat. "I didn't think you would be home until after they were gone."

"Keep talking, because that's only making it worse." She was really angry. Determined. Sexy. "Were you going to take my spare house key like you did with the truck? Just never mention it and see if I notice?"

That was exactly what he'd intended to do. "I called it all in last night. I needed to make you safe here. Do you want to move?"

Her head reared back, making her curls ripple down her shoulders. "What? No."

"This is what I needed to do so you could stay."

She huffed her breath in and out. "David, I'm renting. My landlord is going to freak at all the changes. The door, the wiring for the alarm, the added lights to the outside of the building. It's way over the top. All I needed was a new lock, and I was going to call a locksmith myself."

"I didn't want you to have to."

Her fingers dug into her hips, her nails turning white. "I'm supposed to go through and find what was taken. The cleaning crew straightened everything better than it was before. I don't even know where to look."

"Jewelry. The kid was after jewelry. He got pieces from the other three places he hit, but says he didn't find yours."

She actually stomped her foot. Very cute. "The police told you that? They haven't even returned my call."

David shrugged. "My security director called in a favor. You must have a better hiding spot than most people."

"I don't have any jewelry." Sophie sighed and turned, staring at the front door. Her shoulders rose and fell as she seemed to contemplate something. She turned and walked to him, nestling her way into his lap. "I'm not mad anymore."

As if an outburst like that could mellow so quickly. "Just like that?"

"Life's short. I'll have plenty of time to be mad when I'm dead."

"I think the saying is I'll sleep when I'm dead."

Her smile showed she really was over it. Her anger burned out as quickly as it had been ignited.

"Nah, I'll be exacting my revenge."

"On me? I was trying to be nice. Most women would appreciate it and say thank you."

"I'm not most women," they said in unison.

He wrapped his arms around her and pulled her closer. Her kiss tasted of lemons and raspberries, and was interrupted by the buzzing of the oven timer.

"What are you doing in here?" He released her, watching as she stood and exchanged pans in the oven.

"You mean besides wishing my kitchen were as big as my entire apartment?" She smiled and slipped off the oven mitts. "When I get frustrated I cook. And since Craig and I are working out next season's Deliver-Ease menus, I opted to test out some recipes."

"I pay him for that," David said, popping a mini-muffin in his mouth. The raspberries burst against his tongue, making him grab three more.

"Craig can't cook. I enjoy it." She slid a mountain of muffins into a bowl and set it next to the others. "Good?" she asked, wiping a stray crumb from his mouth.

He nodded. "What kind are those?" He motioned toward the four big bowls.

"Blackberry corn, like the ones that mysteriously disappeared from my fridge the other day." She gave him a pointed look. "Lemon raspberry, toasted coconut and blueberry cinnamon burst. All low fat and sugar free."

"You've always done this for him?" It was almost a year ago Deliver-Ease had turned from being a money sucking in-house nutrition program for Strong Gyms to a profit-generating phenomenon. A success Craig had taken all the credit for, never mentioning someone else had done all the work.

"I enjoy it, and since I get the meals at work, it pays off for me in the long run. Did you eat dinner yet? I'm trying out a couple chili recipes too. White bean and black bean."

"Sounds good. Do you have any beer?" he asked.

"I don't drink, but you could have Craig pick some up on his way over."

David froze. Craig was coming here, to watch them in this domestic bliss he'd never even thought to fantasize about? Craig was going to freak. Freak, and then kill him for messing with Sophie. Take him outside and ask him his intentions. And since they didn't go much beyond dinner, Craig was going to be angry.

"What?" Sophie asked, sitting in his lap again. "Craig lectured you on the empty calories of alcohol too?"

He pressed his forehead to hers. "I'm not ready. For Craig's microscope. I barely know what is going on here. I can't explain it to someone else."

"Me either," she whispered back. "You're here to keep me from eating all this food myself."

Pulling his head back he looked into her pale blue eyes. "You think that will work?"

Sophie shrugged. "It's true, and people believe what they want to believe. Besides, I can handle Craig even if you can't. If he gets too suspicious, just start asking about Daphne and he'll get so wound up he'll bolt. He only agreed to come here because she'll get sick from all the smells and arranged for a girlfriend to watch TV with her."

"For somebody that doesn't lie, you're awfully good at diversion."

"I can be devious, given the right incentive." She snuggled closer. "But I won't lie, David. If he asks."

"I know," he said, shaking his head with a smile. "Too much work."

Craig had bought it. A little too easily for Sophie's ego. Almost as if Craig didn't see it as a possibility. Granted, she hadn't thought it a possibility twenty-four hours ago, but that was beside the point.

A lot had changed in a day. Making love with David was even more than she'd hoped it would be. Almost erasing the fear from the break-in. She was still annoyed about the way David had taken charge, turning her apartment into Fort Knox. But when she saw his bag by the door her anger had faded.

He was going to try, actively attempt to break one of his precious rules. Usually she had to sneak up on him, break the rule before he had a chance to realize what was happening. She couldn't stay mad if he was going to try and make them work.

Them. She was getting ahead of herself. She wanted more, but he'd made it crystal clear that was not in his plan. She couldn't let herself read too much into it.

She'd set the ground rules, promised him that day at the bakery no one would know. Promised him a casual, no-strings affair. And she hadn't let him in on her realization she wanted more before they'd turned the corner. No going back on her word now.

"What are you doing?" His breath was hot on her neck, sending shivers down her spine.

"Cleaning up." She stepped aside, but he moved with her. "If you give me a minute, that's all it will take. If you keep on me, we'll be in the kitchen all night."

His hands came down against the counter on either side of her. "That doesn't sound so bad."

She spun to face him. "David, scoot. Five minutes, I promise."

He cocked his head to the side. When he looked down at her with those big brown eyes cleaning was the last thing on her mind.

"What should I do?"

"What do I look like, your entertainment director?" She held a finger to his lips. "Don't answer that, or I'll never get you out of here. Just give me five minutes to clean and then we'll do whatever you want."

His eyes crinkled in the corners as he leaned in closer. "Whatever I want?"

Her heart skipped a beat. "Whatever you want. Now go, before I change my mind."

Sophie didn't have cable and all of the books in the living room were written a century ago. Or for children. She seemed to have every Dr. Seuss book ever written. David moved to the bedroom and flopped across the bed, the cool cotton of the duvet soothing his heated skin.

Whatever he wanted. If only he could focus on getting the most out of that promise. But she had him so overheated he was going to have to make it up as he went along. He rolled on his side, remembering the books on the nightstand on his side of the bed. His side of the bed, as if he had been there more than once. He chuckled, sitting up and fingering the books.

"What are you laughing at?" Sophie called from the kitchen.

Damn, this place was small. "You'll find out in four minutes." He yelled back. Maybe she'd stay over at his place, where there was cable and more room. But her bed was bigger. He ran his hand across it, still a little intimidated Sophie had chosen the bed with him in mind.

Maybe they could just move the bed to the condo. David shook his head to dislodge the intruding thoughts about closet space and houses. He wasn't going to let himself go down a road he didn't belong on.

He turned to the books again. Her little red paperbacks with half-naked men on the front did nothing for him, so he opened the drawer to drop them inside. He winced, watching them tumble on top of not one, but two vibrators. Which one was BOB? He slammed the drawer shut.

"You okay in there?" Sophie called out.

"Three minutes," he hollered back.

The *Fabulous Fellatio* book had fueled some amazing dreams, but was not on his menu for tonight. The large white Kama Sutra manual was next. He grinned, back to where it all began. This would do nicely. Opening the front cover, he noticed color coordinating tabs sticking out from the pages.

He thumbed through, recognizing the basic positions from week one that had done him in, the female superior positions from week two he'd been fantasizing about, the sitting postures from last week that he'd finally managed to control himself through. Looking ahead he saw how the final weeks played out. Rear entry and standing, then a series called The Perfumed Garden. He noticed Sophie had made notes, listing yoga and Pilates moves to complement the poses.

The corners of his mouth twitched. She'd said anything. He scanned the pictures again. He was like a kid in a candy store, there was no way he could pick just one.

"What are you doing?" Sophie asked from the doorway.

He leaned back against the pillows and leered at her. "Homework. I need a study partner. You know anyone who'd be good?"

"Very funny." She switched off the light and bounced onto the bed next to him.

He reached to the lamp on the nightstand and flipped it on. The red scarf draped over the lamp made the room glow.

He watched the smile dance across her lips as she reached for the hem of his shirt. He lifted up, helping her take it off him. Pulling her onto his lap, he placed the book on hers. "We should practice for next week," he whispered into her ear. She stiffened and tried to push away, but he held her close.

"You know what you might like?" The tremor in her voice grated him like fingernails on a chalkboard.

"Sophie?" he asked, as she reached for her *Fabulous Fellatio* book. He took it from her hand, replacing it on the nightstand. "I'm not going to make you do anything."

"I know," she said, placing her hands on either side of his face. "Just not tonight, okay. I don't want you to be fantasizing about someone else yet."

"What?" He tried to hide his laughter. As if there was room in his brain for anyone else.

"The book says rear-entry positions promote fantasy, which has its place, but not tonight, okay? If you're going to break your one-night rule, I want to know you're thinking about me."

There was no way to not laugh at her innocence. He pulled her against the pillow with him, resting her head on his shoulder.

"I thought rules didn't apply to you," he said, trying to contain himself.

"They don't. Stop laughing at me!" She poked him with her finger.

"I had a one-time rule, not a one-night rule if you want to be technical. Once a break or nap is necessary, I bail. The only time I ever stayed over was with you last week, and then last night."

"Really?" she smiled, pushing herself on top of him. He tried to focus on the conversation as he felt her breasts pressing against his bare chest.

"Really, and believe me I would be thinking about you. And your heart-shaped ass. I swear." He could see she was still not convinced.

Her face twisted. "Those positions seem so clinical. One of them is even recommended for watching television. How can you make love to someone you are not even looking at?"

Make love. Damn. "You're over thinking it."

"I just don't see the attraction," she pouted. "And there are some that won't work for us."

"What are you talking about?" David rose up on his elbows at the challenge.

"Think about it. You are over a foot taller than me. When we're standing we don't exactly, you know, line up."

He collapsed back as the laughter racked his body.

"It's not funny, David. I've been trying to figure out how we are going to manage. The highest heels I can get are only four inches."

He could feel the tears squeezing out of his eyes.

"Stop it." Sophie jabbed at his sides. "Stop laughing."

"Stop tickling me. No one has tickled me since I was five." Rolling over, David pinned her beneath him. "I've been trying to tell you we don't match up for weeks." He caught his breath and watched the fire build in her eyes.

"I'll figure it out. Every one of those positions. I aced physics, I can do this."

He rolled off her as he started laughing again. "The physics of sex. Now *that* is sexy."

"You will like it." Sophie climbed astride him and lifted his hands over his head.

"Sophie," he warned as she slid the scarf off her lamp. With one hand, she held his arms against the pillows, her fingers unable to cover both his wrists at once. "No," he said, wondering if he meant it. It was strange the way this innocent so easily took control of his body and his responses. He'd never given away such power before.

"No what?" Her chaste expression could have fooled almost anyone.

"You are not tying me up."

Her grin sent a thrill through his body. "What fun is that?"

Maddening beeping invaded her dreams. Warm, wonderful, naked dreams. Sophie struggled to free an arm, then slapped the alarm quiet. David had her pinned to the bed again.

Sophie finally felt warm enough. Nestled beneath his body she felt safer than she ever remembered. The way his broad shoulders sheltered her body beneath his, the way one thigh pressed against her while the other was flung over her legs, cocooning her in his warmth. Neither of them could move without the other knowing.

His body radiated heat at exactly the same rate hers sucked it up. Finally, something could warm her. The position made her all too aware of the thickness resting against her backside, a reminder that had her turning around and waking him again and again until she'd finally thought to pull his shirt on. The thin cotton protected him from her, dulling the sensation and allowing them some well-deserved sleep.

David rolled off. "Don't let me do that."

She turned over, facing him. "Do what?"

"Trap you."

She loved the taste of his skin, the feel of his muscles just beneath the surface as she kissed his neck. "I like it."

Squeezing her closer he rolled, pinning her beneath his arm and leg again. She could feel his fingers twisting her curls, almost sending her back to sleep. "Sophie?"

"Hmm?"

"Why don't you lie?" His voice vibrated against her bare body.

"You say that like it's a bad thing."

"It's not, I was just wondering why."

Her hands opened and closed against his chest, her nails scratching him lightly. "Too much work. Who can keep all the stories straight?"

He was quiet for a long moment. "You don't want to tell me." It wasn't really fair, her always pushing him to be more open when she remained closed.

"I can't tell you without asking you to lie for me, and I don't want to do that."

"I can keep a secret."

"I don't know if I can tell one," she said with a sad smile. She'd only said it out loud once, and then it hadn't been the story, just a statement of fact under the safety of doctor patient confidentiality. "Besides, it's too early in the morning for this conversation."

"If you ever need to tell, remember I want to hear it."

She took a deep breath and weighed the risk. "You'd have to lie to Craig, and I won't ask you to. It's better this way."

"You don't trust me?"

To choose her over Craig? Not yet. "It's not that."

"I think it is. Not that I blame you."

Her stomach clenched. "Where do you see this going, with us?" If they had a future she would have to tell him someday.

"Diversion, nice try but you taught me that trick. Did something happen to you?" His arms tightened like a vice. "Did someone hurt you?"

"No, it's nothing like that. It's not even my secret to tell really. It's just a lie that keeps snowballing and I wish it had never started."

"Then end it." His lips were warm at her temple.

"It's not that simple. I can't just burden her with that."

"Her. Now we're getting somewhere. The her you're worried about could only be Daphne."

"David, please."

His body stiffened and he released her. "Oh my God, she cheated on him, didn't she?"

"No!" Sophie grabbed both his hands in her own. "She would never. She loves him completely, just look at all she is willing to do to give him a baby."

David relaxed beneath her touch. "I know. I should give her more credit. I still don't understand why they didn't just adopt. After all, Craig is adopted."

"That's why they didn't."

He rolled back, facing her again. "What?"

"Craig wanted to feel a blood connection to someone."

"That's ridiculous. His parents were great. They adored him."

"But they didn't look like him. And when he couldn't find his birth parents, he put everything into having a baby. When both he and Daphne had fertility problems, he was crushed."

David nodded. "I know, that's why I paid for all the treatments they needed."

"You did that? Even though you thought they should adopt?"

"It was their choice. I wasn't willing to pay for the surrogacy though, even before I knew it was you." His fingers were woven in her hair again, massaging her scalp. "Why did you agree to do it?"

"I wanted to. Daphne has always been focused on having a baby. She'll love this baby as much as she can. And I had a dream the night she asked me. Daphne handed me this tiny baby, and I held him and then I gave him back to her. It was so real. I thought it was a sign." He didn't need to know that in the dream it felt like her insides were being ripped out as she handed him back, had woken up and cried because he wasn't real. There wasn't another explanation for how moved she'd been by that blue-eyed little boy.

"Why would you want to have someone else's baby?"

It was so hard to explain, she wondered if she could even put it into words. "I wasn't thrilled about the prospect, but Daphne was beside herself. It was so important to Craig the baby be theirs, his. That there be someone in the world he could look at and see himself. I got that."

"I'm still missing something aren't I? Were you adopted? Is that why you and Daphne don't look alike?"

"No, I'm not adopted." Sophie whispered, measuring her words. Breathing slowly so she could stay in control, keep the tears making her eyes feel heavy from falling.

"I'm close to it, aren't I?"

She nodded and closed her eyes, focusing on breathing in and out, in and out. She wouldn't lie about it, she'd promised herself that much. But did she want to tell him, or did she want him to guess? Her eyes flew open at the thought of him guessing. He might make it worse than it really was, like he did earlier assuming the secret was Daphne's.

He reached for her, pulling her closer against his chest. It might be easier now that she didn't have to look at him.

"You don't have to tell me, but I want you to."

"Why?"

"It feels like something I should know."

Her eyes closed over the tears. He was right, and if she had as much faith in them as she claimed she shouldn't even have hesitated.

"When I was in junior high I was doing a biology project in my parents' living room with some friends. It was on the laws of inheritance, dominant and recessive traits. We had to do charts on our families. My dad was already sick by then, and so he was home. He overheard I was having trouble with mine. Both my parents were green-eyed blondes with straight hair, just like Daphne. All recessive traits according to the textbook. Which would mean my dark curly hair and blue eyes was impossible." She felt the breath fall out of David's chest as he drew her closer.

"My dad wheeled himself in and explained to my friends his mother had dark curly hair and blue eyes, that sometimes things skip a generation. Which my friends bought. But I knew she didn't. Her picture was in the hallway. After my friends left I asked him about it and he said, "I'm your father. That's all you need to know.""

"Daphne was already away at college, so I couldn't go to her. I assumed I must have been adopted, but as I looked through family albums there were pictures of my mom pregnant with me, pictures in the hospital when I was born. So I asked her. She refused to discuss it while my father was alive. It was an awful thing to sit and wonder about.

"After he died, she explained she had a brief affair with one of the lawyers at her firm. She was fifty years old, and had such a hard time having Daphne she never even considered it might happen again. She didn't know she was pregnant with me until she was four months along. My dad already had cancer by then and there was no way I could be his, and when she told him, they decided to work through it and never tell."

"And what about your biological father?"

"He knew about the pregnancy, but he and his wife never wanted children. They both died in a car accident when I was a baby." She'd researched him as best she could, not liking the person she found. But then, she'd always been a daddy's girl. No one could really measure up to the man who'd taught her to believe she could be anything she wanted.

"Why is it still such a big secret?"

Sophie felt her body stiffen. "Daphne can't know."

"She's an adult. There's no need for you to have to hold onto something for her."

"No. Daphne idolized my parents, and they her. They're dead. They can't explain or defend their choices. I swore to my mother I'd never tell Daphne and I won't." And she wouldn't let him either. "Don't you wish there were things about your dad you didn't know?"

She felt him nod as he tucked her head beneath his chin. "Yeah, I guess so. That's why you don't lie?"

"My whole life was a lie. I have a hard enough time keeping that one straight, I won't add any more."

"And that's also why you'll need to have babies."

That wasn't why at all, but she let that hang, not wanting to hear another argument against them being together, against him holding her right now.

Chapter Thirteen

A bloodsucker. That's what he was. Expecting them to be able to absorb a rent increase every six months. As if any business could withstand that.

Sophie's tiny feet pounded the sidewalk as she marched away from the real estate development office and the disastrous meeting with their landlord. She clutched her briefcase in her hand as she made her way down the block. Just how was she supposed to fix this?

She made it three blocks before she even realized she was headed in the wrong direction, deeper into downtown and the office building she used to work at, further from Working It Out. She tilted her head back, staring up at the skyscrapers. Her problems were taller than any of them. Daphne had been willing to trust her with a child, and she couldn't even keep their club alive.

Sophie tried to run her fingers through her hair, but it was locked up tight in a bun at the nape of her neck. She looked about her, watching the people rushing by. In and out of the buildings—to work, to shop. Spying the Moonstruck Chocolate's store across the street, she smiled. She deserved a little comfort right now.

The smell inside the chocolate café warmed her. Staring up at the menu board, her mouth watered. Cakes and cookies, truffles and candies, espresso drinks and hot chocolate. She doubted there was a single item on the menu Craig would condone.

Her fingers wrapped tighter around her briefcase. Had David meant it when he'd offered to help the other day? Daphne would kill her if she found out, but he did know more about running a gym than either of them.

It was a big favor. She got the biggest box they had, two of each of the twenty flavors. Maybe if he had enough of a sugar buzz he'd agree to look at the books and see something she missed. There had to be something.

As she stepped back out into the cool morning air she clutched the blue box against her. When would she see him? He hadn't said he was coming by tonight. She didn't really have any plans to see him until Thursday night for the class. The guilt would eat her alive by then. And there was no way the truffles would make it either.

She started back toward work, but stalled outside the glass enclave that was Strong Gym's downtown location. How people could get a workout with passers-by staring at them she'd never know. There was even a step aerobics class on display.

The corporate offices were here. She could leave the chocolates with his secretary, and he'd have to call to say thank you. She'd been there before, but that was on a Saturday when the office had been sparsely inhabited. Making her way to the receptionist's desk was easy enough.

Leaving the box seemed to get more difficult at every turn. Odd security rules wouldn't let her just drop it off. As if she was trying to bomb the man into oblivion. Trying to back out seemed to cause even more trouble, so Sophie pressed on until she made it to his floor. There, three secretaries questioned her at once. It was way too much hassle just to drop off a bribe.

"And who have we here?" a booming voice she almost recognized said from behind the fuss. Sophie turned, her eyes widening as she looked up at the man. He looked just like David. Older, and with blue eyes, but the resemblance was still startling. She blinked her eyes quickly to keep from staring. He had to be David's father.

One of the women explained her story at the speed of light. Sophie swallowed hard, wanting to make sure she could speak.

"Sophie Delfino?" the man asked, extending his hand.

Balancing the box and her briefcase in one hand, she took it, hoping her handshake wasn't too weak in light of the fiasco she had created. "Yes. I just wanted to leave the box, that's all."

"Nonsense." He pulled her closer, walking her toward David's office. "You might as well say hello as long as you're here. I've been trying to get him to introduce us for weeks."

Her eyes had to be bugging out of her head as he pushed her into the room. David had talked about her with his father? Was that good? Bad? Ugly?

David looked up from his desk as they entered the office. "Sophie? Dad?" He closed the file he was working on, shuffling it to the side with the others. He looked at his father. "What are you doing here?"

"Tessa wanted me to check the office before she had it cleaned out."

David rose and crossed to them. "Did you?"

"I'm sure it's fine. Aren't you going to introduce us?"

She watched David's lips press into a straight line. He grudgingly made the introductions. Sophie smiled in acknowledgement, and then stared at the floor. She should've thought this through. He was obviously upset she was there. She knew he had a rule about talking business with women he dated; showing up unexpectedly was definitely off limits.

Lance clapped his hands together. "We should all go to lunch."

"No."

Sophie jumped at the forcefulness in David's voice. She held tighter to the box and briefcase. Maybe if she just ran...

His tone was calmer when he began again. "We're not retired Dad, we have jobs to do."

Lance nodded, his shoulders sloping slightly. His hand rested briefly on her arm. "I hope we'll have a chance to talk at the party." Sophie watched Lance leave, felt David retreat back to his desk.

She took a deep breath, ready to apologize and leave. There was no way he'd be doing her any favors now. Turning, she watched as he rubbed his face, staring at the collage of photos on the wall at the side of his desk. They hadn't been there when she was here before. Stepping to the desk, she set her briefcase on the floor and pushed the box toward him.

"A sugar high can cure lots of things. Including me showing up and causing a ruckus. I'm sorry."

His eyebrows rose as he turned and looked at her, a smile slowly crossing his face. "I'm sorry you had to see that."

"What?" Intrigued by the pictures, she walked around the desk, stopping behind his chair as she studied them. David, in every stage of life. There was only one photo he wasn't in, a man and a pregnant woman beaming at the camera.

"That," his hand flailed at the door, "with my father. He can be a bit intrusive."

Sophie's hand rested on his shoulder as she leaned closer. "You have her eyes."

"I wouldn't know. We never met." His shoulder squared beneath her hand.

"Never?" The word came out before she could stop it. Craig had mentioned David's mother was dead, but she didn't know more.

"Aneurysm. Less than a week after that picture actually. They say it's a miracle I survived it."

"I'm sorry." Her arms slid down his neck, pulling him as close as she could in the chair. Was that why he didn't want children? She knew his childhood hadn't been easy, but was it pregnancy that scared him?

"Don't be. You can't miss something you never had."

She couldn't talk, not wanting to betray the tear in her voice. Just squeezed him harder and let him have his lie.

Sophie flipped a switch somewhere in him whenever she walked into a room. Emotions he usually kept in check easily bubbled up. She touched him and every sense was heightened, forcing him to recognize feelings he'd rather leave buried.

Looking at the picture was different with her there, her arms wrapped firmly around his shoulders. His father's words thundered in his ears. *That brief moment of being loved is worth any pain you have to endure at losing it.* How could that possibly be? He was in too deep to let her go now, if she got pregnant and he lost her... He pried her fingers away. That could never happen. He simply wouldn't allow it.

He'd scheduled and rescheduled a vasectomy three times in the last five years, but some emergency always came up and pulled him out of town. He'd call as soon as she left and make the appointment. Not using condoms was an indulgence neither of them could afford to get used to anyway. It was unsafe for his lifestyle, and he didn't want anyone hurting her later. He'd start using them now. He swallowed her hand in his own. Maybe immediately.

They just needed to burn out whatever was happening between them, and she would move on. He wasn't really a person to her anyway, just a fantasy. She already knew he would never give her what she wanted. Soon she'd tire of the game. They'd disappoint each other and it would be easy to walk away.

He pulled her around the chair and down onto his lap, really looking at her for the first time since she'd leapt from his imagination and into his office. She looked so serious with her hair pulled back and a business suit on. Tired, determined, defeated.

"What's wrong?"

"I'm sorry. I shouldn't have come. I really thought I could just drop the box off and leave." Her head nested against his shoulder as her fingers played with his tie.

She'd been there all morning in his head, it hadn't occurred to him it was strange she was there now. He never had personal visitors at work. Because he didn't have personal relationships. Craig worked at SGI. Kelly refused to even enter the building lest the family company draw her away from medicine.

Sophie was an anomaly in his life. A person who crossed so many of his boundaries he wasn't even sure how to categorize her anymore. Friend, colleague, girlfriend? He hadn't had one of those since junior high. Even in high school he kept to older women and one-night stands.

"What did you bring me?" Still holding her, he scooted the chair closer to the desk and untied the gold ribbon. Lifting the blue lid he stared down at heaven. "How many did you get?"

"It's their biggest box." He could hear the smile in her voice. "Two of each of the twenty truffles."

"Two? Are you trying to teach me to share?" The chocolate was tempting but she was so close and smelled even better.

Her hair tickled his chin as she shook her head. "No, they're all for you. It was supposed to be a bribe, but now I made such a mess of things consider it an apology."

Sneaking two fingers beneath her chin, he tilted her face up. His eyes focused on her lips and he couldn't deny himself a quick taste. "For what?"

Her eyes stayed closed as she smiled. "For breaking your no-business rule."

He shook his head. "It's a little late in the game for you to start respecting my rules now. Besides, I broke it first when I asked for help with the accounts."

Her eyes shot open. "I keep forgetting. You should check all the other joint accounts you have with your father for activity you're unaware of."

"What do you mean joint accounts?"

"Two party accounts. Like the one he was depositing the money into."

What the hell was she talking about? "I thought you told me the money was going into his personal account."

"Yes. A personal joint account. A trust if I remember right. I gave you the account number."

His head rolled back on the chair as he processed what she was saying. He'd taken over his own finances when his trust fund started paying at eighteen. The trust was the only joint account left. Or had been, until he had emptied it to pay for his father's buy-out.

"Son of a bitch." David's hand hit the intercom button so hard Sophie jumped on his lap. "Is my father still in the building?"

Two days without so much as a phone call, box of chocolates, oranges, anything. Sophie hadn't heard from David since she left him pacing in his office. She fingered the engraved invitation to Lance Strong's retirement party brought by messenger that morning. For Friday night. It was Wednesday. Obviously an afterthought, but whose? Did David want her there? Lance mentioned something about a party, was he inviting her because he realized David hadn't?

Other excuses for calling him were spread across the kitchen table. The cards for tomorrow night's class and the Working It Out operating statements for the last few months. She really did want his advice about the business, and they'd never gotten around to the homework he suggested when he was over last. Glancing at the clock, she let out a frustrated sigh. It was already eleven. Even David wouldn't be at work now.

Sophie marched back to her bedroom and threw open her closet. If she showed up at his condo he might feel obligated to review the books with her. Fear niggled deep in her belly. What if he was with someone else? What if that was why he hadn't called?

Her breath grew hot as she reached down and grabbed the highest heels she owned. Thigh-high, size four black patent leather boots she'd gotten when she dressed as a vamp one Halloween. The heels were so spiky if he wasn't alone she'd impale his foot and make him wish he had been.

Checking her face in the mirror, she realized the steam from the bath she'd taken earlier to try and relax had curled her hair more than usual. Her eyes were wild. She had plenty of excuses for wanting to see him, but her eyes betrayed the reason. She wanted him.

She licked her lips the entire drive to his condo, letting out a relieved sigh when she pulled in next to the Corvette. If he hadn't been here she'd been willing to try the office.

Clutching her briefcase, she navigated the stairs carefully in the stilettos.

Standing before the door, she realized she was obsessed. Who in their right mind hunted down a man at midnight? He would guess what she'd come for. She knocked with her gloved hand and held her breath. The entire world seemed silent. She couldn't hear a thing. Removing her glove, she rapped again. She'd wake him if she had to.

David's head was spinning as he flopped naked across his bed. He had done nothing but work for the last three days. Work, and try to get his father to call him back. Bastard's voicemail claimed he was on vacation. Lance probably realized his twisted plan had been uncovered when he saw Sophie. She'd been the one to find him out both times.

Sophie. She wasn't going to be happy when she learned he was the new landlord for Working It Out. Exactly how was he going to explain everything without having that evil monster that lived inside her show up? When his team had approached the property management company about buying, they'd been very forthcoming with information about their tenants, especially Working It Out. There was no way she could run a profit with rent that high, no matter what she was charging for classes. He could just give the building to her, but she'd never take it. Probably accuse him of manipulating her with money again.

He rubbed his hands over his face. He needed to shave, and get his mind on something else so he could get to sleep. He sat back against the pillows and grabbed for the remote. The television rose from the cabinet at the foot of the bed. A forty-inch plasma screen illuminated the dark room.

He loved the TV. The way it rose up boxed him in, making his bed seem like his own private chamber. The digital cable provided him with anything he cared to see on demand. He pressed buttons until the program guide came up. Sports, news, movies, there it was. Adult. He hit the button and a list of movies came up. They all sounded pretty tame, but still guaranteed to take his mind off the mess rolling around in his head. He selected one because it was part three in a series of six. Must be good if they made more.

As the music and opening credits rolled he heard knocking. *Great soundtrack.* Nestling into the pillows, he heard it again. He checked the alarm clock. It was almost midnight. He jumped as the knocking grew louder, more insistent. He grabbed a pair of sweats from a drawer and made his way to the front door and checked the peep hole.

What the hell? He opened it quickly. "Sophie? What are you doing here?"

She ducked under his arm and into the dark condo. "Is that peep hole too low for you? Because I know someone who can have it fixed."

"What are you doing here?" he repeated. Did she know what it meant to show up at a man's home this late at night?

"I was going to call, but I don't have your number."

"Yes you do."

She pulled the briefcase she carried tighter against her coat as he approached.

"I put them all in your PDA when you tried to break my back."

Her eyes widened, then narrowed as she dropped her shoulders. "You are such a snoop."

If that wasn't the pot calling the kettle black. "So are you. You went through my SGI statements."

"Maybe you left them there so I would."

Was she taller? "Did you leave your PDA on your desk so I would see how many men you've dated?"

"No! How could I have known you would snoop?"

His eyes took her in from head to toe. Yes, she was taller. She had at least four inches of heel on the boots hidden beneath her coat. Just how high up her leg did they go? He heard the cheesy music coming from his room and his stomach clenched. Caught. He had to keep her from going back there, but the flickering light was already catching her attention.

"Are you alone?" She arched her left eyebrow accusingly.

As if she could be replaced without a full lobotomy. "I thought you said you trusted me."

She narrowed her eyes to slits, focusing on his face, bare chest, finally freezing on the tent in his sweats. Caused by her damned boots, not the two seconds of credits he'd seen before answering the door. Sensing the conclusion she'd jumped to, he grabbed for her arm, but she swung her briefcase at him, nailing him in the stomach.

David sputtered, but kept going, not catching her until she was in his bedroom staring open mouthed at the television. "Where did that come from?"

He closed his eyes in defeat. He wouldn't be learning a thing about the boots tonight. "I can order it directly from the cable."

His eyes widened as she sat down on the bed, never taking her eyes off the screen. Her hand waved at the screen. "Not this. The television. When did you get it?"

He wasn't in trouble? He knew even less about women than he thought. "It hides in the cabinet during the day."

She jumped as a third person came on screen. She turned and stared at him wide eyed, shaking her head.

He tried not to laugh. "Me either, I don't even like to share chocolate."

Her shoulders dropped as she smiled and turned back to the screen.

It was surreal. He couldn't take his eyes off her as she watched. Moving behind her, he stretched his leg around her on the bed. "Do you like it?"

"I don't know," she whispered as if they were in a movie theater and might disturb people. "I've never seen one before. It's not very realistic." She was still whispering as she leaned back against him. "The noises are weird and they're all shaved. Even that guy with hair on his back."

He laughed and leaned his head down on her shoulder.

"Are most women bare like that?"

He wrapped his arms around her before answering. "Some."

Her stomach tightened beneath his hands. "Do you want me to be?"

"No." His fingers found the buttons on her coat and released them one by one.

Her eyes were on the screen as he slipped the coat off. His breath caught as his fingers found the ribbons holding her slip in place at her shoulders. The white, lacy material was all she wore beneath the coat. Except for the boots that came all the way to the hem of the slip. Leather and lace.

He got up and shucked his sweats, not that she seemed to notice. She stayed in her trance as he encouraged her to lift up so he could get rid of her coat. The way she stared was actually starting to bother him as he ran his hands down her sides to her hips. Through the slits on the side of her slip, he found her panties and began to pull them off. But his fingers encountered ribbon not elastic. Some genius had thought to make panties that tied on the side. If that wasn't a million dollar invention. He released her, but she remained still.

"I have a better idea," he breathed against her neck as his hands found the top of the boots. He pushed her legs apart.

Turning her head, she kissed him slow and full. "Me too. This is why they have that position for watching TV. I never thought of it before."

"I don't want you fantasizing about someone else yet." He lifted her up and tossed her back against the pillows, crawling to her as she giggled.

Her hand squeezed around his cock, finally doing something about the pressure building since she had marched into his place in those boots.

"You don't want to try it?"

"Try what?" He untied one side of her slip, peeling it back until his eyes feasted on her peaked breast. His tongue lapped at her sweet skin, carefully avoiding the bud. He wanted all of her attention. Her fingers threaded though his hair as she guided him to the tip. As she arched and moaned he knew he had her, even before he pulled her deep into his mouth.

But as he made his way to her other peak, her mouth started again. "The television position. It's called—" A shriek of delight escaped her as he scraped his teeth along the bottom of her other nipple. As he kissed a path down her stomach she began again. "We have to practice The Top. I have to learn to spin from facing forward to back."

He looked up. She had to be kidding. "Spin?"

Her lip was between her teeth as she nodded.

"I'm right here and you're thinking about textbook positions?"

"I haven't seen you for two days and you've been here, watching porn?"

His head fell against her belly, bouncing as she laughed with him.

"I was trying to give you a break." He crept back up her body, blocking her view with his shoulders. "You're new to this. I didn't want you to be too sore, and I can't be trusted to leave you alone if we're too close."

"I feel fine. I have a very active sex life, just not with other people. BOB and I—" He silenced her talk of the damned vibrator. He would make the thing obsolete if it killed him.

Pulling her arms over her head he whispered against her neck. "If you were satisfied with BOB you wouldn't be making a booty call on a weeknight."

"I'm here for business," she purred.

Dressed like this? He looked down into her face. Eyes closed, lips parted, breath ragged. Business? Hardly. Running him through the positions for real this time? Definitely. He pulled away and opened the nightstand. "Which one's first?"

She pushed up on her elbows. "Which one what?" Her heavy lids opened wide. "What are you doing with that?"

"Which position did you want to try first? I'm not sure if the spinning one works for real, but it sounds like a great show."

She snatched the condom packet from his hand. "What are you doing with this?"

He grabbed it back and stared past her shoulder. "I can't have kids, Sophie."

Her eyes flickered in the light. He hoped it was from the television. "If you *can't*, then you don't need it. And that's not a problem anyway. I told you I'm on the pill."

"Are you trying to get pregnant?" *Why is this such an issue with her?*

"Of course not."

"Then it shouldn't be a problem." He held the packet in the air. "No condom, no sex."

"Fine." Reaching down Sophie lifted and retied her slip against her shoulder. She had to be kidding. She would actually come all the way over here dressed like that and then bail because he wanted to back up their birth control?

He watched her get up and confidently march from the room. *No way.* He got up from the bed as she came back with her briefcase.

"What do you think you're doing?"

"I told you, I came for business." Sitting on the bed, facing the action, she popped open her briefcase and pulled out a file, an envelope and a stack of note cards. She handed him the envelope. "This came by messenger today."

He could tell without looking it was an invitation to the retirement party Tessa had turned into a fundraiser for extra publicity. He handed it back, unsure why she gave it to him in the first place.

"Okay, so it's not from you." Looking down she busied her hands, sorting through the file.

"Would you want to go?" He didn't, why would she?

She shoved the papers back in the folder and stuffed everything back in her briefcase. "This was a bad idea. Forget it ever happened." Slamming the briefcase shut, she reached to the floor for her coat.

Reaching down, he grabbed the coat and held it behind his back. She wasn't going out again dressed like that. "Why?"

"Why?" She echoed. "Because I've had enough rejection for one night."

"I'm not... Where is this coming from?" He sat down next to her on the bed.

She grabbed the packet he'd left on the mattress and flung it at him.

"This is safety, Sophie. Unprotected sex is an indulgence." One neither of them could afford to get used to. All too soon she'd be done with him. She'd realize he couldn't give her what she wanted and be out in the world looking for someone who could.

Her eyes closed and he watched her gnaw at her bottom lip. "You've been with a lot of women, David. I need to have something of you they don't."

Did she ever. But telling her would ruin what little power he still held. He carried the coat with him as he made his way to the table by the door and back. She was still holding her briefcase across her lap when he returned.

She'd turned off the television, the reflection of the lights on the water barely lighting the room. The curls, ribbons and lace make her appear even younger. Joining her on the bed, he handed her the credit card he'd retrieved from his wallet.

She narrowed her eyes as she flipped the card between her fingers. "What is this for?"

"You'll need a dress."

She held out the card. "I don't want your money. And I'm not trying to guilt you into anything."

He didn't take it. "I know. I hate these things. I don't want to go. I've never asked anyone to come with me. I didn't want to subject you to it."

"If you don't want to go, don't."

If only it were that simple. "It's a work thing, and he's my father. It would look strange if I don't make an appearance. And if I suddenly show up with someone, people will talk. Tessa turned it into a benefit for the school district athletics programs. There'll be cameras and reporters and after Colin's column... I honestly thought about asking you to come, but didn't think you'd want to risk it."

"Risk what?"

"Daphne finding out."

Her mouth formed a perfect O as he rose, gathering the briefcase from her lap and stacking it on the chair in the corner. He slipped the card into the pocket of her coat. Circling back to the bed, he stood before her. "If you want to go, buy a dress. If not, then don't." He ran a finger down her face. She turned, placing her cheek in the palm of his hand. "Isn't there something better we could be doing?"

Sophie took a deep breath and wondered how David managed to talk about everything from money to family politics blissfully naked. She was having trouble keeping her mind off the fact that he'd taken off her panties. What she wouldn't give to be that comfortable in her own skin. She gazed up into his eyes while he gently stroked her face. If she could only put her feelings for him into words. Then again, maybe not. Maybe it was better he couldn't read her mind. Not until she could read his.

"What do you like best about me?"

He answered quickly, without blinking. "Your hands."

She was sitting on his bed in thigh-high leather boots and a lace baby doll that left nothing to the imagination. As if he was thinking about her hands.

"Come on, you can be honest. I asked. It's not a trap."

"Your hands. They are my little secret. Hands so tiny and fragile looking, but amazingly strong and powerful." He laced his fingers through hers. "Hands wonderful to touch, and amazing to be touched with."

She cupped him gently with her hands. She wanted to learn everything she could about his body. Not only to pleasure him, but to help herself feel more at ease and less self-conscious.

"You could show me."

His eyes never left hers. "The way I remember it, you don't need to learn anything."

She smiled. "You could show me what you like, the rhythm, the pressure."

"I like it better when you do it."

"You're not playing fair."

"No, I'm not playing show and tell."

She felt him warming and hardening again beneath her hand. Her voice came out low and throaty. "Are you thinking of what you want me to do? Tell me."

"Surprise me."

She began to slowly stroke his growing member. "Maybe I should stop if you don't like it enough to tell me." She tried to pull her hand away, but his held it in place. He stared into her eyes as he lengthened her stroke. He showed her how to twist her hand gently at the top before coming back down. He released his hold on her and himself, and resumed watching her.

She took him first in one hand, then the other. Her hands worked together, one finishing and the other beginning as she stroked the length of him. His breath snagged in his throat as he grabbed her wrists, freeing himself from her sweet torture. Pulling her arms overhead he pushed her onto her back and reached for the condom.

"Let me," she asked sweetly, her greedy fingers contrasting her sweet tone. If he needed it to feel safe with her, she'd let him have it. And besides, she was curious to learn if it felt different.

He took the packet back. "I think I've had about as much of your hands as I can take."

Chapter Fourteen

Something had shifted the moment they had made love. She'd thought it had only been her, that it was the way you felt after your first time. But now she wasn't so sure it hadn't happened for him too. He seemed happier, lighter than before.

It was her turn to be the reluctant one now. Which made her feel extremely guilty for all the pressure she'd put on him. It was obvious he wasn't hiding the relationship from his family, but she was keeping it from hers. Sophie vowed to tell Craig and Daphne as soon as the baby was born. If there was still anything to tell.

Her fingers danced across the racks as she flipped through the dresses. Only three hours until she was supposed to meet him, and she still had no idea what she was wearing. The invitation said black tie but what did that mean for her exactly? Short, long, black, white? Not white. She wanted to catch his eye, to really make him see she could be as sexy and sophisticated as any woman there.

"Is there something I can help you find?" a sunny voice said from behind her. Sophie usually shooed the sales clerks away, but today she could use all the help she could get.

Turning, she smiled, recognizing the familiar face from one of her classes.

"Cindy? I didn't know you worked here."

"Here there and everywhere. The discount keeps Ramon from getting too angry about my shopping habit. Class was great last night, but I have to ask you," Cindy lowered her voice and stepped closer. "Does *The Top* really work?"

Sophie felt her cheeks go up in flames as she nodded. "Just go slow."

Cindy's cheeks pinked. "David mentioned that about ten times." They both fell into nervous laughter. "What can I help you find?"

"What do you wear to a black tie benefit?"

"With David?" Cindy arched an eyebrow.

David's comments in class the night before had removed any doubt the students may have had about them being together. No need to hide it from everyone. She nodded.

"I need something that will make him think how great I will look out of it."

Sophie's credit card was probably melting inside her wallet, but she didn't care. She was not going to take another cent from him. She still hadn't figured out a way to pay him for the SUV—adding to the tab was out of the question.

Still, she hadn't held back. Everything touching her body was new. Even the make-up Cindy had one of her friends apply at the store. Sophie stepped back and wondered at her reflection in the mirror. She'd wanted to look less like the wallflower she was, and more like a woman David would be with. She felt like Cinderella before the ball.

Cindy had piled most of her curls on top of her head, but a few tendrils danced around her neck. Sophie stifled a gasp as she looked down at the dress. The halter neckline pressed her breasts up and out, serving them up on a platter. The bodice cinched her waist before the silk georgette flitted about her legs in jagged asymmetrical layers. The slit on the side was so high she couldn't wear stockings, and since pantyhose never fit right her legs were bare. Cindy had dared her to wear nothing beneath the dress, but she'd chickened out and bought a small red satin thong that matched the color of the dress perfectly.

Red was the theme of the night, from her pouty lips to her spike-heeled shoes, to the quick coat of polish they had brushed across her nails before she'd left the store. Both cars he'd bought her were red, so she guessed he liked it. Maybe it was too much. She'd never worn red before.

Sophie jumped as she heard his familiar pounding at her door. The man did everything at full bore. No polite knocking for David. She slipped on her coat as she made her way to the door, buttoning up quickly before she opened it.

She reminded herself to breathe as he made his way inside. Sophistication oozed from him. Clothes just didn't fit regular people that well. His black tuxedo was obviously designer and expertly tailored, his black coat a wool three times as thick as hers. And he smelled so good. Maybe they should just stay in.

"Ready?" he asked, turning in the entryway.

She could only nod as he brushed his thumb across her lips, then pulled it back and looked at it.

"Smudge proof?"

She grinned as her wits returned to her. "To the average man, but I'm not so sure it would work on you. Feel free to try. I have lots more."

David smiled and shook his head. "I hate the taste of lipstick. Vile stuff." He reached past her, opening the door and ushering her down the stairs.

"Not to worry. This is completely kissable, and flavored too." He didn't respond, just urged her across the parking lot.

"I don't even get to see it?" he asked once they were in the car.

"See what?"

"The dress I bought." He maneuvered the car through the streets as smoothly as if they were on water.

"You didn't buy it, I did." She smiled smugly, pulling his credit card from her pocket. "You can have this back."

He kept one hand on the steering wheel, the other on the gearshift. "What good is having money if you won't let me do anything for you?"

"I told you, I don't want your money. I don't want to owe you anything."

He took the corner so sharp she had to grab on to the seat to keep from toppling out. "Let me do something nice for you. Something to remember me by."

So that's where this was going. "Don't leave, and I won't need memories."

He pulled the car effortlessly in front of the hotel and removed the keys for the valet. "I won't leave you, Sophie. You'll leave me. Everybody does."

He was out of his mind if he thought she would ever be able to walk away. She wanted to argue, but it was all she could do just to keep up with his frantic pace as he dragged her up the staircase and toward the ballroom, obviously forgetting she took almost three steps to his one.

The tension in his body tried to snake its way into hers, but she wouldn't let it. He'd told her he didn't want to come to the party tonight. She guessed because things were tense with his father. It was her job to make sure he enjoyed himself a little, so she stayed calm and hoped to distract him. She got her chance when they paused before entering the ballroom the party was being held in.

He stood stock still as she placed her coat on top of his on his arm. "Aren't you going to check them?" she asked sweetly.

He nodded and retreated back outside while she looked around the ornately decorated room. Green and gold, the company colors. A long bar was at one end of the room, circular tables in the middle and a stage at the other end with a screen running photos. Sophie's heart melted as the pictures changed. There was David, about three, and his father was pulling him on a sled.

Sophie felt him return, though he hadn't touched her. She turned, watching as David threaded a finger beneath his collar, tugging at it as if it were a noose.

"Doesn't your shirt fit?" He hadn't had that problem earlier.

"It fits fine," he ground out, his jaw clenched.

She batted his hand away. "Then leave it alone. You're ruining the effect."

"What effect?"

"You must know. Women love a man in a tux. That's why we make them dress up for weddings. You need to get a new shirt."

He shook his head. "It's not the shirt, it's your dress."

Worth every red cent. "You like it?"

"Every man in this place likes it, a little too much."

"Now you know how I feel." Everywhere they went, women looked at him from the corner of their eyes, sizing him up like a dessert tray. It made her feel possessive and proud. *Dear God, please let it have the same effect on him.*

David rolled his eyes. "That slit is too damned high. Every time you take a step I can almost see, you know. You are wearing underwear, right?"

She waved him off. "You know what I told the sales clerk?" Stepping closer she pulled his head down so she could whisper in his ear. "I said I wanted something that would make you think about how great I'll look out of it."

"It's working."

"Took you long enough."

Where was he? David tried to scan the room, but his eyes kept falling back on Sophie and that dress. Every time he let her out of his sight some jerk came up and tried to ogle her. He'd had to kiss her four times already to keep the trolls at bay, not that he was complaining. She'd found lipstick that tasted like pumpkin pie.

He hadn't expected her to look quite this way. Not that he should be quite this surprised, but still. She was beautiful when her face was scrubbed clean and her curls ran wild. With her face made up and her hair done and her body presented like that, he couldn't blame the other men for looking. She was flawless. And those pale blue eyes pulled him right in. If only he could go there.

But David was here for one reason, and one reason only. To find the old man and get him to explain the game he was playing, with him and SGI. Lance had to show for his own party. Maybe he should check with the desk, see if he and Tessa had a room to get ready in.

Circling back he found Sophie seated at the bar, people watching. He'd warned her about these things. He sidled up behind her, placing a hand on her hip and leaning in to kiss her temple while staring down the pipsqueak who'd been ogling her for the last three minutes. Thankfully the imp scampered away before he had to open his mouth.

"You don't have to keep doing that." She used the straw of her diet cola to stab at the cherries at the bottom of her glass. There had to be at least six. *Is the bartender hitting on her too?*

"I'm not doing anything." He knew it was a lie, but he needed to focus on the task at hand, not have an argument with Sophie.

"You're marking your territory and you know it." She finally speared a cherry and lifted it out, plopping it in her mouth and tugging the stem off.

"If he's not here in ten minutes we'll bail, I promise. I just need to straighten out a few things with him and he hasn't been returning my calls." He watched as Sophie swallowed, then put the cherry stem in her mouth.

"What are you doing?"

Her wicked grin made her eyes flash as she pulled the stem back out of her mouth, tied in a knot.

"Is this what you've been doing?" He swallowed hard. Maybe they'd leave in just five more minutes. "No wonder you have men lined up in droves."

She leaned closer, resting her hand on his knee and gifting him with an excellent view of her ample cleavage. "And to think, you already know you're coming home with me."

Tilting her chin up, he tasted her. The cherry and the cola and the sweetness that was all his, his Sophie, at least for now.

"I'm glad you could make it." David jumped at the sound of his father's voice. Why had he closed his eyes? He felt like a teenager caught necking in the closet.

David caught Sophie's hand, squeezing it, hoping to reassure some of the blush away. "Where the hell have you been?"

"I should greet my guests." Lance spun on his heel and stepped away.

David caught the older man's arm and angled him away from the crowd. "You will not avoid me for another minute."

Lance froze. "Here?"

"There's a balcony. Now." David imagined his father's smile was as fake as his own as he followed him out the doors and into the cold night. "Talk."

Lance dug his hands into the pockets of his tuxedo pants. "About?"

"No more games, Dad. What are you up to?"

Steely blue eyes stared though him. "You should know, I changed my will."

David felt his face contort. This was like a bad movie. "To write me out for firing you?"

Lance's smile was genuine as he shook his head. "The old one followed the stipulations of the prenup, and things are different after the buy out."

"Do what you want with your money. Give it all to her now, for all I care. I want to know what you were thinking jerking me around like a puppet on a string. You created an elaborate scheme to make me think you were embezzling. That's insane. I should have you committed to a mental hospital."

Lance shrugged. "I didn't see another option. You wouldn't buy me out, and I knew you wouldn't slow down until you had majority ownership. I wasn't sure you had enough capital to do it on your own."

"I did. I closed my trust and wired the money you took into Kelly's trust fund. I've removed your access to her account."

Lance laughed silently, looking upwards. "To keep it from Tessa. She's not after the money."

David felt the anger flash behind his eyes. "Would you wake up! The woman blackmailed you into marrying her."

The idiot was grinning. Never would he become such an ass over a woman. Lance pinned him with his gaze. "I wish you'd just give her a chance."

"A chance to sue me too? No thanks."

"It was a means to an end. She's not intimidated by anything. Not the money, not you, not your mother. Tessa knows how special your mother was to me and she doesn't ask me to put her aside, or you. Even as beastly as you are to her. She just accepts you both as a part of me.

"I knew you didn't approve of the relationship, and I'd promised myself never to let another woman come between us. Vicki kept you from coming home all during college, and Gretchen—"

"Spare me the recap of your poor choice in women."

"Tessa wouldn't stand for me sacrificing our happiness for yours when you are determined to be miserable. Suing me was the only way to get my attention. I'm glad she did.

"I want that same kind of happiness for you now. I knew you wouldn't make the time to have a personal life until your professional goals were met, and you refused to buy me out. You didn't leave me any choice but to get creative."

David held up his hand. "Whatever. You're setting yourself up for a fall, but I can't stop you. No more games. Just shoot straight with me from now on."

"Now what?"

"Now I leave." David turned.

"With Sophie?" Lance called after him. "I like her."

"You've barely met her." He did not want to be baited into this conversation.

"I like the effect she has on you. You're happy, and not just because you have SGI."

David took another step for the door.

"Now what?"

From where they stood, David could see the images flashing on the screen inside. The African safari from his sixteenth birthday faded into a picture of him sitting on his father's lap behind his desk. He couldn't have been more than four.

"You always wanted to run SGI."

"I wanted to be you. Hell, I am you." His head suddenly felt very heavy. Until the sound of his father's laughter spun him around. "What's so funny?"

"You may look like me, but you are nothing like me. I jump headfirst without looking, and you have your ten-year plan mapped out in stone."

True. Except his ten-year plan had been to get control of SGI. He needed to rework it. "I still don't understand the need for the charade. You could have done it differently, threatened to sell to one of the shareholders. To make me think you were stealing?"

"Nobody makes decisions for you. It had to be your idea. We thought of it when you said you'd never buy my shares while I was married to Tessa. And it worked brilliantly. I had to stop you from working yourself into an early grave like my father did. Sophie tipped you off didn't she?"

David nodded, pressing his lips together. Sophie was none of his father's business. "She doesn't know if that's what you're worried about. And even if she did, she'd never tell."

"You didn't tell her, and she didn't ask?"

"She's interested in me, not my business." The revelation stunned him even as he said the words with complete confidence. No one had ever been interested in him outside of what he could do for them. Even Craig took advantage of his status.

"You love her."

Did he? Not that it would matter. "It's not what you're making it out to be, Dad. Sophie and I don't want the same things. She should have kids, lots of them. She'll be great at it. Warm cookies after school kind of great." He sucked in the cool air, hoping it would quell the tightness in his throat. "I can't give her that."

Lance's fist came down hard on the railing behind him. "What the hell is wrong with you? It's as if the world is right there dangling at your fingertips and you're too scared to grab on."

That did it. "I'm not scared. I've just learned how it ends. It used to tear me up when Kelly would have to go home after a weekend, and she was just my sister. I don't have it in me, Dad. I've been through enough of your divorces. I don't need to have any of my own."

Lance stepped forward, taking David's arm and spinning him toward the windows. He could just make out Sophie, still at the bar. Thankfully it looked like she was talking to a woman.

"If you don't marry her then don't get married, ever. Or you *will* be just like me. Punishing every woman who comes after for not being her, for not loving you the way she did. Hiding that part of you away that will always belong to her. And you'll hate yourself for it. I didn't have a choice but to let Natalie go. It kills me you are willing to just walk away."

David shook his head, his eyes refusing to focus as he stared into the soiree. "I won't leave, she will."

"Yeah, I'm sure if you push hard enough, even love couldn't make her stay."

"You intrigue me," a deep, breathy voice said from behind Sophie as she leaned on the bar waiting for another diet cola. She turned slowly, not sure what to expect.

She did not expect the exotic beauty who stood before her. With waist-length black hair, wide almond eyes and a neckline plunging to her navel, the woman was stunning. *And she intrigued her?*

"You are not what I anticipated."

"Just what were you anticipating?" And what was she talking about?

"His usual."

Sophie leveled her gaze at the woman. *Just who did she think she was?* Sophie turned away, facing the room once more. She was in the mood to have fun tonight, not deal with some catty woman.

"I'm impressed you got him to teach the class with you. David is usually very private."

This woman didn't seem to get the hint. Sophie blew a few stray curls off her face with a puff of air from the corner of her mouth. She gave a half-smile to the woman and surveyed the crowd. Just where had that man escaped to?

"He works too hard. We were relieved to find out he was enjoying himself."

"We?" Sophie asked, curious but still leery as to where this mystery woman was taking her.

"You don't know who I am, do you?" As Sophie shook her head the woman continued. "Tessa Strong, Lance's wife." Sophie's felt her mouth form an O as she tried to recall the bits David had relayed about this woman. She'd been the one David had suspected of stealing, and there was some kind of sexual harassment suit that didn't make sense.

Tessa smiled, "I see you know my reputation. David thinks me a barracuda, but I promise I don't bite." Her teeth shone like pearls against her deep red lips.

"Sophie Delfino," she said, shaking Tessa's outstretched hand.

"Yes, I know. David is very tight lipped about you. He seems to want to keep you all to himself."

Sophie smiled at the idea. "I intrigue you?" She asked, bringing the conversation back to the beginning.

Tessa nodded. "As much for your effect on David as for the class you teach. *Kama Sutra* is a passion of ours. I wish I'd thought of designing a class around it."

"It was my sister's idea actually. David and I are just filling in while she's pregnant. I still need to talk him into helping with next month's class."

"I'm sure you can convince him. Which positions do you focus on? Do you stick to *The Kama Sutra* or do you also reference *Ananga Ranga* or *Positions of the Tao*?"

Sophie's eyebrows rose at the woman's knowledge. "You're very studied. The class is mainly yoga. We throw in a few positions at the end that complement the stretches."

"So the focus is on touching."

"Exactly."

"Now that Lance is retired, I need to find ways to keep him busy. We'll look into the class once your sister comes back."

Sophie grinned. "I think David would melt into the floor if the two of you walked in."

"Then I shouldn't suggest the sexual reflexology class we're teaching at the chiropractic college. Your students might be interested though. It combines massage and the touch points of Tao."

Sophie's mind sparked to life. Finally, a problem she could solve. "That sounds fascinating. Did David mention you used to be an aerobics instructor?"

He had to leave. Now. Before his father's psychobabble really started to sink in. He shouldered his way through the crowd, keeping his eye on her. He needed to get out of here, get her home and out of that damned dress. Do to her things the men hanging on her all night hadn't even thought to dream about.

His pulse quickened, pounding in his ears as he neared her. Maybe they wouldn't wait until they were home. She was so small they could just—

"David."

He shook his head and kept moving. He was through making nice with people.

"David."

Feeling a hand on his arm, he jerked back like he'd been stung.

His eyes targeted Kia, a stewardess who liked to set him up on dates with her friends. She'd been calling incessantly, no doubt hoping he would pick up the tab for some of her extravagant nights on the town in exchange for a few introductions. He furrowed his brows. Maybe Kelly was right, she really was his madam.

"I haven't heard from you, but I guess now I know why." The leggy redhead tilted her chin in Sophie's direction. "I thought you only did blondes."

He pinned her with his gaze. "Why are you here?"

She shrugged her bony shoulders. "A friend needed some company." She stepped closer, leaning in, her lips almost touching his ear. "If you ever need—"

David stepped back, almost toppling the man behind him.

"He's very well taken care of, I assure you." Sophie's hand slipped beneath his jacket and around his waist, pulling him to her like a possession. Whether she was really jealous or just making a point about the way he'd treated her all night, he didn't care. Her wide eyes sparkled beneath her darkened lashes as she looked up at him. "Did you get what you came for?"

He brought his hand to her face, stroking the soft skin of her cheek with his thumb. "Turns out I already had it. Ready?"

Sophie nodded, taking his hand in hers as she pulled him back to the bar. He suffered through goodbyes to Tessa and his father. Tessa seemed to have charmed Sophie into something, but just what he'd worry about later.

For now, he focused on getting Sophie out of the crowded ballroom before dinner and the speeches began. She was enjoying the entire party far too much. After getting their coats, he helped her button hers up all the way. "Weren't you cold?" There wasn't much to the dress, and what was there just clung to her curves because it wanted to touch her as much as he did.

She shook her head and stepped closer. She slipped her hands in the pockets of his coat and pulled him snug against her. Even with the heels she barely came up to his shoulder. "You've obviously never seen yourself in a tux. It's definitely blood warming."

As she licked her lips, he noticed the lipstick had worn away, leaving just the pink shade he was used to. Almost exactly the color of her nipples. *Ah, hell.*

He pushed her backward lifting her off her feet and carrying her around a corner until he had her up against the wall of the hallway. Not nearly private enough, but it would do. He lifted her up, pressing her body against the wall with his. Plundering her mouth like he'd wanted to do all night. Even before the dress.

She parted her lips to receive him, wrapping an arm around his neck to help keep herself up. As their tongues danced together, his knee slid between her legs until it found the wall. She slid down slightly, never breaking the kiss while the fingers of her free hand busied themselves.

The kiss was too potent, more than he anticipated and he tried to pull away. To breathe. To remember where they were. His eyes opened wider as he felt her hand circle his erection and squeeze. "How did you..." Looking down between them he couldn't even tell she had a hold of him. She'd somehow managed to get one arm out of her coat and was using it as a drape to hide her intentions. He shook his head. "Not here."

"Here, now, fast before someone finds us." Her breath was hot on his neck and her tongue began an assault on his ear that made his entire spine quiver.

"This is crazy." And it got crazier. He moved a hand inside her coat, finding the slit in her dress like it was a homing beacon. He breathed a sigh of relief as he encountered panties. This wouldn't be so easy after all. Her hips shifted and his fingers slid along the moist satin.

"You started it. Finish it."

Her hips rolled again, making him realize he could just pull the scrap aside. His finger glided across her clit as he threaded it inside of her. She squeezed him harder and rolled her hips again. She raised one leg, careful to keep it inside his coat. Her voice rasped against his ear.

"Make love to me. Show me I'm yours, like you did every time you found another man looking at me."

Her hand guided him forward, and he let her. Pressing into her mercilessly. Skewering her to the wall as he plunged in to the hilt. He could tell that he'd taken her breath, but he couldn't stop. Had to hurry. They'd surely be found here. Caught. Exposed. And even then, he might not be able to stop.

He was completely wrapped up in her, and yet he still pushed further, wanting his entire body to be consumed by hers.

"I can't wait...for you." She huffed against his ear seconds before he felt her orgasm clench him, tossing him over the edge as her body pulled him impossibly deeper. He braced himself against the wall and she wrapped her other arm around his neck. "Watch it. Think about what is holding me up."

He had to smile as reason washed back over him. This was crazy.

"Don't move." She whispered, her body stiffening.

They were still joined, being caught now would be worse than being caught during. He listened to her breathe for far too long, until it became even and steady. She reached between them, tucking him away with a sigh and straightening her skirt as she slid down to her feet.

"Okay, now give me a minute."

He spun and looked down the hall in both directions. Empty. "Did you see someone?"

She pulled him closer by the lapels of his jacket. "Relax, you're safe. I kept my eyes open the whole time. I don't know how you do it." She shook her head and leaned back against the wall.

He wrapped his arms around her but then pulled away. He didn't want to risk it a second time. "We should go."

"I know, but just a second okay? I didn't think this through. I usually fall asleep. I've never had to walk after."

He ran his hand through his hair. "I didn't mean to hurt you."

She caught his hand. "You didn't. It's just big man, small girl—takes a second to recover."

His ego couldn't help but jump one cloud up. "Really?"

She smiled, leaning against him. "As if you didn't know. But fishing for compliments will get us arrested before we ever make it home."

Sophie fought sleep as they lay tangled beneath the soft cotton sheets after making love for the third time that night. "David?"

A yawn was the only response he gave before rolling over, pinning her to the bed the way they so often found themselves in the morning.

"What's going on with you and your father?" She'd been wondering all week, since the day she had been at his office. And after what she saw of their heated conversation outside on the terrace at the hotel, she wondered if there were more issues than just what had happened with the company?

"Why?"

"It seems like something I should know." Would he recognize her echoing his words back to him?

"You already know." He kissed her softly, sweetly, more like how she kissed him.

Her stomach clenched at what she wanted that to mean. "It would be nice to hear."

"Dad was just waxing poetic tonight. I'm starting to think there might be something wrong with him. He changed his will and he's been spouting advice."

"You think he's sick?" She wrapped her arms around him, listening to him breathe.

"He seems healthy enough." His breath was forced, in and out. There was something he wasn't saying.

"Are you worried about what it will be like with him gone?" It had been even harder to lose her mother than her dad, knowing that she was alone in the world. If not for her sister, she might feel completely abandoned.

"No."

"You won't be alone. There's your sister, and Craig and me."

"What's your day like tomorrow?" Diversion. He was using her own tricks against her.

"Two early classes and then Daphne's baby shower in the afternoon."

"What about Sunday?"

"No classes, but I have to spend a half day at the club. I need to prepare for a meeting on Monday." With the landlord, which she still hadn't gotten around to asking him about. Though now was not the time or place.

"Sunday night let's go out. I'll finally buy you dinner."

The needy part of her wanted to ask him about Saturday. She hated every moment she spent away from him. But she didn't ask. He was used to his space, and she needed to learn to respect that. She nestled in closer, breathing in the clean sheets, his cologne, their sex. The smell of sweet dreams.

David was beginning to feel silly for showering at Sophie's. He really should have gone home and gotten back into his Saturday routine. He'd stayed longer than he should have, just in case she came back.

He fastened his watch on his wrist and wondered what time Sophie had found him at Diprima Dolci that day. He toweled his hair dry, recalling that he hadn't been in to work yet, so it had to be early.

He felt electricity in the air as he emerged from the bathroom just in time to hear the door click as it opened. His whole body went on red alert as she walked in, her nose and cheeks bright pink from the cold.

"You walked." It wasn't like the truck was burning the ozone layer. Couldn't she just drive and save him the aggravation?

"You're naked." She grinned as she kicked off her sneakers and fumbled with her gloves, scarf and jacket. Her eyes darkened as she walked toward him.

He'd been so smart to wait. Her tiny hands rose to his chest as she pressed against him. His skin stung where she touched him and he jumped back. God, she was freezing.

"You're hot." Her grin was wicked as she made up the distance between him, this time pressing the backs of her hands against his upper abdomen.

Stepping back further into the hallway, he narrowed his eyes at her. "I just got out of the shower. That's not funny."

"No?" she asked, reaching lower this time. Anticipating her move, he ducked inside the bedroom and around to his side of the bed. Her eyes were wild as she stared at him from her side, before collapsing in laughter and rolling onto the comforter.

He stood his ground for a moment. He could never tell just what she might do. A thrill rippled through his spine, straight to his cock. When had sex ever been this much fun?

Erotic, sensual, pleasurable sure. But fun? Not for a long time, if ever. They were past the point of negotiation and awkwardness, finding a security he'd never thought possible. She sat up on the bed and tucked her feet beneath her.

"Fine, have it your way." She pulled the sweatshirt over her head. Even though the sports bra flattened her out, she still looked delectable.

"I will. I'm just waiting for you to warm up first." He licked his lips as her mouth drifted into a circle. He loved it when she did that.

"I'll jump in the shower. That should do it." He was right behind her as she stepped out of her pants on the way to the bathroom. Her eyes were wide, startled as she turned around. "You already showered."

He leaned down, careful to arch away from her frosty hands as he whispered, "I am going to clean every inch of you. Slowly, deeply, completely."

She shivered, though he doubted it was from the cold, and removed her sports bra without taking her eyes from his. "What now?'

He reached behind her and turned on the water. "Now I charm you out of your panties."

"Would you teach the new class with me next month?"

David's smile dropped so fast Sophie could almost hear it plunk on the floor.

"Please, no. Can't you get one of your other instructors to do it? They've got boyfriends right? "

She forced her mouth into a pout. "I thought you liked the class."

"I don't like the way the men look at you, even with their wives right there." David buried his head behind the newspaper she'd brought home with her. She could spend every Saturday just this way.

"Their wives aren't much better." Sophie scooped the creamy oatmeal studded with raisins and apples from the crock pot, and sprinkled brown sugar and toasted walnuts over the top. She barely believed him when he said he'd never had oatmeal before.

"It's all too group sex for me. But if you can't figure it out I will. I don't want someone else, you know."

She set the bowls on the table and pulled down the newspaper so she could see his reaction. "Would you be jealous? It's all very mechanical I assure you. It could be very professional."

He folded the paper and set it aside as she poured the fat free cream over the oatmeal. "I've seen the mechanics of the situation firsthand. Just cancel the classes until Daphne comes back."

Sophie shook her head and took her seat. "It's my most popular course. I was actually thinking of expanding it, maybe offering an advanced class."

David looked at her sideways. "You're a model student, but an advanced class? I've seen the book, Sophie. Some of the positions are downright acrobatic."

"You wouldn't want to try them?"

His spoon froze in mid air, a raisin plopping back down on his bowl. "Not in public, no."

Sophie shrugged. "Maybe I should hire professionals."

He set the spoon down. "Is that legal? Wouldn't that be a liability issue?"

"Not prostitutes, instructors who teach sexually explicit topics. Like Sexual Reflexology and Tantric Sex." She waited, but saw no reaction. He must not know.

"Sounds good, especially if it gets me off the hook." David attacked his bowl, finishing in under a minute. The man loved to eat.

"I'm glad you think so. I know the perfect couple." She scooted onto his lap, wrapping her arms around his neck.

His face went white. "Not us."

"No, not us," she said, nuzzling into his neck. She breathed in his scent, but pulled back. She didn't want to miss his reaction. "It's Tessa and your dad."

Chapter Fifteen

"Marry her." David jumped as his father's voice boomed through the room. "Sophie is fantastic. Beautiful, smart, charming and refuses to talk about you."

David smiled at that. *Good girl.* "You had Tessa grill her last night, didn't you?"

Lance mocked innocence. "Me? They actually get along great, but I was referring to my job interview."

"Right, teaching the classes." David closed his laptop as Lance neared.

Lance sprawled out in one of the chairs opposite David's desk. "I mean it, you know. You should marry her."

"I don't think you'll ever be in a position to dole out marital advice. Though you have plenty of experience."

Lance shrugged. "I'm a slow learner. I made the same mistake three times. But not this time. You'll see." He settled further in to the chair. "Too bad Sophie's busy tonight. Kelly was disappointed she missed meeting her last night."

"You didn't," David moaned. He hadn't invited Sophie to Kelly's birthday dinner because she had Daphne's baby shower. But Sophie might not realize that.

"Didn't what? Ask her if she would be joining us? No, Tessa assumed she wouldn't. I think they must have discussed it last night."

Good, maybe. She seemed fine last night. Better than fine. Her words echoed in his head. *Show me I'm yours. I'll keep you safe. You won't be alone.* He hadn't even bothered to fish the condoms out of his bag when they got home last night.

"Oh good, you're still here."

David snapped back to reality as Tessa glided into the room.

She sashayed to his desk, setting down three sheets of paper and plunking a set of keys on top. "It's perfect for her."

Tessa leaned against the chair Lance was sitting in. David winced as Lance pulled her onto his lap.

"Consider it an early wedding present." They were obviously quite pleased with themselves.

David didn't bother to argue, just set the keys aside and looked down at the papers. A picture of the exterior of a sprawling colonial house was followed by bullet points of its features. Pictures on the other pages showed an enormous kitchen, weight room, master suite, and the view of the Portland skyline at night.

"You think giving me a house will make me want to get married?"

"Not you, her." Tessa said, sending her viper smile his way. "You're a bear. She has to have some reason for marrying you. The house is perfect for her. A gourmet kitchen as big as her apartment, heated floors because her feet are always cold, lots of bedrooms. Just take her up there and see."

How did she know so much about Sophie? They must have talked for longer than he realized. He hated that Tessa was right about this. His condo was too drafty for her, her place too small for him. A house just made sense. But Sophie had a hard enough time accepting the truck, there was no way she'd let anyone buy her a house.

David fingered the keys. Didn't you usually need a real estate agent to see a house?

"We already own it," Tessa explained before he could ask. "I caught it a few months ago and have been decorating it ever since. But if she doesn't like it, she can always redo it herself."

And he thought Tessa's real estate habit was just a cover. "Sophie won't let anyone buy her a house." He shoved the keys wistfully across the table.

"Just take her up there. It's only five minutes from downtown. If she doesn't like it, I'll start looking. If she does, then you can convince her. She swears you're actually rather charming."

"In bed woman, until the guests arrive. Craig will have my head if he knows you got up a minute before." Sophie chided her sister as Daphne applied her make-up in the bathroom mirror.

"The man is obsessed." Daphne pressed her lips together, then pulled back and admired her coral lipstick.

"That he is. But it's just five more weeks. You can do anything for five Mondays right?"

Daphne laughed and rubbed her tummy. "Thanks Dad. I haven't heard that one in a while."

Sophie grinned, remembering how their father used to help them make it through school until the next holiday break.

"Oh!" Daphne's hand molded to her side. "It's her foot!" Daphne reached for Sophie's hand and pressed it to the spot.

Sophie could distinctly feel the heel, the little toes. "It is his foot." She'd felt the baby kick before, but this was somehow more real. Not just a flutter, but an actual body part. "I think he has big feet. We'll have to get him bigger baby shoes."

"She's a girl, Sophie. I just know it." Daphne's head shook as she released Sophie's hand, but Sophie left it there. Just in case. If David was serious about not having children this might be her only chance to feel it.

Sophie blinked the mist from her eyes as she reluctantly took her hand away. He was done stretching for now. "I told you, I had a dream. Right before you found out you were pregnant. You'll see."

The doorbell rang and the guests began to pour in, piling the living room with presents. Sophie managed to keep Daphne seated for most of the party, except for her bathroom breaks and when the guests had to try and guess how many squares of toilet paper it would take to circumnavigate her waist.

After the carrot cake, Daphne dove in to the gifts and Sophie breathed a sigh of relief. The party was almost over, and she was still okay. Sophie snuck to the back bedroom and made her promised phone check in with Craig, who had slipped out to SGI to get some work done.

She'd barely got her message across when the doorbell rang. Hanging up quickly, she skirted the living room and made her way to the door. Laurie, a masseuse at Working It Out, made her apologies for being late, but instead of joining the group she pulled Sophie into the kitchen. She thrust the newspaper at Sophie and said, "You need to see this."

"What?" Sophie asked, plopping the heavy bundle on the countertop. "The Sunday paper?"

"It's the Saturday edition. I get it for the ads so I can plan my shopping. But that's not why you need to see it." Laurie's hands deftly moved the pages. "Scene and Heard." She drummed her hand against a series of black and white photos.

"I know what it is. It's the society column." Sophie turned her attention to the page, and promptly closed her eyes in defeat. David had warned her not to risk it. She opened them again, taking in the four photos of David being kissed by four different women. The only one he was kissing was her. Sophie recognized Tessa and his executive assistant, one of the few people David had taken the time to introduce her to. And then there was that annoying redhead she had pulled him away from, but the angle of the shot made it look like she was kissing him. Sophie had made sure that twit's lips never touched him.

She turned to Laurie. "It's not how it looks."

Laurie nodded. "Whatever you say, but I'm not worried about you. Daphne reads the paper cover to cover every morning. That kiss you are planting on him, that's not a 'we're just friends' kiss. Which is the lie you've fed to your sister."

"I never lied."

Laurie crossed her arms across her chest. "Daphne and I talk every day, she has no idea about you and David. She suspects though, always asking if he's been around and how you are acting."

So Laurie was the one who kept Daphne up on the happenings at the club. *The club.*

"Did they mention Working It Out?" she asked as her eyes scanned the tiny print below the photos. Laurie's finger came down hard.

Strong Gyms CEO David Strong, had multiple mergers on the horizon at his father's, former SGI President Lance Strong, retirement party Friday night. Current plaything Sophie Delfino may want to hold tight to her half of popular women's fitness center Working It Out.

Plaything. She didn't even warrant girlfriend status.

Sophie stepped back against the refrigerator. A picture of her and David followed by him with three other women, and a mention of her club. Daphne was going to freak. Her blood pressure would soar.

"Don't even think about trying to keep her from seeing it. If I found it more of her friends will."

Sophie straightened her spine, making herself as tall as possible. "I have nothing to hide. But I'm not going to rush out there and ruin her party. Once Craig gets home I'll tell them both together. He'll keep her calm."

Laurie's head shook from side to side. "I hope so. If her blood pressure goes up any higher she'll have to check in to the hospital for the rest of her pregnancy." The laughter from the other room spilled into the kitchen. "I better go join the party. Good luck."

Sophie sank down at the kitchen table and stared at the pictures again. The picture of her and David made her smile. His eyes were closed as he leaned down, kissing her as she sat at the bar. He didn't always do that, but it warmed her every time he trusted her enough to close his eyes and enjoy the moment.

Of course, she couldn't enjoy the moment for long. Daphne wouldn't recognize how much that kiss symbolized, how far she'd come with David. A few weeks ago he wouldn't even consider spending the night, and now he found her bed more nights than he didn't, made the effort to understand why she did things and was even beginning to share things with her.

She was winning the war, battle by battle. If Daphne were healthier, Sophie would just take a hard line with her, force her to realize her baby sister was an adult, capable of taking risks and dealing with the aftermath.

If that weren't the joke of the century. As if she had a contingency plan for David balking at her attempts to broaden his mind to the possibility of a relationship. She was walking a dangerous path, one with no safety net for her heart. Every day she fell deeper into the abyss, and while he was at least in the water now, he was still in the shallow end.

With a sigh, Sophie knew she'd need Craig's help telling Daphne. She didn't dare mention the newspaper column until he got back. Craig might know how to make her accept what was going on. Though he was in the dark too. She'd have to tell him first, calm him down, and then tell Daphne.

Once Daphne had the baby, Sophie would never keep anything from her again. Best to tell the little bits as things began, than hit someone with a freight train later.

"How did I know you'd be here?" Craig said as he sauntered into David's office. "I wanted to give you the update on the Deliver-Ease rollout."

Craig slapped a report down on David's desk, much too close to the travel itinerary he'd printed out. Luckily, Craig didn't seem to notice as he plopped back in a chair and rubbed his face.

"Good news or bad news?" David slid the itinerary in a drawer, and then opened the report.

"Good. Everything is right on schedule, ready to roll December one so the bugs will be worked out by January when the world goes on a diet. The managers are a little skeptical though. When you visit, be sure to really push. I have some motivational ideas in the report."

David spent every December and January traveling the country, putting in face-time at most every Strong Gym in North America. He'd spent the last hour reworking the schedule so Sophie could go with him. She'd only been out of the state once. Plus, he couldn't go that long without her. He'd found one of his managers to take over for her at Working It Out while they were gone.

"David!" Craig yelled, slapping the desk. "Do you know when you stopped listening or should I start over from hello?"

David blinked hard. "Deliver-Ease is part of my vision for the new year speech. We'll be nationwide by this time next year. The program is part of my ramp-up at every gym, but I'll look over your suggestions."

"Good." Craig nodded. "I need to talk to you about something else."

David swallowed hard. "Business or personal?"

"Both." Craig checked the cell phone attached to his belt. "Are you still interested in buying Working It Out?"

"I'm not following you." Sophie was the majority owner, and she hadn't said a word about selling. Though there was something she'd come to ask his help with. Of course, he'd been selfishly preoccupied with the fiasco that was his father instead of remembering to ask her what she needed.

"Daphne wants to spend the first year with the baby, and after that, she's thinking she wants a change."

Craig kept talking, but David stopped listening. He didn't give a damn what Daphne wanted. "Have you discussed this with Sophie?" he interrupted.

Craig waved his hand dismissively. "Sophie's just there until Daphne comes back, and if Daphne isn't coming back... Sophie will be happy to get back to her career. She made a lot more money there anyway. Of course, she'll stay in place through the transition."

"You can't make decisions for her." David had seen first hand the ugliness that could cause. He was already nervous about telling her about the house, the trip.

"You don't know Sophie."

He swallowed the words he itched to say. Sophie wanted to wait until after the baby to tell Craig and Daphne. She was putting them first, yet they barely gave her a second thought. David got up from his desk and walked to the wall of windows and stared down at the dots on the street below.

"I'm surprised you're not interested."

So was he. He'd twice offered to buy it from Daphne, hell last week he bought the building. But Working It Out was Sophie's as much as it was Daphne's. That Craig was trying to unload it without talking to her was causing his temperature to rise.

"All Day Fitness made her an offer last year..."

David set his jaw and directed his words to Craig's reflection in the window. "Sophie is the majority owner. You can't make these decisions without consulting her."

"Well, you two sure got chatty," Craig grinned, getting up from his chair. "Sophie is a silent partner. She'll do whatever Daphne wants, and Daphne wants to sell. So we are selling, as soon as possible."

David felt his breath escaping like steam from a teakettle. He just couldn't hold it in. "Sophie bends over backwards for you both, and she never even gets a thank you."

Craig's smile widened. "You're the one bending her over backwards lately."

David's blood boiled in his veins. He spun around and saw the smirk on Craig's face. He grabbed Craig by the shoulders and slammed him into the wall behind him.

"Don't you ever talk about her like that again. I don't care how long I've known you." David unclenched his hands and dropped Craig's body. He turned, taking long strides until he reached the windows again. He didn't trust himself. He needed physical distance from Craig right now.

"My God, man. I was kidding. What have you done?"

He was late. And Craig was never late. The man was as anal retentive about punctuality as he was about calorie counting. Sophie could tell it had Daphne on edge, and she was already exhausted. Sophie had carefully hidden the newspaper as she cleaned the aftermath of the party, tucking it deep in the Tupperware cabinet. Daphne and her belly couldn't get back there if she tried.

"I told you to stay in bed," Sophie scolded as Daphne came into the kitchen. "He'll be here any second and if he finds you vertical we're both going to get it. Scoot."

Sophie gently pushed until Daphne again took her place on her bed. "He's an hour late."

"I know, which means he'll have to pick up dinner on his way." Sophie hoped she sounded cheerful, reassuring. The complete opposite of Daphne's quiet somber tone. Sophie reached for the phone. "I'm going to try him again, and this time I'm putting in our dinner order. He should let us eat pizza for being late."

Daphne's eyes stayed on her as she left a third message on Craig's cell phone. Sophie actually thought about lying, pretending Craig had answered. Anything to take that look from her sister's eyes.

As Sophie set the receiver back on its cradle Daphne chewed her lip. "I know I'm being hormonal, but maybe I should call David. Craig was going to meet with him. Maybe they're still together."

Sophie nodded. It was a good idea, because if they weren't together David could find Craig. Before she could pick up the receiver the phone rang. *Finally.* "Craig?"

"No, it's me. Thank goodness you answered. We have a problem."

Sophie knit her eyebrows together, recognizing the breathy voice. "Tessa?"

The color drained from Daphne's face and she reached for the phone. Sophie jumped from the bed, taking the cordless with her. As different as Sophie and Daphne looked, their voices were almost identical, especially over the phone.

"Yes. There will be some pictures in tomorrow's paper from the retirement party, all completely innocent. Well, except the one of him with Sophie, but that's to be expected. Is she the jealous type? Maybe you could run interference."

"I've seen the pictures." Sophie kept her voice slow and calm. Just what the hell was going on here?

"Has she seen them? Was she upset?"

"She's fine." Sophie didn't know Tessa and Daphne knew each other, but with the way this conversation seemed to be going, it was obvious Daphne knew something was going on with her and David.

"Good. Lance will handle David."

Sophie felt her face contort. She didn't like the idea of David being handled anymore than she liked what this conversation might mean. "So everything is going according to plan." That's what they said in detective books, right?

"Amazingly smooth. If she keeps working her magic Lance should have his grandbaby by next Christmas. I had my doubts, but Lance knew if he cleared the way with the business, David would be forced to reexamine his personal life. Sophie coming along when she did was the lucky break we needed to make this work."

Sophie's jaw dropped open and she stared hard at her sister. *Baby?*

"Did he accept Craig's offer to buy Working It Out?"

Craig was in on this too? "Craig hasn't come home yet."

"I'm sure he will. We got him to buy the building last week, so it's a sure thing. He obviously wants the club."

"Obviously." *David bought her building? Last week? Craig was selling her club?* Sophie plopped down on the bed at Daphne's feet. The room was spinning.

"He still hasn't asked her about December?"

"December?" Sophie turned her body as Daphne grabbed for the phone.

"He will. You should have seen them last night. They were magic. They just need a little push."

"A little push." Sophie echoed the words and rose from the bed. She made her way to the kitchen, snatching the newspaper from its hiding place. No point in sparing Daphne's feelings. She obviously knew more about what was going on than Sophie did.

"It's the only way with David. The man is committed to being miserable. If not for Lance's pushes he'd stay that way."

"How so?" Sophie asked, making her way back to Daphne's room and plopping the open newspaper in front of her.

"You know, becoming CEO, gaining controlling interest. Back when he was bodybuilding, Lance even had his scores lowered to make sure David would stay focused on his studies."

Sophie's jaw dropped open, mirroring her sister's slack-jawed expression. She didn't know who to be angry at. This is where lies took you.

Daphne had only wanted to make something go right for her baby sister. Sophie gave so much of herself to make other people comfortable and happy. She deserved a little happiness for herself.

When Daphne learned Sophie was leading the Sensational Sex class with David Strong, she hadn't been thrilled. After all, David was the man who told Craig not to get married the morning of their wedding. But Craig had sworn for the last five years that was nothing personal. David was just worried because of his father's failed marriages. And if David and Sophie were together, he would stop trying to pull Craig away from her.

The pairing sparked an idea that had snowballed out of control. Sophie had been fantasizing about David for a decade. She deserved to have a couple of dreams come true.

After the first class, Daphne had tried to get Craig to help push David in Sophie's direction. But he'd staunchly refused. And talking with Sophie it was obvious she was hiding something. So Daphne had moved on to plan B.

She and Tessa had worked at the same Strong Gym years ago. A few phone conversations and Daphne had learned more about David Strong's manipulating family than she ever cared to know. No wonder the guy had such issues with marriage. But by then it was obvious something was going on between David and Sophie, so she just played along. Dropping hints, relaying information to Tessa, even helping to pick out a house.

Selling the club seemed like the right thing to do. She didn't want to work as much after the baby came, and to be able to do that she would have to ask Sophie to keep running the club. Daphne had promised Sophie she'd be free to go back to her life once the baby was here.

Daphne only wanted to help, to smooth the way for her sister to live out a few dreams the way Sophie always did for her. But watching Sophie rub her temples, Daphne knew she'd blown it.

"Let me explain."

Sophie didn't stop the slow circles she was rubbing on the sides of her head.

"I just wanted to help, to make things easier for you."

"I'm not thinking about me right now, Daphne." Sophie spoke without opening her eyes or slowing the pace of her fingers.

"You promised Tessa that you would let Lance tell him."

"And I will." Sophie's body seemed to rock with each press of her fingers.

Both sisters jumped as the front door slammed shut and footsteps pounded their way through the house. Craig's angry expression was barely masked as he forced a smile. What had happened to him?

"Sorry I ran late. You must be tired from the party. Sophie and I will talk in the other room." He jerked his head fiercely toward the living room but Sophie stayed rooted.

"You are not telling me what to do," Sophie said between clenched teeth, finally dropping her hands from her head.

"He didn't know." Daphne tried her best to break the glare Sophie and Craig were giving each other, but given her vantage point on the bed it was impossible.

"How could he not know?" Sophie asked.

"What didn't I know?" Craig narrowed his eyes.

Daphne knew the truth was the only thing that could help her now. "Tessa, Lance and I have been trying to get Sophie and David together."

"You what?" Craig's voice roared through the room as his face turned as red as his hair. "Why would you do that?"

"I wanted to help. I wanted Sophie to be happy."

"I can't believe you, Daphne," Sophie yelled, rising from the bed. "You know how much I hate lies. I don't want David to be manipulated into being with me. And I don't want you selling the club without talking to me first."

"I'm sorry," Daphne pleaded, her own head beginning to ache the way Sophie's must be. It was impossible not to rub her scalp and try to ease the pain.

"Why would you try and push together two people who are so wrong for each other?" Craig took Sophie's seat on the bed.

"We are not wrong for each other!" Sophie argued.

"Not you, too. You need to keep a level head about this, Sophie. You and David want very different things from life. When we met with the therapist you said you wanted six kids. David will never have one."

"You can't predict the future. He feels something for me, maybe not as deeply as I feel for him, but in time..."

"It's not love he's afraid of, Sophie. If he loves you now he'll love you forever. But he won't marry you, and he won't let you have his children. He's terrified of divorce, of death, even more afraid of visitation agreements. He knows his limitations. It would break him, and so he won't risk it. Ever."

What had she done? Daphne's head was pounding now. Before her meddling David was just a fascination for Sophie, a harmless fantasy. Now, Sophie was obviously in love with him, and headed for a long fall. Tessa had sworn David could be the man Sophie needed, could give her the family and security she craved.

"Daphne, are you all right?" Craig asked.

Daphne could feel the blood pressure monitor being attached to her wrist, but she couldn't see it. Her field of vision seemed too narrow. The only thing she could see was Craig. But it hurt her head to open her eyes.

Sophie rubbed her tired eyes and checked the clock on the monitor of her laptop. Two hours until David was supposed to pick her up for dinner. She wanted nothing more than to call and cancel, and just crawl under the covers of her bed and hide for the next millennia. But he might need some help getting through what his father had done. And he had some explaining to do.

She was tired of him putting her on project status, treating her as a problem that needed to be fixed. How could he buy the building without telling her? Buy the club without asking her opinion? Unless it was just the club he was after all along.

She shook her head hard to dispel the thought. That was always Daphne's fear, but Daphne had obviously had a change of heart about David. Sophie was just bothered by the way he took charge of everything, as if what she wanted didn't matter to him. She needed to matter.

Sorting the papers into file folders, she let out an exhausted yawn. She hadn't been to bed since Friday night, and there hadn't been much sleeping going on.

"Megan McTavish is here to see you," the intercom squawked. *Who was that?* Sophie had only come in to work to distract herself from Daphne's medical problems. Her blood pressure had gotten so high the doctors had almost delivered the baby Saturday night. Luckily the drugs had brought it back under control, but Daphne was finishing the remaining weeks of her pregnancy in the hospital.

With a flash of fingers on the keyboard, Sophie brought up her planner. No Megan McTavish. Probably a sales call, but on a Sunday? Lifting the receiver of her phone she dialed the receptionist.

"I'm on my way out. Make her an appointment for next week."

"Sophie, she says she's going to be managing the club. Next month."

Her blood was icy cold as it sped through her veins. David had bought her building, her club, and replaced her. Without saying a word. He had a lot of explaining to do.

Sophie had been the one to find the old man out, again. How was he supposed to handle learning that his father was a master of manipulation, Tessa's willing pawn in her plan to control everyone's life? David hadn't slept at all the previous night, even skipping out on Kelly's birthday dinner. He'd made it up to her by having the car he'd bought for Sophie delivered to her apartment.

He just needed to think. To figure out if anything that ever happened to him was real. Lance swore Sophie hadn't known a thing about the scheme to rework his life. That even Craig was clueless. But still he wondered. Craig had set him up to teach the class, and Sophie had been relentless in her pursuit. Irresistible.

More than that, Sophie had found the financial problems at SGI so quickly. Tessa said she bought that house months ago. And the financial issues with Working It Out were perfectly timed.

But Craig had seemed genuinely surprised when David had told him he and Sophie were together. Not in any way he could define, or on any path he could chart, but together. Craig hadn't liked it one bit because Sophie deserved to be in a relationship that was going somewhere. And David couldn't really argue with that. She deserved better, but she wanted him.

Or did she? Maybe she had pursued him so hard because she was after something. She'd done a good job of deflecting his suspicions, fighting his offers to pay for things at every turn. Maybe she was just waiting for a bigger payoff. A reward from Lance, owning the club free and clear, the house, alimony payments for life.

As much as he hated doubting her, it made sense. More sense than any of the rest of it. Except she didn't lie, and she'd been the one who forced them into telling him their sordid scheme. Threatened they tell him everything, or she would.

He could have lived without knowing how far back it all started. Tessa and his dad ought to write a soap opera. They had concocted some crazy ploys over the years. David was forced to realize she and his father were better matched than he thought. All that drama created to propel David's life down the path they thought he wanted to take.

Even though he'd been adamant he didn't want children, Lance never believed him. Lance even admitted to creating an emergency to get David out of town every time he had a vasectomy scheduled.

David didn't really care if he spoke to the old man for a very long time. Every break he thought he made for himself had been designed by Lance. School, bodybuilding, work. He had succeeded at everything, but he'd never gotten there on his own.

It was time for a new set of goals. Things Lance would have no knowledge of or control over. Things he could accomplish and know were his alone. Something more than building the real estate side of SGI and expanding Deliver-Ease. A whole new product, a new direction for the company. A legacy that would be his.

A legacy, but for whom? When he died, the company would be splintered again. His goal of unifying SGI shattered. Unless Kelly had a child who was interested in the business.

David shook his head and pulled the keys from the ignition. Needing an heir was no reason to have a child. A child who, like Kelly, might be raised to call another man daddy, to want little to do with him or the company.

Pulling himself out of the car, he decided to keep the appointment he'd made for tomorrow. If the craziness his father inflicted didn't drive Sophie away now, something would later. He had no choice but to protect himself. Have the surgery on Friday and tell Sophie he was out of town for a week. The class would be over, she'd never have to know. And his heart would be safer.

Chapter Sixteen

Sophie sized him up, his head was contorted by the convex glass in the peephole. It would serve him right to leave him out there in the rain. She wanted to strangle him, had ever since Megan McTavish had walked her tall, blonde, toned behind into her office and prattled on about what a great opportunity it was to manage a club outside the SGI norm.

Sophie had been polite. Megan obviously had no idea what she was walking into. But just like the conversation with Tessa, Sophie had been sure to get more information than she gave. Megan currently managed a Strong Gym in the suburbs. David had contacted her personally and asked her to step in at Working It Out for December and January. Megan was under the impression she was filling in temporarily.

There were a lot of unanswered questions, demands Sophie wanted to make of him as soon as she heard his footsteps up the stairs. Instead, she took a few deep breaths, calming herself. If she got too worked up she'd never get the answers she needed. Her hand vibrated on the handle as he pounded the door again. She could feel metal sliding as the doorknob turned beneath her hand. *Who gave him a key?*

Sophie stood her ground, blocking the entry as best she could. Trying desperately to ignore the flutter in her stomach at seeing the pain in his eyes. Yes, he'd had to face some hard truths, but so had she, damn it. No one else was going to stand up for her, and so she had to do it herself.

"Should I call and push back the reservation?"

Sophie followed his gaze as it swept over her body, still clad in the jeans and sweater she'd thrown on this morning. She'd only gotten home a few minutes before he arrived, but she'd decided against dinner five minutes into her conversation with Megan. Squaring her shoulders, she stepped out of the doorway.

"I'm not going anywhere with you tonight. You need to sit down. Things between us are about to get real complicated, and you don't do complicated."

David closed the door behind him but leaned against it instead of taking a seat on the sofa, letting out a long sigh. "That's an understatement."

Crossing to the living room, Sophie slumped down onto the couch, tucking her legs beneath her and pulling the red afghan over them. *Why is it so cold in here?* "Do you want to talk first?"

Cocking his head to the side he met her gaze. "I don't want to talk at all."

Sophie bit the inside of her cheek to keep from screaming at him. "There is nothing you want to tell me? Are you sure? This is your one shot at explaining."

David shook his head and sucked in a slow breath. "If you have something to say, Sophie, then say it."

Where could she even begin with something like this? "Why did you buy my building?"

David's eyes widened, and then narrowed. "Because it's a good investment. And your rent was so high it was extortion."

Sophie pounded her fist on the cushion. "How do you know how much my rent is?"

"The management company offered the information as a selling point. Why are you upset about this?"

"Were you going to tell me?"

"I made the offer on Wednesday, Sophie. We're not even in escrow yet."

"And I suppose escrow closes February first."

David actually rolled his eyes. "Sounds about right."

"By then you'll own Working It Out, and Megan can help make the transition run smoothly." She was spitting the words now.

"Would you calm down?" David shrugged out of his coat and draped it across a kitchen chair. He looked like he stepped out of a magazine walking toward her in his charcoal suit, the gray shirt and silvery tie doing nothing to lighten the ensemble.

He stopped at the edge of the couch and loomed over her. "I'm buying Daphne's share personally. If you want to sell you can. If not, I'll be a silent partner." He joined her on the couch. "Megan is going to cover for you while we're gone."

"What are you talking about?"

"I make site visits during December and January. It's a great chance for you to see the country."

Emotions bubbled over inside of her. Relief, rage, anxiety, gratitude. She couldn't keep any of them straight. "Do you even think of me as a person? Or am I just a trinket to you?"

"For God's sake, Sophie, don't do this."

"What am I doing?"

"That slanty thing with your eyes for one." David rose from the couch and walked to the kitchen. "And trying to pick a fight with me for another. Do you have any alcohol at all? Because if you keep this up, I'm going to need a drink."

"I'm not trying to fight with you, but any emotional response from you would be nice. Do you care about me at all?"

David stepped out from behind the open refrigerator door and leveled his gaze at her. "Sophie!"

She sprang from the couch. "That's right. In order to speak to me you have to be inebriated." Once she was in the kitchen, she pushed herself onto the counter, standing on it to reach the cupboard over the fridge. Grabbing the box inside, she made her way to the floor again. She thrust the box into David's chest then spun, pulling a glass bottle from another cabinet.

"What's this?" He had the nerve to laugh.

"Liqueur filled chocolates and vanilla extract. I think the vanilla is eighty proof."

"God, you're cute." He was grinning as he sat at the kitchen table and opened the box of candy.

Sophie stomped her foot in frustration. "I'm not trying to be cute. I'm trying to figure out what is happening in my life. Why are you smiling?"

"I'm just waiting for you to get over it, like that day with the door."

She was still annoyed about the swarm of people he'd had in her apartment. "I'm not going to let this go. I need to be an active participant in my own life, not some puppet on a string you can jerk around for thrills."

David's face fell. "I don't do that."

"Like hell you don't. You are constantly telling me what to do, bulldozing over my life, making decisions for me. I can't take it. If we are going to be together I need to be a partner in it."

"I'm not going to consult with you before I make a business decision."

"If they concern me I expect you to respect me enough to care about my opinion."

"Sophie, you're overreacting."

"At least I'm having a reaction. I can't be as indifferent as you. I actually have emotions."

David stood, peering down at her. "Are you trying to hurt me?"

"I'm trying to get any reaction at all. What am I supposed to think? You buy the building and my club, hire someone to replace me all without a word."

There was nothing he could say, no magic answer that would satisfy her right now. What she needed was some time to cool off and come to her senses.

Her eyes opened wide and seemed to peer straight to his soul. "Are you in love with me?"

She really didn't know, which actually kind of stung. How could she not know? That he'd never said the words was beside the point. If her question didn't sound like an accusation he might have answered.

"Well then." Her intake of breath was sharp as she nodded her head furiously. "I don't know what I was thinking. I must be completely deluded."

He stepped closer, still unsure how they had gotten to this point. "Where is this coming from?"

She threw her hands up and stepped back. "I know, you never promised me anything. Hell, I agreed to play by the rules that applied to me. I wanted so badly for there to be more from you. I made it up. I made myself believe that just like I was waiting for you, you were waiting for me. Waiting for me to be ready to have our own life." Her curls swung slowly from side to side.

"Sophie, I—"

"Don't bother." She stepped away, retreating into the living room. "I need some space. I have some decisions to make about the club, my career, us. And since you don't feel the need to consult me on any of your decisions, I'm not going to ask your opinion either."

"What are you looking for here, Sophie?"

She sank onto the couch, wrapping that tattered red blanket around herself as she stared blankly out the window. "I just need a break, some time to get my thoughts together."

"A break?"

"Lance and Tessa are coming to the class on Thursday. They'll do the positions."

"You're ending it? Because I made a real estate investment? Because Daphne decided to sell? Because I want to take you with me when I travel?"

She shook her head slowly, incessantly as if she would never stop. Finally, she spoke again. "The only thing I want to end is not being in control of my own life. I've spent my whole life reacting to everyone else's needs."

"You want me to tell Craig and Daphne no?"

"I don't know what I want, David. I need some time to decide. Please, just go. I'll call you."

He fought the urge to stand in front of her and look into her eyes to see if she really meant it. He wouldn't beg her. Taking his coat off the chair, he took the two steps to the door and left without looking back. Checking to make sure the door locked behind him.

No one touched him. David hadn't even realized it until Sophie was gone. She touched him constantly, incessantly, as if she had to hold him down or he might float away. And he'd loved it. Every pat, stroke, nudge. He was acutely aware of them all, on guard to hide his reaction.

What was it Sophie had said before that first night? The class was all about the touching, that couples came for the closeness the touching provided. What he wouldn't give to touch her again. The way he did when she was asleep and he didn't have to worry about her reciprocating. He would wrap a silky curl around and around his finger and then rub his thumb across the hair. It was the softest thing he'd ever felt.

Now all he had left were the memories and the questions that still lingered. He'd often wondered if he would be able to wrap his hands around her tiny waist. He should have tried. Then at least he would know how it felt.

He wouldn't know how it felt to be touched for a good long while. He wouldn't be like his father and punish some other woman for not being her. And he was just like the old man, manipulating Sophie's life into what he thought she wanted it to be.

Just like his father, he thought he was doing it all for her. The building was a good investment, but he'd bought it to give her a break on the rent, never realizing she was perfectly capable of solving the problem on her own. And he arranged to take her with him on his tour, thinking it would be a way for her to see the country. But really it was about his insatiable need to keep her close so he could glean off her happiness.

She opened him up to the possibility of being happy, of wanting more from life than he ever had. A morbid sense of curiosity had him driving up into the West Hills, to the Forest Heights neighborhood he'd grown up in. He wanted to see the house Tessa thought Sophie would love. To see where life might have led him if he were a better man.

Who would touch him next? A stranger brushing him in the street? Kelly, probably. But even she kept her distance. He'd thought it was strange when his father hugged him. It shouldn't be strange.

It hadn't always been this way. He and Lance had always hugged and played, wrestled, touched and even kissed, until Gretchen. David would never forget Lance's third wife. He'd wanted so much for her to like him, for it to feel like it had with Kelly's mother, Karen.

He tried to be good. Hell, he was a good kid. But she hated how much time Lance spent with him. Said it was unnatural for Lance to sleep with David when the nightmares came. Said all the hugging was going to turn him into a girl. He was twelve. He knew not all the boys were close with their fathers, but they had mothers and he didn't.

He'd never forget his father's face when he stuck out his hand to shake goodnight. Lance had looked as hurt as David felt right now. But he'd taken it.

David had felt himself getting more and more irritable, moody, angry. Who was Gretchen to come in and shake up his world? She'd tried to tell him to do something, who knew what now. He'd mouthed off, calling her a bitch. She'd slapped him. Not that he didn't deserve it, but no one ever struck him before.

Craig had been there. He always was. Had yelled at her as David closed up. Sat with him on the front step kicking pebbles until his father had come home.

"Tell him," Craig nudged, but he'd stayed frozen. "Gretchen hit him. She can't do that." David had heard the words as if they were coming from the television.

He'd never looked up as his father approached, just seen his shoes. Polished black. The briefcase had joined them with a thud, and promptly flopped on its side.

"What do you mean? David? What happened?"

The shoes were really nice. His dad had gotten him matching shoes for his aunt's wedding last summer. Even their ties had matched. That was the day Gretchen had started calling him Clone.

"She slapped him. Real hard. She can't do that."

His father knelt down and David closed his eyes. Tight. Tighter as he felt the fingers where his cheek still stung. Gretchen said boys don't cry.

And he tried not to, really tried as his father had wrapped him up, squeezing what breath was left.

"I'll make it right. I promise. I'm so sorry." The whisper only made it harder. David was grateful his father had held him long enough for him to gain control again. That way no one would know he had cried.

Lance had walked them across the street to Craig's house. Thank goodness the television was on. Lance had tried to hug him again when he left, but David had pulled back.

"I'll come get you right after dinner, okay? Right after. I'll make it right." David had stared at the television. He couldn't nod, or even blink. Boys don't cry.

He never saw Gretchen again. But thanks to her he did have to see a shrink. Not that he said much. At least the sessions taught him about the nightmare.

It wasn't really a nightmare. The therapist thought it was probably a repressed memory. In it he was scared, but he never knew of what, and went into his father's room. He tried everything to wake him, but he was so small and Lance was so big. He just wouldn't wake up. And then the panic would hit, waking David.

Lance had relied heavily on sleeping pills for five years after his wife's death. The psychologist reasoned the event might have actually happened, which was why David couldn't let it go. It tapped into a child's fear of being abandoned by the only parent he had left.

David learned how to change the dream, to walk around the other side of the bed and climb in. It worked. Without the nightmares, David didn't have an excuse to reach for Lance, even in the middle of the night. No one touched him.

Speed bumps were the bane of her existence. Maybe because she drove over exactly sixteen each way to check on Daphne between classes. But probably because everything bothered her right now.

Coming over the seventh bump, she slammed on the brakes. Luckily no one was behind her. She'd know his car anywhere. Not just for its condition, but also for the way he parked it. Always toward the end of a lot, to lessen the chances anyone might park next to it and ding the door.

What was David doing here? On the far outside possibility he was visiting Craig and Daphne, the family birth center was on the other side of the hospital. This was by the clinics, where the doctors had their offices. Was he sick? Sophie pulled her SUV right next to the Corvette. So close to the driver's side he couldn't possible open the door. It wasn't really catty. He had a key and could move the truck. But he'd know she'd seen he was there.

She didn't mind the walk. She didn't have another class for three hours. Maybe she should just sit here and wait. But then she'd have to talk to him, and she had no idea what to say.

Zipping up her jacket, she trudged across the parking lot, into the lobby of the clinic and looked on the wall for the map. The hospital was sprawling. If she followed the maze correctly she could make it all the way to Daphne's room without having to step outside again.

What if he was sick? Or maybe it was his dad? David had mentioned he was worried about Lance. Not that it was any of her business really, but he might need her. Instinctively, she wanted to console him. Guilt still niggled her for not making sure he was okay with the revelations his father had dumped on him before she'd started in about how he treated her. Maybe helping him now would assuage that feeling. Whether they were on a break or not.

Sophie pulled out her cell phone and stepped to the left, surveying the physician's directory. Cardiologists on the fourth floor, oncologists on the third, urology and gerontology on the second. Why the hell was he here?

She dialed his cell phone, surprised when he picked up on the first ring.

"Sophie?"

She warmed from the inside out at the sound of his voice. She cleared her throat and tried to come up with a plan. "I need to see you."

"Yeah? Did you decide—"

"No, nothing like that. Where are you?" Not very well thought out. But she had no idea what she was walking into.

"Oh." Did he really sound crestfallen or had she only imagined that part? "I have a meeting, but it shouldn't last more than an hour."

"What kind of meeting?"

The silence was deafening as she walked into the elevator and pressed two. She'd check every waiting room in the building.

"Are you at work or visiting Daphne?"

"Diversion. I taught you that." she whispered the words as she stepped out of the elevator. Gerontology was out, leaving the urology practice to the left. Her heart raced as she turned the door handle.

Please let him be here. Urology was what, kidney stones? A lot less ominous than heart problems or cancer.

He was standing, staring out the windows lining the waiting room. She watched as he rocked back and forth on his heels. He was nervous. About the appointment or the phone call?

"David?" She snapped her phone closed and crossed the waiting room. She watched his shoulders tense, his hand clenched into a fist at his side, but he didn't turn.

As she stood next to him and looked up at his face, she saw why. He was white as a sheet. Terrified. Of the appointment or her? She wrapped both her hands around one fist.

"Are you okay?" Her voice was quiet, and not because she was afraid of making a scene in front of the receptionist and two other men in the lobby.

His eyes closed and he nodded slowly.

"Why are you here? Are you waiting for your dad?"

His head shook as he squeezed his eyes tighter.

"You won't tell me?" She didn't bother to disguise the hurt in her voice. Not that she deserved to be told after the way she'd treated him, but she needed to know he was all right.

He shook his head, differently this time, as if he was clearing his thoughts. His voice was quiet, but the low tone showed his anger.

"Why are you here? How did you find me?" He splayed his fingers, shaking off hers and sliding his phone in his pocket. "Did my father send you?"

Sophie looked down at her hands, open in front of her. The void where he had been was gaping and noticeable. "I saw your car. I thought you might need me." The only need seemed to come from her voice.

"I don't need you." Vile, bitter, an absolute lie. Good God, why was she here? Now? And why did the doctor have to be running late?

David heard her slump into the chair next to him. He had to stop hurting her. He could physically feel it every time, as if it was happening to himself.

"Why are you here?" she asked again. "Is there something wrong?"

He didn't want to share the conversation with the room, so he sat next to her. Purely out of practicality. Not so his knee could touch hers. Not so he could breathe in that sweet almond scent. Her eyes were so blue.

"Sophie, it's none of your business."

"David." The hushed whisper of his name sounded just like it did in the morning when they would talk in bed. "If you're sick, if you have something, I do need to know."

He rolled his eyes. She thought he had an STD. As if he would have ever risked hurting her. "The only time I've ever," he made circles with his hand as if that explained anything, "is with you. That's not why I'm here."

"Then why are you here? Kidney stones? Prostate?"

"Vasectomy." He watched her face as he said the word. He doubted she would look this pained if he slapped her.

Then she narrowed her eyes and all her features sharpened. He knew this look. This was the mean Sophie, the nasty side of her he never wished to see. The only part of her he would not miss. Realization washed over him. He'd always thought she did this when she was angry, but it was when she was hurt.

"You asshole."

He was pinned to his chair as her icy blue eyes froze him in place. Her voice was still a whisper, but he could hear the rage.

"How dare you? I have been spending every waking moment trying to figure out a life where I would be okay with not having children of my own. I thought maybe if you explained why, maybe if I understood, I could be okay with it. I'm willing to change everything I am, and you don't even trust me."

"I trust you," came out automatically. Should have kept his damn mouth shut.

"Then why are you doing this? Without even talking to me? This isn't just your decision, David."

"No one makes decisions for me."

"Of course not, that's your job. You know what is best for everyone." She took a deep breath, her pale throat undulating as she swallowed. "You could change your mind."

"I won't."

"How can you have so little consideration for my feelings? You weren't even going to tell me. I deserve better than that."

He set his jaw against the strain in her voice. He was doing the right thing. "Yes, you do." His eyelids slammed shut as she choked on a sob. This had to stop.

"I do."

He heard her rummaging in her bag. She must be crying, looking for a tissue. Tears wouldn't change his mind. He needed to do this, should have a long time ago.

"David." Her voice was deadly calm, crystal clear.

He opened his eyes. She wanted to cry, he could feel it. But she wouldn't, at least not in front of him.

"I should thank you for making this easier for me. You really are a bastard."

He saw the keys dangling in front of his face. She dropped them and he instinctively reached out and caught them without thinking. A profound sense of deja vu swept through him. He'd done that to her when he tried to give her the car. He shook his head. "I don't want—"

"I don't care what you want anymore, David. I deserve better than this game you're playing with me. I deserve someone who wants to love me without any qualifications. Who'll be honored, not burdened, to have children with me. Have a nice life, David." She grabbed his face, kissing him hard and purposefully. There was no romance, no regret, just goodbye. An end so bitter he couldn't watch.

"God damn you," she choked, pushing him away. "You closed your eyes."

"Daddy, wake up," the familiar voice pleaded. Tossing to his side, David knew he was dreaming. He'd had this dream so many times. *Just walk around to the other side of the bed and get in.*

"Daddy!"

Walk around, he told himself again. But something was different. Usually he was staring at Lance's sleeping face, but now he couldn't see anything.

"Daddy!"

The dream would go on forever if he didn't get in the bed. If he couldn't see, he'd just feel his way in. David stuck out his arms, reaching for the edge of the bed. His fingers touched warm skin and his eyes shot open. There he was, maybe three years old.

"I went potty all by myself. You have to tuck me in."

His hands cupped the little face in awe, focusing on the pale blue eyes. Sophie's eyes. He pulled the boy as close as he could, the soft skin and fuzzy cotton of the pajamas beneath his fingers, the short cropped hair against his cheek. He pulled the boy's scent into his lungs until he thought they would burst.

"Daddy, no. Not with you. In *my* bed. Mommy said you would."

Mommy. Releasing the boy David turned, looking at the other side of the bed. But it was empty. His bed, in his condo. He looked back to where the boy had been, but he was gone too.

David felt so empty he thought he might vomit. He fell back on the pillows and slammed his eyes shut. It was just a dream, but it had felt so real, so warm. The sheets had been white like Sophie's, not gray like his. That meant she was there, right?

It could be real, he could make it real. He could risk it. He could risk anything just to feel that sweet-smelling hair against his cheek. Soap, peanut butter and grass.

He tried to imagine it again, tried to relive the moment. He tried to concentrate on every subtle nuance of the dream, but the tendrils snapped and evaporated as he wakened more and more. Maybe if he fell asleep the dream would come back. This time he wouldn't let go.

"It's a girl." Sophie spoke softly, setting the flowers in front of the grave marker her parents shared. "Kinsey Dawn, but you probably already know that."

She rambled on, wishing they were really listening. Wishing there had been someone to hold her as she'd left the hospital room this morning, fresh with the realization her sister had a family that didn't include her.

She wanted to kneel, to throw herself on the ground and cry, scream, kick, at how selfish she felt. But the ground was wet from the morning dew, and cold from the November air. She should feel blessed Daphne had a baby a month premature who came into the world pink and screaming. But instead she was envious she didn't have a family of her own, angry with David for not being the man she wanted him to be, furious with herself for allowing her happiness to rest on other people.

"I messed up." Her eyes closed as she purged her heart in the early morning silence. "I'm trying Mama, I'm trying to find that full life you were talking about. But I'm afraid if I run to him because I want to now, I'll regret it later. I'll regret not having a baby. When I held Kinsey today, I just ached. She is so pretty and she knows Daphne already. Daphne picks her up and she relaxes."

Sophie wiped a tear away with her glove. "I don't understand why it feels like this. I shouldn't hold my sister's baby and want her to be mine. I should be happy after all they went through. I shouldn't have wanted him to be there with me. But I did. How long does that last? How long until I can have a moment where I'm not wishing he were with me, that he actually loved me the way I loved him?"

She huffed out a breath. It was ridiculous to be looking for answers here. Opening her eyes, she blinked away the tears until she could see clearly again. Her heart stalled in her chest as she saw him, so far away he was merely a figure atop a hill. She knew it was David as surely as she knew she should go. She'd ended it, she'd decided it was too much and walked away.

But as she watched him drop to his knees, her legs had a mind of their own. She'd handle the rejection somehow. She needed to get to him, just in case he needed her.

Her eyes never left him as she made the hike. It was barely eight in the morning, her footsteps the only sound. He didn't turn as she neared him, stayed on his knees rocking slightly. Sophie carefully stepped closer, until she could read the headstone in front of him. Natalie Davidson Strong. Her eyes stalled on the date. Today, Kinsey's birthday, David's birthday.

He didn't move as she stepped closer, didn't flinch as she laid her hand on his shoulder. "David?"

His hand covered hers. "Are you real?"

Sophie pinched his earlobe with her other hand. He laughed, pulling that hand forward and kissing it. Looking down, she realized he was kneeling on one of the yoga mats she sat on so she could see when she drove the truck.

"Did my dad tell you where to find me?"

"No, I came to congratulate my folks. They're grandparents today."

His head nodded slowly as he tightened his grip on her hand.

"You're officially mid-thirties now."

How did she know not to say happy birthday? "I've missed you."

"You saw me two days ago."

It felt like years had passed since that morning at the doctor's office. "I'm not doing it. You were right, I changed my mind. You changed it."

She stepped closer, so close he could press his head back against her stomach, feel the buttons on her long wool coat.

"That wasn't why I was upset. I should go."

He tightened his grip on her hand. He wouldn't let her go this time. "Just listen and let me try and explain. It feels like you are always with me, like what would make me happy would make you happy, so I never think to ask. It's hard for me to think of you as separate from me. But I promise I'll try.

"From that first night we spent together, I changed. I became the man you wanted me to be, and I'm still getting used to the feeling. It scares me to trust you, because when I trust people they disappoint me. My father has a real knack for it."

"He does mean well, David. He just goes about it wrong."

"I know, and this isn't about him. Remember that night in your bed when you said we matched? You were right. You can feel it when I need you, like at the clinic and today, and I can feel it when you're hurt or happy. We can't let that get away."

"David." She was crying in that silent way she did, so he pulled her arms tighter around him.

"Have you decided anything yet?"

He felt her struggle to control her breathing. "You can have the club."

"You know that's not what I meant."

"I want my truck back."

Laughing, he let one hand go so she could wipe her eyes. Taking the glove off the hand he had left he splayed her fingers between his. Even with her fingers stretched out her hands were smaller than his palms. He'd wondered about that.

"Don't laugh. There's no point in you selling it so I can buy it again. But I want to pay for it."

"It's in the south parking lot. You want it now?"

"Why are you driving it?"

"The Corvette is my mother's. I never drive it today. When women I love leave me they seem to leave me their car. It's very bizarre."

She must not have heard him.

"Your mom's maiden name was Davidson. Is that where they got your name?"

"We don't know my name." He took a deep breath and reveled in how easy the words came. He never talked about it, never explained, not even when his father pressed, or to the shrink as a kid. "She wanted it to be a surprise. Dad looked everywhere to see if she wrote it down, but never found it. Davidson was all he could think of."

She hugged him close, which wasn't why he'd told her, but he liked it anyway. Liked it so much he held her tight as she tried to pull away. "I won't let you go."

"I won't let you treat me like I don't matter."

"Good." He pulled her around in front of him. "Teach me. Teach me to love you like you deserve to be loved."

Her mouth twisted up as he wrapped his arms around her waist and pulled her close. Pressing his head against her chest until he could hear the pounding of her heart.

"I should go."

"No, not yet." He couldn't let her go, not now, not ever. "Tell me." Anything to keep her talking, to keep her here. "Tell me about the baby."

Her breath was catching in her throat as she tried to calm down. "She's tiny, but perfect. They named her Kinsey Dawn. She's almost five pounds and eighteen inches long, what there is of her hair is red."

David looked up and stared into her big blue eyes. "Red hair, Craig will like that. I thought you said they were having a boy."

"I dreamed it was a boy, but Daphne always knew she was a girl."

"You dreamed about our boy." He held tight as she tried to wriggle away. "I did too."

"It was just a dream, David."

"Make it come true."

Sophie sank to her knees and kissed him softly, pushing away when he tried to deepen it. "It's not about babies, David. I need to make my own choices, have my own life. You have to let me."

"I will, as long as you choose me."

"You're not a choice. You're a part of me. I need to go, to think, okay?"

He nodded slowly, reluctantly releasing her. Watching as she put her glove back on and turned to go. "I love you, Sophie. Remember that when you're deciding."

He watched her feet stop, waiting before she made her way down the hill. He watched every step as she became smaller and smaller, fading away behind a hill. He turned back to the headstone and did what he did on this day every year. Planned the rest of his life.

Chapter Seventeen

Sophie had said she wanted the truck, so he brought her the truck. To the last class of the Sensational Sex series. Even though she'd told him not to come. He'd promised to finish out the classes, and he didn't disappoint. She might be angry he was there when she'd told him not to be. But he couldn't sit still thinking someone else might be putting her in the *Perfumed Garden* positions.

He'd taken the Kama Sutra manual she used to plan the classes from her apartment when he snuck in to set up for tonight. *The Perfumed Garden* was a fifteenth century North African guide to sexual fulfillment. There were eleven numbered postures, but David couldn't tell which Sophie had chosen to focus on in class.

Reading about the first posture had made his decision for him. The basic man-on-top position was designed for couples with significantly different builds. It was very straightforward, lacking the creativity of the positions she used for the class. Still, he wondered if she'd planned to include it.

Making his way to her office, he heard voices and paused. Lance and Tessa were already there, running through the format with Sophie. She wouldn't look at him, but from the way her shoulders tensed he knew she felt his presence.

"Can I talk to you for a minute?"

Lance and Tessa both turned to him, their eyes widening. David hadn't spoken to either one of them since his father's forced confession. He was still angry, but in a twisted way he understood. They just wanted him to be happy.

Sophie looked at the clock and at her hands, anywhere but at him.

"Dad, why don't you go check out the studio. I already set it up."

She finally looked at him, narrowing her eyes. He waited until Lance and Tessa left before responding.

"I'm not running things. I just wanted to talk to you."

Her face relaxed as she leaned back in her chair.

"I figured some things out and I wanted you to know what I learned." He pulled the bag from behind his back and set it on the table.

"You like presents, easy fun presents like fruit and chocolate." From the bag he handed her the box of chocolate-covered strawberries. Her smile was wide, dimples pressing into her cheeks.

"You want to have the fun of picking out major purchases like a car," he handed her a toy truck, "or a house." Pulling the folder out of the bag he handed it to her.

"What is this?" She narrowed her eyes again. Not good.

"I think we need to buy a house."

"David." The warning in her voice was as blaring as a ship's horn.

"I'm not going to just lie down and let you run my life either. I want a partnership. If you don't think we need a bigger place, then we'll argue about it."

Sophie slowly shook her head and cracked the folder.

"And if you are still trying to figure things out career wise I have some ideas too. I need someone to handle Deliver-Ease full time when it rolls national. You could stay on here, or work in the accounting department at SGI."

"David," she warned again, slamming the folder shut. He'd pushed too far.

He held up his hands. "Whatever you want, I just want you close."

"That's good to know." He knew that smile. It was her teasing smile, the one that always pulled him in.

"What positions are we doing tonight?"

"*The Perfumed Garden.*"

"I know, but which ones?"

"I've already gone through them with Lance and Tessa. You don't need to worry about it."

"We should do the first posture."

Her lips twitched as she eyed him. "There's not a lot to learn about a bent-knee male superior."

"It's designed for people of different sizes. I learned a lot from it."

Sophie didn't want David to stop being in control, she just wanted him to share the control with her. It had been almost impossible for her to walk away from him yesterday, but there was still a power imbalance she wasn't comfortable with. But maybe, if he understood about the postures, he might understand her too.

The Perfumed Garden postures were all male dominant, so it might be hard to show him, but she would try. She would teach him there's more power in giving up control than in maintaining it.

"We're going to do something a little different tonight because it's our last class," Sophie began after the warm-up and the couples were together on their mats. "This is our last chance to make sure every one of you takes away something from the course."

Walking around the room, she handed each pair two note cards and pens. "Completely anonymous, I want you to write down a problem you're having sexually, maybe the reason you are here or a physical compensation you need to make. We're going to try to answer that problem with a position from *The Perfumed Garden.*

"Texts like *The Kama Sutra* and *The Perfumed Garden* were written centuries ago to answer questions just like the ones you'll be writing. The works have endured because the solutions work.

"While you are thinking about it, I'll give you an example. As you may have noticed, David is a couple of inches taller than me." Sophie hoped the laughter from the class meant they were warming to her idea.

"In *The Perfumed Garden* the first posture compensates for this." Sophie returned to the raised platform and lay on her back, pulling David down with her.

"In the first posture, the woman lies on her back with her knees pulled back. The man kneels between her legs, his hands at her sides. She then presses her calves on either side of his hips. Because he is on his knees there is less pressure on her body to support his. The man also has a lot of control over the depth of penetration. Thinking about what makes your partner comfortable will help you relax and perform better."

Sophie kissed David pertly on the nose and rolled him off of her. "Now that we've thoroughly mortified David by making him simulate sex in front of his father, I'll collect your questions and see how *The Perfumed Garden* can help you."

The students loved her idea, almost as much as they loved Tessa and Lance's announcement about an advanced class. Their questions were endless tonight, but Sophie had stayed out front, answering them all.

Closing the door behind the last of them, she retreated to her office, expecting to find David with his feet on her desk like he owned the place. Which he now did. Instead she found the keys to her truck on top of her desk and the words *see you at home* scrawled on a note.

Chuckling to herself, she bundled up and collected her things, noticing he'd swiped the folder with the houses and her strawberries. He'd better not eat them without her.

Her SUV was right outside the front door, the yoga mats already on the seat that had been pulled all the way forward. Climbing inside, she noticed a sticky note on the stereo panel. *We need to get a song* written on it.

God he was cute, too cute really. Sophie smiled to herself as she started the truck and made her way back to her apartment. They were going to be okay. Maybe she'd go with him on his trip. As long as they could make it back for the holidays. She didn't want to miss Kinsey's first Christmas.

Spending every day together they could really talk, figure out just where they wanted to go. She still needed time to figure out what she wanted to do with her career. With the money from the sale of Working It Out she could go into business for herself, or take him up on one of his offers.

Sophie knocked before letting herself into her apartment. Opening the door, her eyes widened as she took in her living room bathed in candlelight. Tiny tea lights flickered from every surface. The room seemed warmer than usual and filled with an amazing cinnamon aroma.

Her grin stretched while she peeled off her jacket and gloves. As David stepped out of the bedroom wearing his tuxedo, Sophie noticed candlelight flickering in there too. She'd heard make up sex was supposed to be good, but this was going to be exceptional.

"I'm underdressed." She smiled as he approached.

"You can change if you want, but not into that red dress. That thing short-circuits my brain. And if you take off your clothes, I doubt I'll let you put any back on."

She loved the way the light danced with the desire in his eyes.

"Why didn't you dance with me at Daphne and Craig's wedding?"

Where is that coming from? "I told you, I had to take care of my mom."

"How long is a song, Sophie? Three minutes? Why wouldn't you dance with me?"

She looked at the floor. *Not now.* "I don't know how."

"I thought you said you didn't lie."

"Really." She looked into his eyes. "I don't know how. I never went to school dances or out to clubs or anything. It was never a priority."

"I'm not buying it. I've seen the way you move. You teach aerobics classes."

"Ah," she raised a finger, "I teach yoga and Pilates, neither of which requires rhythm."

She had him there. "So you'll learn."

"I could, I guess. I didn't know you liked to dance."

"I don't. I only dance at weddings."

"Another rule?" she teased, stepping closer. "You know what I think of your rules."

"I think you'll want to leave this one unbroken." He looked down at her, framing her face with his hands. "Take off your shoes."

"What?" she asked, shaking his hands free.

"Take off your shoes."

"I heard you," she said, kicking off her sneakers. "Why?"

He lifted her up, setting her feet down on top of his own.

"What are you doing?"

"Teaching you to dance," he said, wrapping an arm around her waist.

"I thought the object was to not step on your feet."

"This is how I taught Kelly to dance. I only know one way," he said as he began to guide her around the living room floor.

"That's sweet." She stretched to wrap her arms around his neck.

"Nah, it was purely selfish. If she could dance at family weddings I could avoid my dad's sisters. This is selfish, too. From now on, you can dance with me at weddings and save me from the bridesmaids."

From now on. She liked the sound of that. Whether he meant it like she did or not.

"I'll get some really high heels."

"I got you a present."

"I like presents." Especially now that he understood the difference between a present and a major purchase.

"It's in my pocket."

"I really like that present," she said, reaching her hands into his pants pockets and rubbing her hands along his hard thighs. "Hey, there really is something in here!" she squealed pulling the box from his pocket and stepping back.

She tried to breathe as she stared at the tiny burgundy box. *Earrings,* she chanted to herself. Don't look disappointed. She closed her eyes and swallowed hard against the lump in her throat. She didn't want it to be earrings.

When she opened her eyes he was down on one knee. For a change, she was looking down at him. He reached for the box. She pressed her hands together, realizing that without the box they were shaking.

"Dance with me at our wedding, Sophie."

Her eyes filled as her emotions swelled within her. *When did he change his mind?* The world blurred before her as she blinked, meeting him on the floor. Her mouth found his as she tried to communicate all the sensations coursing through her body.

He pulled back, framing her face with his hands. "You've got to say it, Sophie."

She opened her eyes as his thumbs brushed the tears away. "I'll dance," she breathed more than said.

He smiled. "Close enough."

Epilogue

"Daddy, wake up," the familiar voice said. Tossing to his side, David knew he was dreaming. It had been so long since he'd had the nightmare, he'd almost forgotten about it. *Almost.*

Just walk around to the other side of the bed and get in.

"Daddy!"

Walk around, he told himself again. But something was different. He couldn't see Lance, the room was too dark.

"Daddy!"

The dream would go on forever if he didn't get in the bed. If he couldn't see he'd just feel his way in. David stuck out his arms, reaching for the edge of the bed. His fingers touched warm skin and his eyes shot open.

Tyler. He wasn't dreaming.

"I went potty all by myself. You have to tuck me in."

His hands cupped the little face in awe, focusing on the pale blue eyes. Sophie's eyes. He pulled the boy as close as he could, pulling the boy's scent into his lungs until he thought they would burst.

"Daddy, no. Not with you. In my bed. Mommy said you would."

Mommy. Where was Sophie? Without putting the boy down, David checked the bed. "Where's Mommy?"

"Feeding Bella. She said you would tuck me in." David breathed in the smell that was Tyler—soap, grass and peanut butter. The boy loved to eat.

Finally, David set him on the ground and let himself be led through the home they'd built together over a decade ago. He could hear Sophie humming softly in the nursery. Isabel was almost one. Sophie should really let her cry it out the way the books said to. *Like that was going to happen.*

Tyler pulled him past Natalie and Phoebe's room with the matching canopy beds, to the last room at the end of the hall. Tyler's eyes closed as soon as he was tucked beneath the tattered red afghan on his race car bed. Before leaving, David stepped across the room and kissed Dustin's smooth cheek. Shampoo, grass and grape jelly.

When they slept only Sophie could tell Tyler and Dustin apart. Everyone thought they were identical twins, but doctors claimed they were fraternal. Their eyes the only tell. Tyler was the only one of the kids to get Sophie's eyes. *So far.*

Closing the door softly behind him, David saw her coming out of the nursery. Sophie must have caught the look in his eye because she ran to their bedroom. By the time he locked the door, she had rounded the bed.

"Isabel's asleep?"

Her eyes narrowed as he approached the bed. "David, I told you earlier. Not tonight, I'm ovulating."

He smiled wide. "I know what you said. You said six." And he wanted to give her everything she ever wanted. And more.

She was fighting a smile. "I'm the one home with five kids under the age of ten."

"Tyler's the only one with blue eyes. I need another shot at it."

"That's your argument?" Her quiet laugh was sexy as ever.

David shrugged. "It worked last time." He put a knee on the bed, but she backed to the far end of the room.

"It was a weak moment. You were wearing a tux. It short-circuited my brain."

Kelly's wedding. That was when they'd conceived Isabel. "I could change."

"No. If you take off your clothes I doubt I'll let you put any back on."

Thank goodness, she was considering it. He rounded the bed to her side, but she scampered over the top. Standing on top of the bed, she was taller than him. Barely. "Two more days, then we're in the clear again."

Sophie and her rhythm birth control method. Phoebe was proof of how well that worked. He hooked his hands behind her knees, pulling her legs out from under her. As she landed on her back, he climbed on the bed, keeping her there. He bent his head, tasting the skin just beneath her ear.

"Diversion. I taught you that." Sophie giggled, turning her head to grant him better access.

"What have I taught you?" he whispered, finding the place on her neck where he could taste her pulse as it beat faster.

"You want to play show," reaching her legs up, she slid her toes into the waistband of the pajama pants he'd started wearing when Natalie learned to walk and slid them down his legs, "or tell?"

About the Author

Jenna Bayley-Burke is a domestic engineer, freelance writer, award-winning recipe developer, romance novelist, cookbook author and freebie fanatic. Blame it on television, a high-sugar diet or ADD; she finds life too interesting to commit to one thing—except her high-school sweetheart, two blueberry-eyed boys and a perfect baby girl. Her stories, both naughty and nice, are available everywhere. To learn more about Jenna Bayley-Burke, please visit www.jennabayleyburke.com.

GREAT CHEAP FUN

Discover eBooks!

THE FASTEST WAY TO GET THE HOTTEST NAMES

Get your favorite authors on your favorite reader, long before they're out in print! Ebooks from Samhain go wherever you go, and work with whatever you carry—Palm, PDF, Mobi, and more.

LaVergne, TN USA
30 September 2010
199115LV00003B/32/P

9 781605 043128